· *Saraband* ·

· *Saraband* ·

PATRICE CHAPLIN

Methuen

First published in Great Britain in 1991
by Methuen London, Michelin House, 81 Fulham Road, London SW3 6RB

Copyright © 1991 Patrice Chaplin
The author has asserted her moral rights

A CIP catalogue record for this book
is available from the British Library
ISBN 0 413 63290 3

Typeset by Deltatype Ltd, Ellesmere Port
Printed and bound in Great Britain
by Clays Ltd, St Ives Plc

· One ·

When he said he was having an affair with the young girl she didn't quit. When her eldest boy went back on drugs she didn't quit. When the agency said she was no longer young enough to do glamour commercials – in other words her looks like the rest of her life were going downhill – she still didn't quit. Then one day she went to the sink, started washing up and as she scraped the golden fleece scourer around a blue and white striped cup, she quit. She turned off the taps because she was an orderly person, even in despair, took her ripped leather jacket from under the gaunt cat and left the house. She turned right and crossed into the chaos of the morning traffic. Unhurriedly she entered the goods yard and climbed the steps to the railway bridge.

Alexis was thirty-three; her face gave nothing away, not even happiness. The horror she'd gone through, sometimes bordering on the purgatorial, was never allowed to show. It had taken eight years to dim her love of life. She hadn't once thought of running away. You did your best, you brought God into it – what you couldn't handle you left to Him. Alexis had tried doing deals with God: let my husband come back to me; give me recognition for what I am; let my son stop doing coke, it's killing him and me. And I'll do good. Put good energies and thoughts into this world, beautiful but ruined by people. But God, she saw, disliked too personal a relationship. Perhaps it was too human and therefore belonged to sin. Nothing changed.

She leaned over the tarnished metal bridge and watched the trains writhe around the curve towards King's Cross like speeding snakes. Her head felt too full of blood, her legs were weak and shaking.

On this Monday morning, shortly after ten o'clock, she saw that nothing much *had* changed. She knew that to progress you had to cut away the dead wood so new shoots could push through. Only then was change possible.

Her husband had been having an affair with the young girl but he'd never actually said so, not in words. Everything in his behaviour screamed that this was the one, total, consuming passion in his life, one for which he'd give *his* life if necessary. He'd never felt that way about Alexis; they'd got by on sex and her desire for him that had sometimes come near to adoration. The girl wasn't someone you'd notice unless she was stealing your husband. But she was mysterious and no doubt made the most of it. She had the utter ruthlessness of the very young; she was out to get him but also to get him away from Alexis. She was settling some past unhappy parent business – love didn't come into it. The girl wanted power not love. Alexis knew you couldn't have both.

The night she knew for sure her husband was having sex with the girl, Alexis had left the house, quite steadily, and made for the bare wall in the high street next to Sainsburys. The following day everyone in the area, walking, driving or passing the wall in buses, laughed as they read, 'Paula Strong – Home-Wrecker'. Paula Strong saw it on her way to her first class at the Polytechnic behind Sainsbury's. Her pale face turned paler, towards green. The letters were huge and scarlet like an advertisement; the paint on 'Paula' had dripped like blood. William Darby saw it as he went in to teach. As usual he was late and carried a huge carton of expresso coffee from the Italian shop. They always gave him a double for the price of a single because they, like most people, succumbed to his charm. As he looked at the well-formed scarlet letters, flagrant in the sun, he knew his wife hadn't done it because her handwriting was usually incomprehensible. Or did jealousy make you neat? And how could she know about Paula? He was far too canny, he prided himself on that. That vile public message was the work of one of his other students, jealous because of his preference for Paula. He doubted that his sons were involved: the eldest couldn't spell 'Home-Wrecker'. Even when William Darby got the Polytechnic porter to repaint the wall the letters showed through.

It was around the time of her gynaecological operation that Alexis knew the girl was pregnant; Paula Strong sat in the kitchen, pale-faced, silent, her long hair hanging over her breasts like a Madonna. She was untidy, her nails were dirty and that was a surprise. She looked around the kitchen as though it ought to be hers. Seeing Alexis watching her, she explained her visit to William Darby's home: she needed an extra tutorial.

Paula was cool in life but the reverse in bed. She gave her lover hours of a sensation approaching ecstasy. She also knew at what point to remove her yielding, greedy body and not answer her phone. She would come back. Her condition? Marriage.

William Darby would not leave his wife, not when the boys were so constantly getting into trouble. But it was a cliché, and he loathed those, so he told the girl other things – fairytales, lies, a promise or two. They would share a house in Italy; he'd go there and write a book. She would assist him.

His friends were appalled by her. 'She's so common. Even her name.'

'But, William, she's a Woolworths shop girl.'

Wasn't that what he liked? How he liked Paula's common touch!

The eldest boy hadn't gradually gone to the bad. He'd always been there. He gravitated towards low life with an inevitability that defied even prayer. He would find pushers even on a glacier. The speed with which he located 'gear' in a straight place was legendary. On his home patch, which seethed with drugs, he used his energy to locate money. To begin with he did glue, mushrooms, dope, dropped acid, popped blues – he wasn't fussy. He denied taking anything. So his eyes were crossed, voice slurred. Wasn't that his age? Hadn't his mother heard of adolescence? William stayed out of it, preferred to take the boy's word.

Before he started seeing things that weren't there, the boy had got the other kids rolling joints and freebasing smack. The younger one, Rick, got hooked. Alexis understood it was to do with an over-developed pleasure centre in the brain; not every kid who used the stuff in the neighbourhood got a habit. During the eldest boy's crack-up, doctors, private and National Health, paraded through the house but the boy refused all treatment. He had the arrogance of the insane. Both her kids refused help. She was the only one who would accept it, would have taken it gladly. The GP said she was a typical London user's mother. There was one mitigating factor – the boys took it in turns to go wrong. They didn't do it both at the same time. As she stood half hanging over the bridge, Alexis saw that was ironic, even merciful. Of course her children were a product of London, of new-age freedom, of the dictates of their peer group. William had been loath to see trouble: trouble kept him at home. He too, she saw, needed pleasure.

Domestic life had put lines on her face. The candy-floss glamour, the pink blonde baby hair and dewy eyes were suited to seduction and good times, not age. Her face wasn't tough enough for the life she had to lead. The agency said that clients thought she'd outgrown her sparkle and she was replaced. The only things remaining that betrayal, heartbreak and failure could not affect were her songs. She would sit upstairs in the dusty attic with the old cat and write about urban paradise in the mornings and sing in the alternative culture clubs at nights. Her voice was like a bird escaping from a cage; free, soaring, deep, wonderful, thrilling. It was absolutely sure. One of the alternative recording groups put her on tape and she cut one disc. Virgin planned to give her a contract but nothing came of it. Perhaps because Alexis was hard to categorise.

Steeped in sorrows, pierced with injustice, she caught sight of a grey-haired woman with a white stick moving with confidence towards the traffic lights at the junction. For a moment Alexis' attention was taken: would the woman stop? Did she know about the traffic swinging round from the north? The woman listened to the silence from the west but wasn't fooled. When the northern flow passed and the lights finally changed, she crossed unaided to the traffic island. She was confident and smiling – in spite of everything life was good. Alexis couldn't believe it, that smile in a dark and dangerous world. She felt sickened with guilt. She was, with all her faculties and gifts, standing on quitters' bridge.

'It was just one fucking dirty cup too many.'

She leaned further over and the balance shifted in favour of death. She quit right there on the railway, in the city she had loved in her songs. The last sound she heard was the tap tap of the blind woman's stick. The last thing she saw was the new poster on the goods yard wall: Angel Lupez, Spanish flamenco dancer, Royal Festival Hall.

Before she fell she clawed her wedding ring off and it tinkled onto the electric rail with a cheap metallic sound.

Kay Craven couldn't believe it. 'She had such a marvellous voice, didn't she? Really extraordinary.' And she stirred the lamb stew, tasted it, added freshly picked herbs from her garden; a stew should not be bland. Her dumplings were kneaded and ready to go in the moment the last unseen grease rose and was skimmed from the juice. Cooking for Kay was predominantly a visual art; things came together at the right time. Cooking involved all her senses and skills and was the job she did best.

'So many have gone over that bridge,' said the Irish cleaner. 'They'll have to put up a barrier now. It only takes one depressed day.'

Kay didn't know Alexis personally but was sure she'd seen her. She wanted to have seen her. 'She had children didn't she? Two?'

'Three,' the cleaner corrected her. Her performance with the Hoover might be slack but the quality of her gossip was impeccable. 'She must have been Irish with that voice.' She put away the Hoover and its attachments. 'I'll leave the underneath.'

By that she meant under the table and most of the floor. The cleaner hated housework.

Kay was sure Alexis was the one with strawberry blonde hair and a movie star's face. She had used to wait with a group of mothers outside the primary school in Hampstead. She had dressed to please men and her eyes showed that women were rivals and never to be trusted. Kay had the idea Alexis was a model and had an exciting life.

This had been in the old days when the mothers had gathered together and shared looking after their children. They had given spontaneous tea parties that turned into dancing in the evening. Life had seemed free and on your side. The kids played in the streets until after dark and were safe; it had been a community. Then the kids grew up and the mothers grew apart. It had been an optimistic time, before Thatcher, before the weather started going wrong. On hot afternoons the mothers used to drink in the Hampstead pubs, the ones with gardens. There seemed to be a lot more music then and it was in one of these pubs Kay had first heard the woman sing.

'How old was she?'

'Thirty-three.' The cleaner had got it direct from the bouncer of one of the Camden Town clubs where Alexis had occasionally sung.

'So young?' Kay was nearly forty. She had supposed they were about the same age.

'He said she'd never really got started; and it upset him to say it because she was so special. But then it all comes down to luck.' The cleaner looked at Kay, thinking her success was definitely down to luck, and her good looks and fortunate marriage. For a short weekly column in a Sunday newspaper Kay got paid a fortune. Now she was a celebrity and appeared on television. What the cleaner refused to see was that payment rarely bore any relation to quantity: although short, her employer's columns were gritty and often profound. She set trends. People talked about what Kay Craven wrote. Women identified with her.

Kay had long bright hair tied back with a ribbon. Her eyes were intense, and she had a slow smile that men loved. She looked as though she liked sensual pleasure. She had a statuesque body – large breasts and a small waist, long shapely legs with big thighs. Some people said her nose was too large but that could be out of jealousy; it was a Roman nose with flared nostrils. Her voice was soft and lovely to listen to. She was a woman in a feminist society and she disliked equal rights. Men were different from women and she wanted it to stay that way, enjoy the advantages. Her husband Joel said she'd been born at the wrong time. He never tired of looking at her. Lately it gave him the same heightened pleasure as eating her food. The two were becoming uncomfortably connected. Everyone said Joel and Kay were lucky; they had a good marriage that their friends clung to like a raft in a sea of divorce. The house was always welcoming. It had a country atmosphere.

Her cleaner said Kay had breeding, the true kind, not all distorted vowels and silly manners and showing off, but a class she was born with and could never lose. The cleaner also said Kay's airs and graces would be her downfall. She knew these things because she was Irish and her people were all mad or fortune tellers.

Kay's breeding was not hereditary; her daughter Sophie had none. She kicked open the back door and threw her school bag on the floor, leaving a trail of academic implements as she stamped to the sink and drank noisily from the tap. Kay could see her lips were stained from a forbidden lipstick.

'You pick up germs doing that,' said the cleaner. 'Use a glass.'

Sophie mouthed an expletive and grabbed Kay's purse from the table. 'I've got to get a really short skirt. I did tell you!'

'Ask her to pick up her things. Catch me picking up after a spoilt – ' The cleaner bypassed 'brat' and chose 'article like her'.

Sophie screamed, 'Don't you start ordering me about. What's it to do with you?' She searched for money but found only a few pound coins. Disgusted, Sophie threw the purse onto the floor. 'I want it now, Mum!' she whined. 'Don't expect me to go to Julia's party and be the only one in a long skirt. D'you want me to look a fool?'

'Bit late for that,' said the cleaner.

Calmly Kay put the dumplings into the stew. She turned the kitchen mirror to the light and powdered her pale matt skin with a huge pink puff. Her mouth was big and sensual; she rarely used bright lipstick and applied a muted gloss.

'Well, do you?' Sophie stamped her foot, eyes blazing. 'Listen for once!'

The cleaner winced and got ready to leave.

Kay decided to speak to Joel about their daughter. The girl needed a stricter school; Catholic schools, she'd heard, had the best discipline. Joel was an elitist in many ways, but not where his daughter was concerned; he wanted her to have the advantage of classlessness. Their son, Tom, had just been shoved into Harrow and from there he would go to Oxford.

Kay soothed the cross, adolescent girl with promises. The cleaner would have preferred to throttle her. She left saying, 'You can't reason with an angry rat!'

'Why don't you get rid of her?' said Sophie. 'A cleaner? She's the dirtiest thing in here.'

Kay explained the woman needed the money. Her dependants were endless. 'We've got it, so why not give it?'

Sophie put a finger into the foaming crust of the lemon meringue pie. 'It's better than school dinners, I will say that. But I can't bear the boring men Dad brings round.'

'It's business, Sophie.'

'Phoney, you mean.' Suddenly excited, she said, 'You'll never guess what, Mum. One of the boy's mothers killed herself this morning. She threw herself in front of an express train by Kentish Town.'

The first lunch guest opened the gate. Kay sent Sophie upstairs to watch television. She used a bribe; skirt money. Her son Tom had passed through puberty as though it didn't exist, but then he was like her – harmonious.

She served the stew and dumplings, cooked to perfection. The professors ate noisily and talked about Kant. They could have been eating tinned muck for all the notice they took, thought Kay.

The development and juxtaposition of ideas was what counted, not sensation. Joel poured his second-best wine; he knew what he was dealing with. He made a swift interjection in Latin and the professors bellowed. The chemical corporation chairman sat silent and impressed, he was completely out of his depth. The minister from the Board of Trade ate little. He was disconcerted by Kay, by her sexuality and beauty. She didn't eat but served the men, cleared the table and made coffee, to which she added a touch of cinnamon. She said suddenly, as though to herself, 'A woman threw herself from the railway bridge this morning.'

'Really, darling?' said Joel. 'What did she do?'

'Jumped.'

'No. I meant, who was she?'

Kay, amazed at the way his snobbery could flourish on any occasion said, 'She was a housewife.'

Joel muttered something appropriate. The professors just stared; they couldn't think of one thing to say. Neither did they want to hear about it. A tragedy required an emotional response and they disliked emotion. That was woman's stuff.

Joel was forty-four, dynamic, competitive, even in his sleep. His dreams were marathon experiences of contest and he awoke feeling insecure. He was an executive director of a multi-national chemical corporation and travelled frequently. In spite of a large sexual appetite he did not take advantage of the temptations on offer during his travels; he stayed loyal to Kay. The purpose of this lunch was to intimidate his employer, the corporation chairman and give him a taste of a world he could never enter. Money and power meant nothing when the brilliant and the academic got together.

Once the chairman had left, Joel shooed away the professors, who were settling in for an afternoon's drinking. His employer knew that Joel was ambitious. He thought Joel wanted his immediate superior's job; Joel wanted *his* job. The chairman was known as 'Chief' on three continents. Joel despised him because he hadn't had a classical education, he did not have even a

second-class brain, he was a football fanatic and he never seemed
to know where the enemy lay in wait; he believed it was outside
the company. It would never occur to him that the enemy could
be his host.

Kay put the crockery into the dishwasher and turned on the
radio. Joel passed swiftly across the kitchen and kissed her. He
had a sturdy, power-packed body, every ounce exuding energy,
and he looked invincible. Neither illness nor over-drinking could
get him down. Bereavement and rejection didn't even touch him.
But unbeknownst to Kay he was a disappointed man. He'd
wanted to be an academic; highly-paid executive company
director was a second choice.

'Good lunch, Kay. I could eat it all over again, I really could.'
He had yellow eyes, the eyes of a cat. He filled his briefcase,
found his raincoat and wondered why his wife, so sought-after
and clever, should have made such a nebulous impression at
lunch; mention of a suicidal housewife, in front of his employer?
What had *that* to do with his career move? Joel had expected her
to be at his side using her skills and subtly showing off her media
triumphs, not brooding privately over local disasters.

'Did you know this woman? The one who died?'

'No.'

He stroked her hair. He had lovely hands, clever and quick.

Bewildered, he left the kitchen. A taxi waited to take him to
Euston Station.

Kay called after him, 'We've got to talk about Sophie. It can't
go on.'

Joel wouldn't even discuss it. Sophie was the one part of his life
that didn't enter his ambitious world. His best gift to his beloved
Sophie was the freedom to be herself. Public schools? Not a
chance! Why? He'd been to one. As he left the house he heard
part of a song on the radio; the singer had an unbelievably lovely
voice. He got into the taxi knowing he could never be the person
he should be. Not revered or immortalised. Just rich.

Kay checked her latest Sunday column before the bike came to
collect it. The radio announcer said, 'That was "Inner City

Blue" written and sung by Alexis Scott who died tragically in London this morning.'

It *would* take death to make her famous, thought Kay. She tried to recall the group of mothers waiting outside the primary school. Why did the memory of a woman she hardly knew so preoccupy her? Why had it been valuable, that time? Waiting for the children. She had never thought about it before, and now it seemed like the best time, quite natural and lovely, and it had gone unnoticed in Kay's life. It had taken a woman's death to make Kay even remember it. Were the valuable times hidden and forgotten so she couldn't sully them with her up-market media perceptions? Kay clearly saw chubby Tom running out of school, pleased to see her, carrying a drawing of a tiger with yellow and red stripes and the same eyes as Joel. It had been tricky – getting him to school. He'd cried all the way there on the first morning. When Kay went to fetch him in the afternoon and asked how he'd liked it, Tom had said, 'It was all right. But I wouldn't like to have to go there again.' Persuading the child that school was an ongoing business had been the bane of Kay's life. The other children were so easy to love, too. Now she couldn't even remember their names. That was in the days when she had simply been Joel's wife. The image of Tom running towards her made her suddenly cry. It was like belonging to a very special club, that time. Everyone wanted the best for everyone else. It was the children who brought them together.

· *Two* ·

On impulse Kay crossed the road, its houses bristling with media people and minor celebrities, to Roly's house for dinner. Joel was spending the night in the north and Kay didn't feel like being alone. This was unusual.

Roly was a highbrow TV personality, traversing the world of medicine, philosophy, music and current affairs, somehow making them all sound the same. His programmes, she thought, were like dinners out of a tin. He had a bright toothy smile that only appeared on television. At home, his face fell into sad folds.

As usual the television was on loudly and he didn't reduce the volume because a guest was present. The television, she saw, was the real host; it paid for the dinner. It wasn't a house she liked visiting anymore, but – unaccountably – she couldn't stay alone. Roly chastised his wife Liz about the food. 'Kay hasn't just crossed the road, but a whole continent: you'd have to go to a suburb of Calcutta to eat this badly.' He forked around his spiced noodles pre-packed by Marks and Spencer. Any other evening they would have been perfectly acceptable. 'No wonder you stay in, Kay. In your case there really is nothing like home cooking. I can't forget that lemon mousse you made on Sunday. I dream about it.'

His long, sad, horse face looked more gloomy as he described the chemical structure of an E additive. Kay didn't understand a word. Then one of his programmes came on the television and the women were expected to sit in reverent silence. Liz immediately collected the plates and clattered out to the kitchen. When she didn't come back Kay joined her.

'He's a real crasher.' Liz sat on the table swinging her legs and eating trifle.

'He certainly doesn't go in for small talk.' Kay opened the fridge and helped herself to ice-cream. 'Philosophy, politics, current affairs, Verdi. But he's not too good on women.'

'It's only a matter of time. He's in the fast lane now. He'll trade me in.' Liz sounded bright about it. 'First the car, then the club, then the wife.'

Kay thought of the group of mothers outside the primary school. The ones she still saw – how they'd changed. But not Liz. Not even in appearance. She had got plumper; she liked pleasure, drink, cigarettes, compliments, laughter, dancing. She was bright and sharp and well-qualified in French history. But Liz had never made use of her intellectual attributes. She was more concerned with her children, keeping the house going, dealing with Roly's success.

'He's in to change like a weather vane, but I don't think he's found the right model yet. He's tried plenty of wrong ones – I get the phone calls.'

'What do they say?'

'They hang up.' Liz laughed merrily. Not much got her down. 'But over the years, those long, poor years, I've managed to put by a little nest egg. My family allowance, a bit of the housekeeping. I invested it properly, so don't worry. I call it my "flight fund". I think when he does get straddled over the vehicle of his choice, my lawyer will boost the flight fund quite significantly. I won't just fly, I'll take Concorde. She's a ball-breaker, that lawyer. Looks like a cockroach. Of course, *you'll* never need her.' Liz poured Kay a generous measure of Spanish liqueur. 'It's got forty-one herbs concealed in the alcohol: medicinal. Good for the digestion.'

Kay liked it and asked where she could get it.

'Some Spaniards brought it. They came to see Roly about one of their clients. He's a gypsy dancer or something – '

Kay took her shoes off and put her feet up on the table. 'I've never thought about money.'

'Oh, you do when you haven't got it. How often I've lain there in that lonely bed wondering where the media star is. Then I've been practically lulled to sleep counting up my flight fund. You have to know when to quit, that's the secret. Otherwise you become a loser and a victim.'

Kay felt quite cold: another dramatic weather change? Roly had just told them the polar caps had melted by several inches. Liz cut herself a slice of Marks and Spencer's Swiss roll and covered it with ice-cream. 'Did you know that a famous singer jumped from a railway bridge near here?'

Kay shivered – yet it was a warm night.

Roly came into the kitchen and searched around for some pudding. His exits and entrances were always noticeable and these days he was disconcerting. He said to Kay, 'Next time you go on the box, remember rule one: always keep your sentences short. Otherwise you get into the middle of one and think, where the hell does it end? What am I saying? Short and effective.' He patted her on the back. 'You had a frontrunner's lunch again. I counted three Oxford luminaries – '

'Oh do shut up!' said Liz. 'You're only jealous. Why let on you snoop?'

'Why does Joel have all those academics over? He has a more privileged dinner table than I do.' Roly discovered there was no more ice-cream and chucked the box away, a tantrum beginning.

Kay said soothingly, 'He needs their research. He taps the new stuff at its source.'

'So he gets the latest.' Roly's teeth were long and wolf-like as he smiled. 'It makes him feel like the latest, does it?'

'He *did* go to Oxford,' said Liz. 'He *did* get a double first. He's not some pharmaceutical salesman trying to be clever.'

'I'll have to come across to your house for a decent dessert.' Roly stroked Kay's hair with his thick, unfeeling hands and went back to the television. The news was on.

Liz said, 'I went past the very spot where she jumped, just before lunch. The police were there. I must have just missed it.

There was a funny atmosphere today, as though something bad were going to happen.'

Kay realised only women had mentioned the suicide so far. And from 'housewife', Alexis had become 'famous singer'.

'She wasn't famous at all. She'd made one record.' Kay told Liz about the primary school mothers waiting outside the small Hampstead school.

'I was one of them,' said Liz as she tried to remember seeing the singer; she always wanted to be part of anything going on. 'She had black hair, was thin, wore black – '

Kay corrected her impression.

Liz said, 'It's funny you can live so close to someone and never know who they are. Inner City isolation.'

'At least being a mother allows you to be part of a group. At least when the kids were young. That was the best time, wasn't it?' Kay remembered Alexis walking in Camden Town: short skirt, leather jacket, beautiful, weird. When punk was in she'd had spiky hair. Then she became what she had always been – very female. Kay remembered seeing her buying healthfoods in the high street.

The TV news was full of disasters but none of them were given much detail; there were too many to fit in. Fires, bombs . . . What did one woman's suicide matter compared with those?

When Kay went to bed she turned on the radio to Alexis Scott singing 'Firechild'. The voice rose almost unbelievably, touching nerves, senses, feelings that were not appropriate in Joel Craven's academic territory where only empirical thought was acceptable.

No one, Kay realised, had asked why Alexis had done it.

· *Three* ·

'Innercity Blue' became an overnight success and it seemed to
Kay that was all it lasted – one night. By the following week it was
forgotten. And the suicide was forgotten. It hadn't even made the
London evening paper. The local journal gave it one paragraph
on page three.

Kay had wanted to write about Alexis and the mothers waiting
outside the primary school in the early seventies. But the subject
had died down and another drama took its place: contaminated
food. Salmonella in eggs, glass fragments in baked beans. Was
nothing safe? Kay wrote instead about food hazards. The editor
hadn't been keen anyway – a local suicide wasn't topical.

Kay was surprised to learn from her daughter that Scott was
not Alexis' real name and that she had been married to an
academic; as William Darby only taught in a local polytechnic he
wouldn't be known to Joel or his group. Alexis had had three sons
and everyone said they were good kids. Sophie said the youngest,
Rick, was in her class and on the day of the death, his father had
come for him and broken the news. Apparently Rick had just
said, 'Yeah yeah, yeah. That's a bad one, Dad. Heavy.' And he'd
gone back to finish his lesson; everybody said he was a very cool
guy.

'But why did she do it?' said Kay.

Sophie didn't know.

Alexis had been a regular customer at the Camden Town
healthstore. When Kay called in to buy cracked wheat and lentils,
the salesgirls were talking about the death; how Alexis had stuck
with natural remedies and refused anti-depressants.

'Perhaps sometimes you've got to go over to the other side if it's really bad,' said the youngest salesgirl.

'The other side of life?' asked another.

'Orthodox medicine, Dumbo!'

When Kay asked why Alexis had needed anti-depressants, the girls shut up. After paying for her purchase Kay asked if Alexis' family was all right, if they needed help. She meant financially. The young salesgirl said the family was self-sufficient, all of them, like Alexis had been. But if anything came up she'd let Kay know.

Kay always went to the market for her vegetables and fruit. She shopped at the same stall and they let her pick out the best. She made it a rule that if she couldn't handle the produce she wouldn't buy it. The stall owner said he had used to drink with Alexis in 'The Elephant's Head'. He said she'd always wanted to be a star and she'd tried for a recording contract but not got anywhere. She'd even done commercials on television.

'I told her if she wanted to make it she would have to give it everything she'd got. She'd have to go all the way – she'd have to die for it if necessary.' Realising what he'd said he shut up. 'You know what I mean, Kay. Stardom demands total sacrifice.'

'What was she like?'

'Hard to know, she was hard to know. I just saw him – the husband. Really cut up.'

As Kay wheeled the food basket up to the house she thought she'd write William Darby a letter. Alexis had been glamorous, then punk, then very feminine, but it was her presence outside the school that Kay remembered.

The house was empty. Kay became so much more herself when she was alone and she felt so good on her own. She drew the silence up around her and the house, in exchange, filled with peace. The rooms were thick with peace. You could almost lie against the air. She was loved, complete, unscathed by tragedy. She was good and attracted only good things. Because she was harmonious she enjoyed being herself.

She was setting out the ingredients to make a duck pâté when

Liz arrived and the calm was shattered. The din of Liz's scurrying, unsettled mind was almost audible.

'I met a French duke last night. He'd been on one of Roly's programmes. I liked what I saw and he liked what he saw, let me tell you!' She pulled back her shoulders so her breasts swelled. 'Roly got wind of the action and was strangely jealous. But I said you can't have double standards. Don't you ever fancy going off?'

'No,' Kay said simply.

'Why not?'

'I suppose I'm all right with Joel. I get everything I want with him.'

Liz stayed to watch Kay make the pâté. She made it very physically, moving around the table, touching it from several angles, getting her hands right into the mixture. It looked more like making a sculpture.

'You're alone,' said Liz suddenly.

'Of course. Joel's in Milan.'

'No, *really* alone. Your soulmate isn't with you.'

Kay was amused. 'How will I know him?'

'You won't be able to not know him.'

Kay disliked the fanciful and changed the subject. The primary school, what did Liz remember?

Liz couldn't say. 'Of course I know I went there every afternoon and every morning. But I can't remember anything about it.'

'It's where we met, Liz.'

And Kay remembered how Liz had always looked like a tart, whatever she wore. The other mothers accepted her because they were a caring group, concerned with children and doing the best for them. They wouldn't accept her now. She had a provocative way of showing off her body, her hair was always uncombed. A cigarette in the corner of her mouth, she looked as though she'd just got out of bed. She had a contemptuous, selfish way of moving. But she was bright, her voice clear and precise, however much she'd drunk.

'Don't you remember meeting me?' said Kay.

'All I remember about that time is pushing Baby Dolly up the hill; the squeal of the pushchair wheels made my hangover intolerable. And there was a woman with a face like a pudding who accused me of sleeping with her husband.'

Liz then remembered the birthday parties and how the fathers came around to get their kids and drunken wives. 'I liked that bit. There was one I fancied a lot. Taught at the Poly. Brian or William – I didn't have an affair with him. I wished I had! That, I'm afraid, was a time of regrets. Although I looked as though I was doing it, I wasn't; for some incomprehensible reason I was faithful to Roly. And hasn't *that* paid off!'

'You don't remember Alexis?'

'No more memory lane please. Too depressing. You're always so reassuringly of the moment. We did used to drink a lot then, all of us.'

So Kay didn't put the story in her column. She didn't write to William Darby either. Other things took her interest. A London tragedy lasted half a day at most, and soon Kay too forgot.

On the spur of the moment Joel brought the head of the diagnostic division of the drugs department home for dinner to plot the downfall of their chief. Kay stood barefoot by the stove; she hadn't even had time to put on any make-up. All around her mixers whirred, blenders sloshed and shook, graters shredded and extractors squirted the juice of many vegetables. The dinner was unexpected and she literally whirred it together. The diagnostic director said it was one of the best he'd tasted – in London. Kay thought her beignets a little overfried. He disagreed – he adored Provençal specialities.

The spring night was cool so she lit a log fire. Although it was normal for Kay, the director was thrilled: how often did you find something real these days? She agreed with him that London had changed. She didn't like Sophie going to the pinball arcade in the high street. She liked Sophie to be in touch at all times.

'So you don't like London?' He wanted her to agree with him.

'I like my house and my life. But not the outside. Not as much as I did.' As Kay poured liqueurs she saw Roly leaving his house.

'Oh shit!' said Joel. 'He's coming in here. Has his television broken down?'

Roly was accompanied by a dark man with a leather jacket slung over his shoulder. He wore one small gold earring.

Roly came in first and murmured, 'I don't know what to do with him. I thought I'd better bring him over here. Liz is out, I don't know what to talk to him about.'

'Well who is he?' said Joel, expecting a mass-murderer.

'A gypsy.'

The man had a certain quiet arrogance.

'This is Angel Lupez. He's a flamenco dancer and guitarist. He's performing at the Festival Hall.'

Joel was amused. How had a gypsy got into Roly's house in the first place?

'Oh he's one of the very best. His people want me to do a programme on his show.' Roly lit a cigar. 'Liz is away so I had to – come over here.' He implied gypsies were a woman's sort of thing.

The diagnostics director was very impressed by Roly. One thing about Joel Craven's house – it was always stimulating. You wouldn't find the like of Roly in the chief's dining room. Just football stars and club sponsors.

Kay began putting fresh plates on the table. Roly said, 'I suppose you wouldn't have any of that mint sorbet: the one you make yourself?'

· *Four* ·

Kay hadn't noticed the gypsy. She'd served him the leftover soup that she'd prepared for the diagnostics director. He'd eaten hurriedly and mopped his plate with hunks of bread. She had not noticed his face because she didn't look at it. She couldn't remember him saying one word.

Roly held forth on falling house prices. He had a solution and he made it sound like splitting the atom. He used obscure words and his sentences were convoluted. Only Joel had the remotest idea what he was saying. The diagnostics director pretended to.

Kay said, 'Is this important Roly? It just sounds like someone trying to sell his house.'

'Oh, women,' said Roly. 'Why do they make everything so simple?'

'You know a lot about it,' said Kay as she laid out a spread of cheeses and cold meats. 'Are you thinking of selling yours?'

'He wasn't saying that, my sweet,' said Joel. 'If you'd been listening you'd know what he was saying.'

'I doubt it.' She wanted to include the gypsy in the conversation somehow but she wasn't sure gypsies lived in houses.

Roly then spoke more simply so women and gypsies could understand: 'House prices have fallen into the abyss of what has to be called political mismanagement. Thatcher could put a stop to it. All these people who shouldn't be together are stranded, literally chained together because they can't get rid of their house.'

'All? Perhaps just two.' Kay smiled sweetly. She sensed the gypsy was looking at her.

Joel said, 'People were too greedy. They asked too much, got it and blew up the market. The only hope is to sell to – '

'The Arabs?' said the diagnostics director with assurance.

'The Arabs haven't got money anymore,' Roly said energetically, as though addressing his TV audience. 'The Japanese.'

'Are you trying to tell us you're selling your house?' said Joel.

'No,' said Roly. 'But I'd hate to think I couldn't.'

When the gypsy had gone a fragrance lingered. It smelt better than aftershave. Kay thought it was an essence that he'd rubbed into his hair.

Joel locked the kitchen entrance and back door. 'Roly's got house sales on the brain. I presume Liz knows?'

'He doesn't sleep with her anymore.' Kay turned out the lights.

They climbed the narrow wooden stairs to their bedroom. Joel said, 'Roly spends his life watching himself on TV. That's how he gets his kicks now. We'll soon be the only couple left in this street.'

She put a hand over his mouth. 'Ssh! Don't give your luck away.'

Joel fell back across the bed and watched her taking off her clothes. 'You are so lovely. I noticed the way they look at you – other men. I noticed it especially tonight.'

She laughed and asked in what way.

'With reverence, Kay.'

He wanted her to get on top of him. She wasn't entirely in the mood and as they did it, this act which they'd performed and succeeded in making satisfactory thousands of times before, she looked out of the window. She noticed the moon, a mere slit of subdued silver in a busy sky. She thought how it was obliged to change its shape in monthly cycles, how female it was, the cause of much melancholy and speculation. The stirring in the trees against the windowpanes seemed important. For once she noticed things about a night that was usually shut out. She couldn't quite pin it down, this fascination with the obvious. She felt excited and it had nothing to do with the sexuality being provided by her husband.

'You didn't come,' he said. He turned her onto her back and made sure she did. Only her body was involved; her mind, most of the time, was alert and occupied with life on the other side of the window. Why were the moon and night sky so noticeable?

She thought about the gypsy. Someone had told him he had beautiful hands. She hadn't looked. She thought his name was Juan. She had not noticed that when he came in, the room seemed lighter.

The woman from the local mental hospital phoned before eight. 'You did get my letter?'

Kay said she had. All three letters.

'There's nothing wrong with me. You do see that?'

Kay had to admit she seemed sane enough.

'I'm phoning you before they change the staff. The day people are much more alert about phone calls. Can you help me?' She had a warm voice and Kay immediately liked her.

'I'll come and see you.'

'You're my only hope.' The woman sounded so relieved. 'God bless you.' The phone was disconnected abruptly.

Kay received many calls from readers asking for advice. Quite often women identified with what she'd written in her Sunday column or wanted to share an experience, or meet her personally. Occasionally a letter was abusive. Men invited her to dinner, their clubs or country estates (probably false). She was a goddess amongst other media women who were all too available. Occasionally her admirers put her on the track of a story.

The letter from the mental hospital had touched Kay. The woman was intelligent, perceptive and trapped, and every move she made only tightened the trap. Her family had had her hospitalised because of recurring incidents that were open to interpretation. The family had succeeded in persuading the authorities that their version was correct. There was a lot of self-interest involved. As far as Kay could see the woman was a victim of circumstance. Also she was too rich. Because she had resisted forcibly being hospitalised, and threatened suicide, she was held on Section Two. 'Who wouldn't want to get out one way or another if forced into such a hellish place?' she'd written to Kay. 'You don't have to believe me. But please could you just listen.'

Liz, still flushed from an aerobics session, came into the kitchen. Her cheeks were the same flame colour as her pink towelling tracksuit. 'You should always keep your door locked. Anyone could walk in.'

Kay shrugged. The world outside might not be safe but the inside of her house was.

'You should carry a gun that squirts a nerve-paralysing acid: get them before they get you.'

'Then I join them,' said Kay. 'Why should I become brutal?' She set out the paper, notebooks and typewriter and waited for Liz to go.

'Well you've got an admirer,' and Liz flopped onto a chair. She wanted breakfast, gossip, consolation.

'Who?' Kay sounded sharp, almost frightened.

'It's your cooking: men love women who cook. I don't want to be like you, cooking all the time. Every time Joel gets in from some high-powered meeting you've got to start a gourmet dinner, whatever time of day or night. He expects it. I've got to say, feminists have got something after all.'

'Who's the admirer?' Kay rolled sheets of paper interspersed with carbon into the machine.

'Roly, of course. Who did you think?' She looked longingly at the coffee percolator. 'Don't you ever see a guy you fancy? Come on, be honest.'

'Stop challenging me, Liz.' Kay was irritated.

'It's a serious question. Not a frivolous enquiry. I've thought a lot about you. How can you go on the same, with the same guy, year after year?'

'Because I adore him.' Kay stopped. 'It's more than that. With Joel I go through a sort of process of self-renewal, it doesn't get dull. I can't imagine our lives becoming stagnant. I'd never be unfaithful to Joel. No one could be better for me than him.'

Liz' eyes were narrow and predatory. Someone else's

happiness rarely did her any good. Snappily she said, 'Does Joel feel the same?'

'Ask him.' Kay typed the date and title of the article.

'I can tell he is a very good lover. Joel. But my God, an elitist.'

Kay knew that Liz was angry with Joel because she couldn't have him. Married men were supposed to be bored and available.

Liz got up unwillingly. 'Perhaps the ideal *is* the faithful couple after all.'

The phone rang. Would Kay appear on a live TV chat show? Only if she knew who the other guests were. The phone rang again. The Irish cleaner was ill and couldn't come in.

Liz stayed around waiting for the calls to end. 'Self-renewal for me would be a frequent change of scene and partner.'

She looked sulky and Kay supposed the dalliance with the French aristocrat wasn't going well.

'Liz, I do have to work. Is there anything – well, that I can do?'

'Just squash Roly.' Liz picked at the towelling cloth of her exercise suit, her eyes not meeting Kay's. She looked like a child in disgrace. 'He's trying to get me on some trumped-up adultery charge.'

'The Frenchman?'

'If you ask me, Roly set the whole thing up so he can grab everything: house, cottage, cars, assets, kids. Well, not the kids. He doesn't want *those*, oh no. Whereas he's playing around all the time and I never get one thing on him. Try and get some dirt, he talks to you. Stick his head in a rice pudding with lots of nutmeg and vanilla or whatever it is he likes so much over here.'

'Does he talk to you?'

'The only time he opens that mouth, which must be one of the busiest in the land, is to argue about money.'

'He was over here last night. Said you were out. Actually, he brought a Spaniard over – why?'

'Because he didn't know what to talk about. And Roly has to talk. Talk for him is like breathing is for us.'

'I don't want to get into it, Liz. People's domestic lives.'

Liz couldn't be scathing enough. 'But you're *always* in it.

That's what you make your money out of. Contemporary life-trends alias the women taking over so men can't get it on anymore.'

'Not my friends. I won't interfere. Sorry.'

'Well you're lucky. One of the lucky ones.'

She still didn't leave. How Kay wished the phone would ring.

'Don't you want to know what Roly caught me doing? With the Frenchman? It was in the kitchen and I was sitting up on the kitchen table eating some ice-cream. He told me how he loved my breasts; he wanted to look at them, he told me to take off my top. I could tell he'd been wanting to see them all evening. So I took my sweater off and he got a hard-on. He took it out and dipped it in the carton of whipping cream and rubbed it, rolled it over my breasts. It felt very exciting. It could have gone on to be very exciting indeed but Roly came in. Have you ever had that done to you?'

Unexpectedly Kay laughed.

When Liz had gone, Kay thought, yes, I am lucky. She's right. And I thank God for that. Nothing bad will ever happen to my marriage.

She phoned the hospital and asked why the woman who'd written to her was being kept on Section Two. The hospital was understaffed and the administrator's assistant looked at the patients' notes briefly.

'I can't give you any information. You're not a member of the family – '

'I am,' said Kay. 'I'm her cousin and she's written to me. The way she's been admitted seems irregular to say the least. She's asked for help. There's probably been some misunderstanding.'

'But she's an arsonist.'

'Fires happened around her. That's not quite being an arsonist – '

'On three occasions she has set fire to the room she was in. She could have caused a serious accident. Her daughter was trapped and had to jump from a window. On another occasion she was seen setting fire to a table.'

'Putting it out. She explains it in her letters.'

'As far as the doctors are concerned she's suffering from a mental illness and needs to be hospitalised. On a confined basis.'

'What illness?'

The assistant said Kay would have to visit the hospital personally and talk to the doctor in charge of the case. He only attended the patient's ward on a Wednesday. Kay insisted on making an appointment to see him immediately.

She sat at her typewriter. The phone rang continually and was picked up by the answering machine. Sophie clumped down the stairs, late for school. 'Nothing ever happens in this house,' she snarled. 'It's so boring.'

Kay asked for a kiss. Sophie replied with an expletive.

'That's boring,' said Kay, 'the way you speak. It's the most boring thing in this house. I think you should go to a private school. I'm going to insist – '

'I'm not making new friends. Not now. And there's drugs in those schools too. You can get drugs anywhere if you look for them. And Dad wants me to stay in the comprehensive.'

Joel believed in motivation. If a child wanted to do something, he would. A comprehensive school represented urban life and he saw it as a logical aquarium. Sophie would swim to the top and be stronger and better-muscled than if she'd been in a protective environment. He didn't put his son through it, Kay noticed.

She started typing.

'You never listen to me, Mum,' the girl shouted.

Kay stopped typing. Quite smoothly she said, 'I'm listening.'

'All Dad thinks about is outsmarting his boss. He thinks about it day and night and grinds his teeth. He never looks at me – not *really* looks. And you – you let all these creeps in. Don't you think I'm embarrassed to let my friends come in and see what you've got sitting at the table? I hate NW1 if you must know.'

'Where do you want to live?'

'NW5, obviously. That's where Rick lives. In a squat.'

'Rick?'

'Surely you haven't forgotten Rick? His mother killed herself last month. He's moved into a squat and I'm going with him.'

Before Kay could say anything Sophie stamped her foot and the forbidden earrings hidden behind her long hair jingled. 'It goes in, you churn it around and turn it out. Like meat going through a mincer.'

'What?'

'Life.' And she stormed from the house. The reverberation of the back door slamming made several things in the storeroom fall down. It used to be countries in *my* adolescence, thought Kay. We wanted to run off to Paris or South America. Now it's postal districts. But now, everywhere's the same.

Before she had finished typing the 2000-word obligatory Sunday article, the back door opened. First there was a gentle knock. Upstairs Joel's private line gave its piercing cheep, like a trapped bird. Footsteps sounded in the passage, but she took no notice. She smelt a fragrance: was it orange blossom? The gypsy was in the room but she, Kay, had to finish the last line. Then she turned off the typewriter and looked up. The gypsy leaned quite casually ·in the doorway. He said, 'I wanted to thank you for dinner last night.'

Kay gave him a smile, the one people told her was enigmatic. She was thinking about the article, how you had to catch the reader in the first twenty seconds. The obligatory twenty-second hook irritated her. The same rule applied to TV.

'I thought the way you flavoured your soup was unusual. You have a balance in the way you make things, it's wonderful.' He made the 'wonderful' sound like a caress.

She was surprised he knew so much about it. 'Do you cook then?' She tried to suppress the image of a rabbit in a pot on a camp fire.

'Just essential things.'

She thought the rabbit image was probably correct. She almost looked into his face, couldn't. It seemed forbidden. She shuffled the pages of her article and said, 'Are you – do you – I'm sorry, I don't know quite what you do.' All she knew was he came from Spain.

'I have my show on at the Royal Festival Hall – I'm on for five nights – I'm a flamenco performer.'

'Is it doing well?' she asked. She couldn't remember his name and wished she could be at ease.

'It's all right.' He sounded as though he were comforting her. He got up to leave.

'Thank you for calling. Please come round again, but phone first. Roly has my number.' And then she looked at his face. It was in shadow, as he backed along the passage to the door. She thought the shadow was deceiving her – no one looked that good. He smiled slightly, keeping his lips closed. He had a sensual, well-shaped mouth, the lips not large but beautiful and etched, fine, classical, almost perfect. The mouth was determined and showed he got what he wanted. She learned a lot from mouths. His eyes were dark and sombre and utterly still. They rested on hers and she felt the slightest sensation stir in her chest like a mild electric shock. His black hair was quite long and glossy. He wore a red knotted scarf. He waved, turned deftly, was gone. She watched him run up the steps to the gate. He had a physical attraction that was very obvious when he was still. Then when he made the smallest movement he was riveting.

Quickly she looked at the entertainments page of the newspaper. All right? He was doing better than all right. He was the sensation of London. Angel Lupez, the greatest flamenco artist in the world. More than just all right. The show had been a sell out. He was a master of the understatement.

She stayed at the typewriter, just sitting, still hearing the sound of his feet going light and fast to the door. He had an optimistic walk. She hoped he would not visit again.

· *Five* ·

The consultant wasn't free to see her. The duty doctor was prepared to look up the woman's file. Kay still claimed to be a cousin.

'All I want is to be sure. It seems her daughter is responsible for admitting her – '

'We admitted her. She's suffering from a mental illness.'

Kay asked its name.

'Paranoid schizophrenia.'

'You wouldn't be at *your* best if you were committed against your will and no one believed your story – '

He put away the file.

'It's a nightmare,' Kay insisted.

'I think we can tell the difference between paranoid schizophrenia and a nightmare.'

Kay asked if she had a history of the illness. He said they'd not uncovered anything so far. 'We haven't got her early notes. It's probably been there since adolescence, it often starts then. Sometimes it may not recur for years.'

'So what will I see so I will know she's ill.'

'What do you know about this illness?' the doctor asked.

'Persecution, violence, hallucinations, delusions of grandeur –'

'Look out for those. Delusions of grandeur.'

Kay thought he was mocking her because she was wasting his time. She didn't have the usual modest manner of a relative. He was called to an emergency and Kay gave up waiting for him.

The day room was full. Only in a mental hospital perhaps were people so diverse. Only the disturbed could be so individual Kay thought. They were able to take their personalities to the furthest point and beyond. But Sarah Prince was different. Kay could see that as soon as she came in.

She looked younger than forty-nine. In fact there wasn't a line on her face and she could have been any age. Her strong fair hair was layered and casual, she had good skin and an attractive face with a charm and energy that reminded Kay of women in French cafés. She looked gamin, French, could have been an artist or art student. Strangely she seemed very alive.

The first thing she did was apologise for the way she looked. They'd taken away her clothes and shoes and she wore a cotton hospital gown. Her voice was soft, intimate. There wasn't a hint of madness, not in her expression, her manner or what she said.

'I read your column every Sunday. You should be a politician.' She spoke quickly.

Kay almost laughed.

'I'm serious. You care about things and you've got good ideas. And the courage to come out with them.'

Kay said she was glad to hear that. 'I would have brought you something but I didn't know what – what you need.'

'To get out,' she whispered. 'I can't bear it in here.'

Kay offered her a cigarette. The simple act drew every eye in the room. There was a stampede to reach Kay. She gave the cigarettes out. The patients who hadn't been able to get one stayed very close to Kay. She said, 'I'm sorry I haven't got any more, perhaps you could ask someone else?' She struck a match and lit Sarah Prince's cigarette.

'I can do it myself.' Sarah took the box of matches. Nothing could have moved faster than the nurse towards that box. She gave it back to Kay.

'Now, Sarah, you've got your cigarette. Be a good girl.' She indicated that Kay should put the matches away.

'I used to worry about lung cancer,' said Sarah. She laughed bitterly. 'Not in here. Everything's relative. They tell me if you're mentally sick you don't know where you are or what's happening.

· 31 ·

You just don't know. But I am aware of everything. Some days I long to go mad so I don't know, I don't see.'

She seemed so soft and broken. Anna held her hand and said, 'You hang on. We'll sort it out.'

'I'm not even allowed outside into the grounds now. They're not going to let me out. It's all a mistake, terrible. I've been to the registrar, the administrator, the district medical officer. You read my letters. It's all to do with the money. I get a quarter of a million when the family trust is dissolved in the summer. My daughter wants the money. Finding out she hated me was a terrible shock – that she'd go this far, tell these lies. I still can't believe she'll go on with it but – '

Kay waited. Sarah Prince was looking down, trying to decide. 'It's her or me. She's a heroin addict. She's twenty-four and needs that money.'

'Have you told them here that she's on drugs?'

Sarah shook her head. 'I can't do that to her. Her boyfriend, that's his front – he's really her pusher, is putting ideas into her head after the fire in my kitchen, and that happened because the chip pan caught fire and of course throwing water on the flames instead of putting a lid on was crazy; what had been one foot high became six feet high. The second fire was at my aunt's house up north. She had one of those old-fashioned tea services on wheels – is that what you call them? She placed it too near the fire and the legs scorched. I tried to put it out but I always seem to make things worse when I try. The sofa caught and all the furniture that belonged to my – and the fire brigade came.' Sarah sighed. 'She was my father's sister.' She stuttered slightly on 'father'. 'It was his stuff. He always had a lot of stuff. Even though it was up north *they* heard about it. The third fire *they* started – '

'They?'

Sarah Prince looked at Kay, disappointed. 'Yes, *they*. My daughter and her boyfriend. It got completely out of hand and I was burned. They got the doctor to call in a shrink and they said all sorts of things about me. Of course at the time I was distraught. They nearly burn your house down and murder you, how are you going to behave? And I was terrified of them. They said it was because I was sick. They turned everything around. Then they planted certain things in my room: paraffin, lighter fuel, fire lighters. They let my GP find them and he put me in here so I wouldn't do "it" again. And I know what's going on: she's taken over. She's my executor and she'll get everything. Of course I sound crazy sometimes. The situation makes you crazy.'

Kay liked her. She was being open, even if it showed her at a disadvantage. Kay said she'd get help. She would go to the right people.

'Will you get me out?'

Now Sarah looked panicky and pale. Kay stopped by the door. She could see into the canteen and the food had the smell and colours of her worst nightmares. The dark brown of the gelatined gravy would look better as shoe polish. The pastry on the fruit tart had a ruched design and came up in points like Plantagenet hats. Kay averted her eyes from the overcooked vegetables. Canteen food always upset her, she distrusted the green of those beans.

Sarah came up behind her and asked if anything was wrong.

'How do you know they started the fire in your house?'

'They rewired a plug so it was faulty and caused a fire. That's why I went around afterwards and took out all the plugs. They said that it was a sign.'

'You must come from a wealthy family to have this trust fund.'

'Well yes, I do.' She sounded ashamed. 'Yes I do.'

Kay said gently, 'You don't have to tell me. It's not my business.'

'It's not where you're from, it's who you are.'

Kay couldn't see any 'delusions of grandeur'. A quarter of a million wasn't excessive these days. Roly would call that a slump price if he was offered it for his house.

Kay was determined to see the administrator. If necessary she'd wait all afternoon. If she left now, who knew what would come up urgently? An interview with a dying politician, the AIDS campaign, lunch with a movie star who wanted to meet her;

Sophie's problems and Sarah Prince and her plight would recede. Sarah Prince would be lost in madness. Kay saw enough of the patients to sympathise completely with the woman's desire to leave. In such an atmosphere of disquiet you never knew what would happen next. A woman suddenly started screaming and banging her head with fury against the corridor wall. An old man wandered up and down not knowing, not there; his body continued to function but he, like a raggy bird, had long since flown the nest.

Kay looked away from the horror of the head-banging woman and covered her ears. Sitting at the very end of the ward she felt terrified, sad and exhausted. How did the staff manage?

Assaulted on all sides by the horrors that life could throw up, she no longer believed in the idea of continuing normality. Steps should be taken, preventative measures. Why expect life would go on as it usually did? Only a smug fool would think that. She needed to do something active to strengthen her resolve to be normal – meditation, prayer, life-affirming thoughts. She thought Liz had sense. She made sure she laughed. Liz was as good an example of survival as anyone she knew.

A well-dressed man in a pinstriped suit told Kay he was dealing with her case. She was fooled and thought he was the administrator; she started on her problems. 'You'll get used to it.' He patted her kindly. It seemed after all you *could* tell the pretend doctors from the doctors – the real ones never had any time. She found a nurse and asked how much longer she'd have to wait.

'He knows you're here,' said the nurse and sped past.

By the time Kay got into the administrator's office she felt shaken and stressed. It was worse than that: she felt her very being was torn and in rags. She wanted to howl with grief, run with fear, defend herself, throw up, attack God for letting such suffering exist.

The administrator gave her five minutes. He didn't have time for journalists unless they were interested in the staff shortages, lack of beds and the threatened hospital closure.

'Do you know how many letters Sarah Prince has sent?' he asked.

Kay was taken aback. She hadn't thought of that.

'To media people, celebrities, the church, MPs. Most people disregard them as outbursts from a sick woman.'

'I was the one who listened,' said Kay.

'Listen all you want, Mrs Craven, but at the end of the day you're going to find she is as diagnosed, and a danger to herself and others. We have to keep her in.'

'Perhaps you're in it too.' Kay realised that this sounded inappropriate in such a place. Quickly she corrected herself. 'Perhaps you've been persuaded by the unfortunate coincidences and the attitude of the family. Apparently the daughter has a lot to gain if her mother's hospitalisation is made permanent.'

'I don't approve of journalists pretending to be patients' cousins but I can see you've been sucked into a woman's desperate attempt to get out. A lot of the patients think they shouldn't be here. Don't waste your time.'

'I think she's logical and very clear.'

'Thank you, Mrs Craven. It means the medication's working.'

'You won't object if I have her case re-examined? If I bring in an independent psychiatrist?'

He gestured total acceptance. 'We don't need to keep well people here. We haven't got enough beds for the sick.'

As Kay left the building, several patients gathered around her. 'Please take me with you,' said one. 'I won't be any trouble.'

Another said, 'I'm allowed out, so just give me a lift to the North Circular will you?'

Kay experienced a definite moment of apprehension. But Sarah Prince looked sane, smelled sane. As Kay saw it she was the victim of a conspiracy and it was up to Kay to get her out before she became too damaged. She'd act for her because happiness made her generous. As Liz had said, she was one of the lucky, and she'd share that with those who weren't.

· Six ·

Once a week Kay made a batch of bread using real brewers' yeast which she got from a baker's off Camden Market. She was a traditional cook and disliked taking short cuts. Only real ingredients and pure flavours were allowed. Into her mixture she added a teaspoon of olive oil which gave the loaves a slightly holed texture, a little like Italian bread. The smell of the baking would, on occasion, cause Roly to stand in the street and stamp his feet with joy. For a change she sometimes made milk bread or huge farmhouse loaves, crisscrossed on the top or plaited, that belonged in a harvest festival. Kay's baking was a celebration of life.

Joel watched her put the last baking tins into the oven as he tasted an asparagus mousse. 'The way you cook you ought to be married to a millionaire.' He was off to a conference in Paris.

She asked if he knew the procedure for getting a committed patient reassessed.

'Try the BMA, her GP or ask your editor.'

'It's not for publication.'

'Roly should know. He knows everything. He's given us tickets for the flamenco show at the – '

Kay declined immediately.

'These tickets are hard to get. It's a sell-out.'

'Take Sophie.'

'But Roly said it's worth seeing. Phenomenal, that was his word. Not a Roly word is it?'

So she said she didn't have time to go.

'He was here the other night. He didn't say much. But then

performers are often unexciting off stage,' Joel said. He held her tightly and promised what he'd do with her when he got back from France. Her body flared in anticipation. She readjusted his shirt collar and tie, not because it needed changing but because she wanted her hands on him, owning him. With this man she felt complete intimacy. His flesh belonged to hers. They could do anything to each other. She wanted to go on touching him, to keep her hands on him, but he reached across to the table for his overnight case. His movements were all deft and sure. He was a tactile man and his hands – how they could give pleasure. He saw they way she was looking at him. 'Not now,' he said.

'You can't go like that, with a hard-on.'

But nothing, not even sex would keep him from the business jungle. She watched him leave the kitchen. He was power-packed, agile, sometimes graceful, and he moved silently, not unlike a big cat. He moved as though he enjoyed being in his body. He opened the back door, then turned and mouthed the words, 'I need you.' There was nothing more to say. They'd both said it, all of it, dozens of times. He'd told her he couldn't be with someone else. His reasons were selfish: someone else would change his view of sex, make his performance different. It would alter the chemistry between Kay and him. He found their intimacy so compelling he didn't want to lose it. It was his own pleasure he was protecting.

She took out the first batch of bread and tapped each loaf, waiting for that satisfying hollow ring which meant it was baked. Then she stacked it to cool. She kept the week's supply in the freezer and used a loaf a day. Their friends took the rest.

Why did she care about Sarah Prince? Because she'd hate to feel trapped, without choice, it was her worst fear. Sarah Prince had written to her MP, her church, various smart London clubs and the BBC – even Roly had received a letter. It seemed inconceivable to Kay that in the twentieth century a woman could be shut away in an institution for material gain. All that belonged in the ignorance of centuries past.

Liz brought over some samples of a new French beauty range.

· 37 ·

'I got them from my healthclub. They're the best you can get. So pure, if they were one degree purer they'd have to be on prescription. That's the sales pitch. Some of the treatment creams cost a fortune. Have all of them, I can get as many as I want. I simply say they're for you.'

Liz sniffed deeply. 'Always cooking. Those suffragettes did have a point: why should you slave away making his meals.'

'I like cooking,' said Kay.

'No you don't. You do it because men find it attractive. They love women who cook. In fact, they think it's a sign of being a real woman. I'm always having it thrown in my face. Prepacked quickies, takeaways, I don't know how to please a man etc. But be careful it doesn't turn you into just another mother-figure. You'll have every weakling at your door.'

'I had the gypsy at my door.'

'Oh he's spoken for. They're all after him according to Roly. He doesn't need a mummy.'

'What do you think of him?' asked Kay casually.

'Me? I haven't seen him. His impresario's been round. I saw him. He's after Roly to give his flamenco show the top Sunday slot. Why? Is he attractive?'

Kay changed the subject quickly. 'If cooking is such a turn on, why don't you do it? You do everything else.'

'For those men! English men! They don't even like women. They stand at parties unsmiling, uninterested, two-dimensional, up and down like cardboard cut-outs. Cook for them? Listen Kay, I've got a superb pair of tits and I'm good-looking and I like to eat out and be paid for. I've been looking at a map – that's my in-house activity: I'm looking for the right place. Well, you know I'm going to leave him before he leaves me. The flight fund is ripe to bursting and I'm off. A new life. Where there are real men. Of course my lawyer wants me to start proceedings because of Roly's playing around. But that's a depressing business and I don't think I'll get anything on him. And he's definitely got the French count on me. But he's got to cough up for those kids.'

· 38 ·

Kay, for once, didn't know what to say; Roly and Liz seemed so discontented and each blamed the other. 'What if it's a mistake?'

'That's weak talk, Kay. I'm strong now. I'm strong enough for it not to be a mistake whatever I choose to do. There's a lot I want to do.'

And Kay thought Liz would be better off on her own. She'd brought up her kids and stayed loyal to Roly, then his success had changed everything, threatened her. So she'd gone back into herself, built up her spirit, stamina and bank account and planned to leave. However unhappy he made her, the plan acted like a salve. In some ways, out of all those mothers that used to wait outside the primary school, Liz, without seeming to, had changed the most.

The next morning the cleaner had an infected toe so Kay went out to get the household shopping. As she wheeled the shopping basket across the high street she saw a blind woman in a smart coat also walking across to the opposite pavement. Kay didn't know whether to help her: was she better left to her own instincts? Kay watched her. She had trust. How rare that was. Kay decided some people were looked after and some weren't.

When she got back, Liz, in her early-hour tracksuit, was reading the notes on Sarah Prince. 'Why get tied up in all that?'

'I hate injustice.' Kay left the basket unpacked. She thought the cleaner's toe would hardly prevent her putting the shopping away. Wrong. An Irish voice said, 'I can't stand on it, Kay. It all has to be sitting down today.' She turned on the Hoover. Irritated, Kay left the basket where it was.

Liz quickly read the letters. 'You'll have to get all sorts of people in. It's a long exhausting business. Could we have some breakfast? I could bring over some Spanish sausage that gypsy left.'

'Sarah Prince is as sane as I am. Why should she be shut away in there? Greed. They want her money. It's not a far cry from Roly, is it? He'd do just about anything to get what he wants. Hearing him talk reminds me of that woman's daughter.'

'If you get the feeling he's trying to put me away, let me know. With any luck the commercial channels will put *him* away. He went on live to talk about Verdi and thought for one wild moment he was meant to be on about Italian cooking. He can't get food out of his mind; it's living opposite you. He wormed his way out of that one – just. Strings of spaghetti, octaves of opera; he makes it sound all the same anyway.'

'He does,' said the cleaner. The Hoover was off. 'I can't understand a word he says.'

'It's only a matter of degree,' said Kay, 'all of it . . . Crime, madness, destruction. We're safe because we never go to the edge: Roly might think of putting someone away but he wouldn't actually do it.'

'I know Roly automatically comes to mind when one talks about zeal but what about your husband? He's pretty merciless in the ring. It's no secret he wants to take over "Drugs inc". He'll be grabbing Roche next. You thought you married a well-educated executive, content to excel in a specialist area, but you married a magnate in embryo.'

Kay stirred the kedgeree and gave Liz a plateful. She cut bread, poured freshly-squeezed orange juice. The coffee was percolating. They sat down to breakfast. Liz thought Kay was one of the few cooks who enjoyed her own food.

Again Liz asked about Sarah Prince. 'I think you're making a mistake. Why do it?'

'Because no one cares about anybody else. We step over people dying in the street. It's getting like New York here. People don't want to know, don't want to be involved. It's a backward step, all of it, and it means this is a city in trouble: I'm all right, my corner's nice.'

'They ought to ban television.' The cleaner winked at Kay. 'Then people would have to speak, and go out.'

'People don't get involved,' said Liz, 'because it takes too much time. And if you're a witness the police give you too much hassle. It's easier to walk away. Let the ones who get paid for it deal with it.'

· 40 ·

'So you wouldn't stop to help someone lying in the road?'

Liz could see Kay was angry. She'd never seen her so over-sensitive. She was turning into a *quasi* Jesus.

'In Camden Town? Of course I wouldn't. There's so many lying down out there, sometimes I'm the only one standing up. I'd like it better if I thought you were doing all this to look good. Why don't you go on television and support the NHS and get something out of it?'

Kay gathered up the letters and held them away from Liz.

'If you take her on it's a relationship,' said Liz. 'You'll have her living with you next. You know the rule, Roly told you: if you answer their letters never give a home address; never agree to see them, they'll be on your doorstep; never let them in, you'll never get them out.'

Kay could hear the cleaner punctuating the sentences with savage grunts of agreement.

'What about that singer you were going to do a piece on? What was her name? She sang "Inner City Blue". She killed herself. You remember – you were going to write about her.' Liz tried to sing the tune.

'Oh yes,' said Kay. 'I was going to write to her husband.' She couldn't remember his name.

'You always get involved then you cut off.'

'Liz, that's what a journalist does, surely? You can't carry all that suffering in your head.' She felt guilty that she hadn't written to the singer's husband. Darby, William Darby. It was over a month since the suicide.

Kay thought of Sarah Prince in the hospital ward, wandering up and down, shoeless, with the hospital stamp visible like an ad, front and back, on her official nightgown. There was only death or acceptance, unless you kept fighting. Sarah was getting tired; Kay, because she was free and had the luxury of choice, would take over for her.

· *Seven* ·

The GP was honest and the first to break: with Kay's help he found he had doubts, and she quickly uncovered them. 'Of course, Sarah's disturbed state of mind could have resulted from the fires themselves. The last one badly burned her house and could have killed her daughter.'

'She says the daughter started the fire.'

'Then she could have chosen a lower window to jump from. She was hospitalised for ten days.'

'Perhaps to add weight to her allegations,' said Kay.

'The daughter said she'd shown signs of a personality disturbance for some time. Which came first? The fires or the illness? Is that what you're asking?'

'What can you do?'

'I'll have a word with the registrar, get his opinion. He's a good chap.'

'Did you see Sarah Prince before?'

He said he had, on occasion, and she'd seemed quite normal. Kay asked about the trust but he knew nothing about that. She asked what the daughter was like and was surprised to hear she was a social worker.

'So what she said would be taken seriously.'

'Oh look, she might be able to spot symptoms in her mother that other people wouldn't notice, but she has no power once her mother is admitted.'

'Could it happen that Sarah Prince was put away mistakenly?'

'Well, it could . . .' He hated saying that. 'But the mistake would soon be realised. When I saw her she was definitely in need of psychiatric assessment.'

'Perhaps because she found out her daughter hated her! Wanted her shut away. That's terrible.' Kay shivered. 'That would make her lose control. She admits that.' Kay showed him the second letter. He glanced at one page.

'The most disturbed patients can appear sane if they're about to be put into a mental hospital.'

'What about the daughter's boyfriend?'

He looked at Kay, dumbfounded, and she wondered if she'd offended him.

Kay didn't mention the daughter's drug habit. Drugs like viruses were the true democrats. They went everywhere.

The early May sunlight seemed to go on forever, slanting in at Kay as she sat at the table, taunting her, not letting her work, wanting her outside. She was writing an article on living in London for a glossy magazine, but memories of the visit to the mental hospital cut across any dainty pictures of nearby Regent's Park. She saw only the woman banging her head against the wall, the sound of those screams was not too forgettable either. She thought mental illness was like broken glass – you saw life through a jagged, shattered pane. Kay supposed she should be sitting, head in her hands, weeping for the lost and desolate, but once on home ground she was optimistic. The atmosphere soothed her, gave a respite from the world. Her house had a rare quality – peace, and although she spent nights on her own she was never frightened. The house was like a good parent, even visitors felt its influence. They felt at ease, able to speak openly, their appetite improved; they left as though healed. Even Joel's edgy, clever talk didn't spoil it. A guest had once told Kay the house had been blessed and Joel remembered finding a crucifix in one of the cupboards shortly after they'd moved in.

She thought she should make some phone calls, decide whether to appear on the live TV show, prepare Sophie's dinner, but she did none of it. A sudden joyous urge sent her out into the

street. The evening sunlight had the innocence she remembered as a child and she felt young and excited. She turned the
corner into the market. Even her body felt different; her legs
strong, as though they could walk great distances effortlessly,
her stomach flat, the rest light as though set for some splendid
adventure. She wanted to buy some flowers, some token to
mark the moment. Unexpected happiness – it had come out of
nowhere – was rare. Along the side of the stalls the gypsy
walked towards her, his bag slung across his shoulders like a
slain animal. She wanted to run away – there was still time – but
she stayed her ground. Kay Craven had survived everything in
life. Except ecstasy.

As he approached she looked into his face with its classically
beautiful features. He was good-looking. No, it was better than
that: there was nothing weak or self-indulgent or sentimental in
this man, she saw it at a glance, but there was a touch of
bitterness. Did he know it showed? He held himself beautifully,
with a natural grace, unstudied, not like a professional dancer.

The gypsy said he was going to Roly's house because they were
going to do a TV film on gypsy flamenco and its origins. His voice
was harsh and sometimes faded away or broke as though he had a
sore throat. She said something about the film being a sure thing
because flamenco was very popular.

'Not flamenco: gypsy flamenco. That is what I do.' He
suddenly smiled at her. A front tooth was broken. His nostrils
were flared. He was the sort of man never to fall in love with. His
eyes lit up as he spoke, telling her about a gypsy song. How a man
went to the city and met a golden-haired woman. She was beyond
price. But he had captured her with his songs and gypsy magic.
He could never take her back to his family because his people
wouldn't accept her, and hers would never accept him.

'So what did they do?' Kay said.

'They used to meet every week at the market.' He indicated
the stalls around them.

'You're making that up,' she accused him.

'Why?' He exaggerated the word playfully. 'The song has been in my family for generations. They couldn't be together. It was a blood thing.'

Again she couldn't look into his face and it infuriated her. Why couldn't she meet his eyes? As though guilty, she said, 'I'm very busy.'

He made an attractive gesture as if to say, who isn't? 'Where are you going?'

'I came out to buy some cigarettes,' and she gestured towards the pub opposite. How she resented the intrusion of this man, his attractiveness.

'Would you like a drink?' And he was in her life.

When they got to the pub she realised she had left the house on a happy impulse which had not required money. He bought the cigarettes and knew she'd told a lie. She was upset because from now on, for always, the happy free moment she'd experienced would always be associated with him. He'd simply walked into it, become part of it.

'You speak very good English,' she said.

'So do you.' As he reached across for the ashtray, she could smell the fragrance. It was on his skin, his jacket, not necessarily something he applied. Some people had a naturally strong smell. He was fortunate that his was so evocative. She thought he would talk about the show, its success, but instead he asked about her. 'They tell me you're a very well-known person.'

'They?'

'Roly, and I've heard it since. You have your own column yet you don't have the usual availability of journalists. They have to be available to get information, surely?'

'I'm not a reporter in that sense. I write my view of what's happening. Or about a situation that interests me. It's personal. I choose my subject.'

'Yes I can see that.' He asked questions about her everyday life but she said little. Then she asked why he was walking.

'A star like you should have a chauffeur-driven car to take you to Roly's. You're not getting what you should!'

'Oh yes I am,' he said. 'I am.' Now his eyes were on hers. They were certainly marvellous eyes, full of delight. In fact they filled with delight like a child's. They were almost black eyes, the whites slightly blue.

The sunlight, like an obstinate child, still played in the street, flickering against the windows.

'I like to walk and know the city I'm in,' he said. 'You don't get to know much in a chauffeur-driven car.' He finished his drink and stood up. So Kay finished hers quicker than she'd have liked and they walked towards Roly's house. Usually a man waited for her to finish a drink and asked if she wanted another before leaving. She didn't see Angel's rush to leave as a sign of rudeness, just something he was used to – when he finished drinking so did the woman.

They stopped by Kay's gate. She said, 'What did you mean when you said, yes I can see that? We were talking about my choosing my subjects, remember?'

'You have choice. That's what I meant. Or you seem to.'

'I do,' she assured him. 'Not about what happens, but the way I see what happens.'

'Quite a deep lady, then?'

She couldn't tell how the remark was meant and she certainly wouldn't ask. A neighbour passed and greeted Kay. She looked twice at the gypsy. Kay thought he was worth a second look. In her whole life she'd never seen such a marvellous face. 'I must come and see your show.'

'Be quick, because I am not going to do more than eight more performances. I have to go to Paris, then New York. And I have to be back in Seville for fiesta. Tell me which day you want to come and I will leave you a ticket. Two tickets.' He sounded very practical.

Then he smiled at her and she smiled back. There was no particular reason to smile. Again she felt that happiness, that had driven her into the street in the first place. It needed some expression. If she could dance, sing, she would have. On impulse she said, 'If you want, I'll cook you something. I've got to feed my daughter. It won't be much. Or perhaps you'd prefer to eat with Roly and – '

'I'll eat with you and pretend to eat with him.'

· *Eight* ·

The gypsy stayed by the open French windows with his face to the sun while she placed dark mats on the pinewood kitchen table. Kay poured him a strong gin and vermouth and asked him to choose a wine from the rack in the storeroom. Effortlessly she put out the hors d'oeuvres. They agreed the sun was staying longer than usual, that it was an odd kind of day. There was a definite smell of adventure in the air.

'I like your house,' he said. 'It accepts me. I feel at home here.' He opened the wine.

She thanked him as though he were paying her a compliment.

'I mean the house, Kay. Not you.' He laughed.

It was the first time he'd said her name – she felt valued. She didn't, however, want to acknowledge the feeling or think about it. She decided not to bother with the meal she'd planned but keep all her attention on her guest; she'd whisk up a few omelettes.

'It's a big house. How many people live here?'

She told him.

'So you're here on your own most of the time?'

'I love being on my own.'

'So do I,' he said.

She put an asparagus mousse into dishes and asked if he still lived in Andalusia.

'Of course. Where else?'

'The first thing people do when they become successful is to leave home. Putting an instant separation between yourself and the past seems to be a prerequisite of fame.'

He turned away and she knew he was laughing at her.

'The famous go and look for the house of their dreams,' she continued.

'I don't have to look.'

She loved the way he touched the cat, his hands moving, caressing. She sliced the bread. 'Why are you laughing at me? Just now you were.'

'You got all tangled up with what you were trying to say. All those long words. I'm not sure about prerequisite. You start one of those long clever people's sentences and you're not sure how it ends.'

Roly had told her that. On TV, keep the sentences short. 'You seem to know about languages.'

'I know about rhythms, cadences. I can feel when a phrase is getting out of control. I imagine you don't write the way you speak?'

She said the two things weren't the same. He said, 'You tune in to another part of yourself and another voice comes out. I expect you're – caustic.'

Kay was surprised.

'You seem so harmonious in your house, your everyday thoughts. There would not seem to be much to write about there. So the other voice doesn't live in the house exactly.'

And yet he wasn't criticising her. 'Caustic. You know a lot of words – ' She nearly called him Juan.

'I love words. That's why. And my name is Angel.'

Did he read minds too? 'I thought your name was Juan. That's how you made it sound when we were introduced.'

'Angel. Arn – hell.' He taught her how to say the name so he was satisfied with it.

Instead of calling Sophie, she sat near him by the French windows. 'So you have a beautiful caravan?'

He laughed. 'House.'

'And it's beautiful?'

'Not especially. It's where I was born. I will always live there.'

Everything that happened in the kitchen had an importance:

· 49 ·

the cat moving, clock ticking, Aga gleaming. Life had put Kay on stage. It was her turn.

'I feel as though I've known you all my life,' he said.

And all the years with Joel were just stripped away. All the dark sexuality and desire extinguished, like snuffing out a candle. The pot on the stove fizzed sensationally in warning, and the clock ticked like gunfire.

Now Kay could really look at him she felt light and fizzy as though her body had turned to sherbert, all effervescent and thrilling. She was no longer restrained by human functions but like a character in a fairytale. 'I really do feel strange. As though my flesh has changed to sugar. It must be something to do with the day. It's been odd.' She got up and blamed the sky for her happiness.

His hand was near her wrist and she thought he was going to grasp it. She waited. When he didn't touch her she went quickly to the stairs and shouted for Sophie. And then it occurred to her that he'd spiked her drink. She went to the stove, to safety. He followed her.

'So you think gypsies live in caravans and travel all over the place?' he said.

'Well, yes, I did. That's what I hoped. Don't they take to the road? Go where they like? They're free.'

'Without wishing to kill off any dreams, Kay, you are more free than we are. Everyone has their own idea of a gypsy.'

Be careful, she thought. Calm actions, deep breathing. Think of something else. Since when has this body felt full of sherbert? And why am I so happy? He's tipped an acid tab into my beer. But of course I'm afraid to feel too happy. Isn't everyone? 'Do you like English food, Angel?' She sounded tough.

'I haven't had any.' He watched her swiftly core and stuff the large apples. He opened the oven door. Before putting them in she added more sugar. 'What they serve in restaurants isn't exactly English and sometimes not food. I hate powdered soups. But there are places where the fish and chips are good. I like eel pie.'

She didn't want to call Sophie again. She wanted to stay with the gypsy.

'So tell me about yourself, Kay.'

He stood close to her and again she could smell the fragrance; his clothes were full of it. He seemed taller than he was but that was because he held himself well. His body was taut, his thighs and buttocks tight. Yet when he sat down he was as relaxed as a cat. He'd make love well. Superbly. It was just there a part of him, something he had been born with.

'English people usually say, tell me *all* about yourself.'

'I expect you mystify them,' he said.

'Why?'

'You seem so receptive.' His voice changed, became sharper, 'And yet you're not.' He reached across her so their arms touched and took some bread. 'Have you any olive oil? And a large tomato?'

She couldn't move. He didn't move. They stayed as they were. If she didn't watch it the next movement could only be a caress. Quite wildly she went to the stairs and shouted for her daughter.

He'd noticed her agitation. 'This house is – *muy simpatico*. It's impossible to translate into English.'

She gave him a large tomato and a bottle of Italian olive oil and he sat at the head of the table. He poured olive oil onto a hunk of bread, smeared it with tomato, sprinkled salt generously and ate as though it were his last meal on earth. She stayed by the stove as he poured some wine. 'I'd be a disappointment to you.'

She was shocked. 'In what way exactly?'

'We live in houses. We have HP and savings accounts, televisions and pension schemes. We're more bourgeois than you.'

Kay laughed.

'Of course, I don't tell that to everyone. It would kill off the romance.' He gave a small private smile.

'I won't write about it, don't worry.'

In spite of what he said and how he seemed, he was sensual, full of colour, he loved variety and he was wise. He belonged to the night. He walked across deserts. He knew life's little secrets and its big tricks, he saw behind death. He could be wild. She knew him – absolutely.

She broke the eggs for an omelette. She got a skillet and while it was heating she beat the eggs with a balloon whisk, added black pepper, chopped herbs. He watched her make the omelette. The underneath cooked immediately and she drew the omelette edges into the middle; the outside formed a crust and with the omelette still runny in the middle she served it.

'You serve it while it's not cooked?' He was puzzled.

'It goes on cooking in its own heat.' She put a warmed plate in front of him and sat down with hers. He poured some wine, she passed the bread, the salad. She'd forgotten about Sophie.

'So where is your bourgeois house?' she said.

'Originally my family came from Triana. But they threw us out.' He offered her some olives. 'It was the gypsy quarter for ages.' .

She asked where Triana was and he described it as a neighbourhood of Seville. 'I remember my grandfather singing in Triana. He was – beyond measure.' His voice was almost a whisper. 'Flamenco would break out in the streets between one moment and the next and we'd dance all night. We'd dance and sing with high glorious energy, a song from here to heaven, and when they threw us out my grandfather had to live in a soulless tenement. He said it was his punishment for singing as gloriously as an angel. He said to go back to Triana he would willingly cut off the fingers of his hand.' Angel held up three fingers. 'My grandfather's voice could drive you to ecstasy, it could draw out your very spirit, it was so hypnotic and dangerous.'

Kay thought his voice, just speaking, was a little like that; it took you with it, carried you along on the story. She listened like a child, with rapt attention.

'I lived in Utrera, a village near Seville. I am gypsy from every possible side of my family, to the core. When a gypsy sings out it cannot be bettered. So listen . . .' He paused. She knew he was going to do something sensational, and her mouth opened slightly, waiting.

Then Sophie stomped in. 'What the fuck is going on?'

The girl's entrance jarred Kay and shocked her back from the world Angel was creating. The slap she gave was automatic. Sophie, hurt, yelled and the magic was quite gone. Suddenly furious Kay turned to her daughter. 'Don't you *ever* speak like that!'

Sophie eyed the stranger; he didn't look like a school inspector. She ungraciously dragged out a chair. 'You've heard "fuck" before – I say it enough. You said dinner was ready. Well, where is it? Don't say you've torn me away from *Top of the Pops* for nothing.'

Kay hit her again.

'But it's Rick Darby's début, for crissake! Can't you see I'm emotional? I've just seen him playing drums in front of the whole country.' She kicked her chair over.

Angel moved quickly; he picked the chair up and sat the girl in it firmly. 'So you like Rick Darby?'

'Did I say that?' Sophie turned on him, her eyes huge and blazing.

'So what about Michael Jackson, or is he all over now?' He went through a list of famous popstars, then the less famous as Sophie watched him suspiciously; this wasn't the usual kitchen-talk. Sophie chose one of the names and challenged him. 'So what do you think?'

Angel shrugged. 'I think he's all right, but not great.'

Sophie made a strange noise – it was approval. 'I've found a friend: I'm the only one in my entire school that doesn't think he's from another place. I mean he does it with the hair and the image but – '

'He's not a star,' said Angel.

Kay placed a new omelette, small and neat, in front of Sophie and gave her a measure of salad.

'Where's the chips?'

Kay stared at her, another slap on its way.

'No, I mean it, Mum.'

'Yes, I would love chips,' said Angel and he smiled at Kay, putting a great deal of charm into it.

Kay went to the stove. She loved the way he said 'love'. His voice was broken and harsh, yet it could be so soft and seducing.

'Do a lot,' said Sophie. 'I'm hungry.'

Kay worried about her chips: they were not as good as those she'd tasted on the Continent. Some people worried about meringues. They were difficult. Kay sailed through a meringue session, but her chips could let her down. She also worried about her daughter; this evening's entrance was as bad as it was going to get. She would try slaps and discipline. If that didn't discourage Sophie from copying the behaviour of her peer group she'd take her out of school. If Joel didn't agree to a Catholic school she would have Sophie tutored at home. Kay did not go along with the view that bad behaviour had to do with age.

Behind her, Angel and Sophie talked about music passionately. The phone rang twice and she let the machine pick it up. Then she remembered her husband: he'd call from Paris before going out to dinner. She served the chips with a mayonnaise sauce and as she turned off the boiling oil she thought of Sarah Prince; all her choices taken from her because of a mishap at the stove.

Angel said, 'Did you hear a song, "Inner City Blue"? Was it a hit here? I heard it the other day on a car radio. The singer was – ' He couldn't remember her name. 'What a marvellous voice.'

'Don't get to like it too much because you won't be hearing it anymore,' said Sophie. 'She's dead.'

Kay could see he was having trouble with that one, he thought dead was current slang for out-of-fashion.

'Really *dead*?' He didn't believe her. 'How?'

Sophie told him about the suicide and Kay thought the young could be so cruel. Angel's chip-eating slowed. 'Did she make any more discs?'

' "Firechild",' said Sophie promptly. 'Now *that* is truly fabulous. But I don't know if they will release it. I heard it at

Rick's place. He's my friend. He's joined a group – it was his début on TV tonight. *Top of the Pops.* I was nervous for him, actually.'

Sophie sounded sane, even relaxed. Kay watched them and thought about Spain, how each part was so different and kept its individuality. She was really thinking, 'He is the most exciting person I have ever seen.' She appreciated the harmony at the table. For once Sophie approved of a guest and now there was a nice easy feeling between the three of them. They seemed to bring out the best in each other. Time was forgotten. It was an utterly unplanned episode in an otherwise ordered life.

'I will make the pudding. I will prepare for you an Andalusian speciality.' Angel went to the cupboard and to the fridge. Sophie helped him. 'Don't look,' he said to Kay. 'A surprise.'

At the end of the surprise, which seemed to Kay to consist of a caramel sauce with a toasted sugar top, he said, '*Hostia!* It's ten o'clock and I've forgotten all about Roly.'

· Nine ·

She felt unlike herself, as though baptised by the songs of his grandfather; they had filled her ears, taken her soul, making her joyous. She felt strong and full of laughter, everything was all right and always would be. She understood many things during those nocturnal hours with the gypsy.

Everything that happened in the kitchen was special, heightened, never-to-be-forgotten. It was an elation she believed mystics experienced. She couldn't stay inside, so went barefoot into the street. The trees and the smell of the night intoxicated her more. He followed her out as a south wind started up.

'Ah, a wind from the south,' he said, and Kay felt fierce with happiness. He broke off a piece of blossom and gave it to her, presented it rather formally. She closed her eyes because the happiness was now too much, and she didn't have the constitution to contain it. She was built for peace and not eroticism, and the beauty of the night only inflamed her more. The only act she could think of that might do justice to the way she felt was to fly.

Three o'clock and there was a strange whirring in the kitchen. Kay realised it was the quiet of the night which she rarely heard. Angel had left hours ago and she had sat at the table, too full of feeling to go to bed.

She drank some mineral water and looked for signs of the dawn, then walked into the park fearlessly: nothing could touch her because she was no longer Kay Craven. She was part of the grass, the stars. 'It's all me and I'm all it. Part of life, the past, the future.' She thought that moment was the ecstatic fusion with life that drug addicts searched for, that Buddhists experienced, that some poets wrote about. She heard God's voice say, 'Take what you want now, pay later.'

Angel called for her early. He brought a bottle of Spanish liqueur containing forty-one herbs, the one she had enjoyed at Roly's house. He also gave her some white flowers. She could see that he, too, hadn't slept.

'I found a part of London that impressed me very much. I'd like to show it to you. Would you like that?'

She nodded.

'It has a very special atmosphere and I think – ' He looked into her eyes and forgot what he was saying. 'I often think that strangers show you something about your neighbourhood that you would normally overlook.'

'You're not a stranger,' she said. She was about to make Sophie's breakfast: fried potato and bacon. The potato was already cooking in the pan.

'No, let me show you something.' Angel jumped up and took the pan away. He beat some eggs, added some olive oil, a lot of pepper, a little water. 'Have you a pimento? I'm going to make you a tortilla.' She noticed he stayed by the stove and watched his cooking and didn't walk off during the easy bits – that was the sign of a good cook. 'I liked what you did with the omelette,' he said, 'but it was too bland. This is more substantial. People put all sorts of things into a tortilla but traditionally it's eggs and potato.'

He was rougher in his approach than she was. His handling of the ingredients lacked refinement; he didn't coax, he insisted. It was a greedy man's meal. However, the tortilla was quite a *tour de force*, she had to admit that. Solid, firm, yet not overcooked.

'I expect your wife cooks for you,' she said.

'No.'

'Because you are such a good cook? You should hide your skills or she'll have you doing everything.' Her voice was provocative.

'Why don't you just ask me what you want to know: have I got a wife?'

She stared at him. 'People's domestic lives are their own business.'

He laughed, then mimicked her. She smiled and suddenly they were both laughing, unable to stop. She thought it had nothing much to do with what she'd said.

Sophie rushed into the kitchen. She was in a bad mood until she saw Angel. 'What's the matter, Mum?'

'The matter?'

'You don't normally laugh.'

Kay was surprised.

'You always laugh quietly.' She looked reproachfully at her mother.

Angel coaxed the girl into a chair. 'I've saved you some tortilla. Come on, eat. You need nourishment or you'll laugh like a lunatic too. Eat!' He put the food in front of her, poured some apple juice. It was obvious he was used to dealing with children.

'And these are for you.' He showed Sophie some castanets. She reached for them. 'When you've finished your breakfast.'

Angel took his new friend to York Way which she thought was a funny part of London to be impressed by. He walked down from the Kentish Town end along a blind wall, sullen, dark, not even adorned with graffiti.

'This part reminds me of mad houses,' he said. 'The other night I drove past this wall and thought, it is the last wall in the world, the most forlorn barrier. After this, anything goes. I thought that here I could lose my mind. I felt quite depressed.'

'Well don't – lose your mind,' she said firmly.

'What about my heart?'

She didn't answer.

'You can lose such a lot: health, mind, heart, life. From your first cry on, it all diminishes.' He pointed out the way the road curved down towards King's Cross. 'Now it is evil. Animals were killed here, I can smell their suffering.'

She wasn't so moved by the area. At best it was bleak – the chimneys, the expanse of sky. Windows were broken, the remaining splintered glass glinting in the sun, reminded her of madness.

'It is well – it's depressing,' she said.

'Merciless.' He crouched down and lit a cigarette. 'Like the desert, it's a challenge. Spiritually speaking.' He looked at the view as though he were surveying the Dolomites. She wanted to move on, have a drink, a coffee, be somewhere softer.

Further down, an effort had been made. 'The yuppification of York Way,' he laughed. 'They can't get rid of the smell of the place, too much has happened here. I wanted to show this place to you because you should be here.'

'Thanks a lot!' She was astounded.

'In this place you would write like crazy to get out of it. It would give you energy you can't even dream of. You would do anything to be away from here. The place must have quite a history.'

He leapt up, wiped his hands, started walking down towards King's Cross and Kay followed.

'Perhaps the plague?' She suggested.

'No no. That comes *upon* people, not from them. When you cook meat you must use certain spices and herbs to neutralise any fear the animal felt in dying, otherwise the fear is retained in the meat. It's bad for you. Sometimes animals are slaughtered in a very bad way and the terror they go through changes the structure of the meat. Why eat terror?'

'Are you a vegetarian?' she asked.

'If you knew what I know *you* would be.'

'And I thought you were going to show me London Bridge at night. That boat lit up on the banks of the Thames, pretty with lights and – '

'I don't like pretty.' He flicked the cigarette away. 'That's what Alexis Scott's songs were about; this area, these feelings. Why did she die?'

Kay shrugged. He waited for her to catch up. 'You're tired?'

'I didn't sleep.'

'Nor did I.' He took her hand and pulled her along. 'Someone

· 59 ·

must know why she did it.' His voice, in spite of the harshness, was expressive, caressing. 'I'm going to find her other songs.'

Kay said she'd get Alexis' address and talk to William Darby.

It was a high, beautiful day. They walked to the City, along the river. Being with him changed London. It was no longer the same place, nor she the same woman.

· Ten ·

In the late afternoon Kay sat at the side of the stage while Angel tried out a new song. First the other gypsies beat out a rhythm, then the guitar began, then he started to sing. The sound pierced the roof as it flew out of him towards glory. It took her very soul with it, up on an endless, ever increasing high. In response she muttered a prayer. Then he started to dance and she thought, I'll remember this in my moment of dying.

Afterwards he wiped his face with the red scarf as he asked for some changes from the group – he wasn't getting what he wanted. They listened to him because they respected his grandfather who was a legend, and Angel was said to be his natural heir. All the songs were now in him, like birds come home to roost.

An old man with a black hat watched Kay with amusement. He said something in a dry croaking voice and several people laughed.

'What was that?' she said politely.

A guitarist who spoke English said, 'Pepe says be careful, English woman. Angel has *duende*.'

'What's that?'

He shrugged indicating it was hard to define. 'Some gypsies have it. You cannot get it, it's something you're born with.'

Angel showed the female dancer how he wanted her to move and when to join in and sing. Then he turned to Kay. 'Solea is the purest, oldest flamenco. It has to be serious, formal and angry. Then he sang and the guitarist translated for Kay. 'If this is living, then a thousand times I ask to die. I would follow you, even in to

Hell. Being with you I am covered in glory.' After the last note there was a silence. It was the silence of respect given to a master.

He came across to Kay. The excitement had made her sweat, her hair was untidy. 'So what do you think?' he said.

'If I never have anything else in my life, that was it, enough.' She couldn't do justice to how she felt.

'I meant the song. It's about her.'

'*Her*?' Kay sounded in pain.

'Alexis. It's about her songs of the city. And the way the city let her die.' He reached for Kay's hand as they walked down to the street. He seemed quite normal. She was still euphoric. Then she saw that it was dark.

'What time is it?' With horror she realised Joel was in the world, in the house, by the empty stove. She hadn't left a note or even phoned him. 'I can't go back like this.' She felt as though she'd spent a day with a lover or been somewhere exotic and forbidden, or taken ecstasy pills. Whatever – she wasn't tidied back into the Kay Craven that belonged in Joel's world.

'So let's go and look at pretty London. What was that you said about a lighted boat near a bridge?' Angel leapt into the street and hailed a cab. They went south. He was in London, she in a dream.

She saw that they were 'familiars', she had seen it from the first. She thought it was a good thing, an unexpected gift from God. She had known him from the day of his birth, that well, and yet they'd never touched, except for his hand resting in hers. With him she watched each moment unfold with new eyes, and yet she knew nothing of his practical life. So although she knew him in one way very well, his everyday behaviour was all discovery. Being with him made her weightless, unlimited, unafraid. She was elated and at one with the world, she did everything at his speed, ate when he did, drank when he wanted, went to the places he chose. He liked the streets, looking at people, and he kept the experience to himself. He rarely said, 'Look at that,' or 'Isn't that marvellous?' He wasn't a sightseer and he allowed her to think what she wanted, see things her way. She felt she flowed into him, reinforced him, was absorbed by him. They were one.

She arrived back home with no real idea of what she was doing. When she was with Angel no one else existed. He put her into a taxi and it was like banishing her from paradise. He gave her address to the driver and it was a death sentence. He touched her face with a cheap gypsy caress that he bestowed on his fans, and the cab pulled away.

She arrived in the kitchen and it was slightly less than paradise. Joel said, 'Where the fuck have you been? I haven't had my dinner.'

She lay on the bed and the roar of her heart filled her ears, shook her body, the room. She recognised that she was careening about up there above the safety line of consciousness, with ideas and images inappropriate to her life with a man who had known her for eighteen years and expected her to be reliably the same; change was what Joel dreaded most. Her head was full of the sound of Angel's feet tapping and trickling and thundering out those rhythms, their meanings unknown, wild, angry, menacing, arousing, always in control. However out of control he got, the rhythm held him like a corset. She could see the narrow streets of his neighbourhood near Seville. Her inner eye flew along those cobbled alleyways and courtyards where the gypsies lay in wait with their magic that created a charmed life, that turned cats into dogs, faithful wives into harlots, tin into gold, the barren into the fruitful. She could see them gathering with their black hats and their songs and then in her mind she swooped up over the sea, up to the moon, and there she rested like a bird of the night enjoying its white light, feeling cleansed and strengthened, and she thought, My God! Maybe the sound of his song has stolen my soul.

Joel said, 'That quiche was not quite right, darling. I've got indigestion.'

She could see Angel's face as he had come out of the tunnel near London Bridge. His beauty made her cry out. 'So this is the lighted boat,' he said. 'Like a stage set. All right for the Americans.' His expression was mercurial, open, guarded. Hundreds of years of breeding had made that face. She kept thinking, They only ever go with their own kind.

'Flamenco must be very old,' she had said.

'Not at all. It started in the last century. In 1860. Before that it was country dance. It used to be unaccompanied – the gypsies rapped out a rhythm on the bar or with a stick on the floor, or hand-clapping. The guitar came later. You must understand, Kay, that there is much so-called flamenco around but very little is profound or pure because it does not come from the gypsies. Our way of expressing it is different from *payos* – the non-gypsies. Of course the *payo* can sing very well, some say he sings as purely, but the gypsy is more profound. When a gypsy cries out it cannot be bettered.'

She'd asked about the non-gypsies and he had mentioned some flamenco stars. 'They're good, they make a fortune, but they are *payos* and nothing to do with us. Mexican music, pop, all kinds of influences come in.' He had sung a song of how the gypsies suffered persecution, always had, and would do gladly to keep their blood pure. 'We were born with profound grace. We are aristocrats. We have purer blood than you.'

She didn't disagree. He was as élitist, in his way, as Joel. He was proud of his origins and upbringing.

Joel lying beside her said, 'You're very restless. And hot. Have you caught a bug?'

'I've caught something.' She was back in that cold white light. The stars were huge and never-ending; swarms of them, like insects.

· *Eleven* ·

On Kay's second day of ecstasy she suddenly remembered Sarah Prince. They were walking across the heath towards Kenwood and she noticed how he touched the trees, their trunks and leaves, as he passed. Things he liked he kept to himself; he wasn't forever trying to get her to share everything as Joel did. He picked a flower and gave it to her – it was better than that. By giving her the flower he took her up, up, and the heights were dizzying. Being with him was not unlike being at the fairground. She could have screamed. Instead she laughed, a small excited laugh. She couldn't do justice to what she was experiencing. Life gave her ecstasy and her response was that of a housewife – she was found wanting.

He only spoke when he had something to tell her, they could be silent together, without awkwardness. In retrospect she remembered little of what was said, only of how she'd felt. Angel wanted to feel good, he wanted her to feel at her best, and he wanted them to be in touch. When she failed to see what he was saying he felt he'd lost her. He jumped up and down, gesticulating, making her see the point of it all – the 'it' – the supercharge. And she wondered again, 'Has he drugged my drinks?'

He loved standing on Parliament Hill, looking over London. 'It seems so small, vulnerable and silent.' He looked at the hills beyond and wanted to know what they were. He told her about an evening he'd spent with a South American writer, how they'd so disagreed, their view of life had been so imcompatible. Angel was ironic when he wanted to hurt. Kay suddenly wanted to defend the writer.

'All right he is famous and ignores his fame, so you blame him for that. Yet you'd blame him if he flaunted it.'

'Listen,' said Angel, 'I wouldn't care if he carried it in that stomach of his, bulging like a pregnant woman. That's not what it's about. You don't understand, and I thought you did.' He chewed a blade of grass and looked away from her.

Later he said, 'I thought you would have understood.' He shrugged.

So she supposed the South American was labelled an intellectual fraud, his images were all shit, his visions tacky because he was richer than the gypsy. When she met the South American writer several months later he said the gypsy was one of the most perceptive men he had ever met.

'He is the true executioner of flaky ideas, pseudo-beliefs, over-used myths. Funnily enough he doesn't mind his, as long as they have their own truths. And he's so well read – for a gypsy.'

Kay thought, So that's it. He tried to patronise Angel.

They sat on Parliament Hill and looked across London and she knew she must do something about Sarah Prince or the woman would be lost. He put his arm around her shoulder. His first embrace. That of a friend or a lover? She told him she had something to do.

'Then I'll do it with you,' he said. 'Would you like that?'

'It's not going in front of a TV camera exactly.'

He said that whatever she did was fine with him.

'When I went to school I was so clever they let me go to the *payos'* school – there is still segregation against us. Then I learned a trade: animal doctor. But by then they saw I was a star and could make a lot of money.'

'You've left a lot out,' said Kay. 'I can hear when the story is cut, then stuck together. Clumsy editing, the first clumsy thing I've seen you do.'

He laughed.

'Where did you learn your English?'

'In America and by reading books.'

'Do your family mind your being away so much?'

'Kay, I haven't time for a wife.' He took off the chain around his neck and put it around hers. It had a small stone in the centre.

'For luck?'

'Protection.'

'Who from?' She laughed.

'You know.'

They started back down the hill. The day seemed darker and she came back down to earth as they did. She had been absent from all sense of responsibility towards herself, caring for herself; as he said, protection. Here was a man who would leave tomorrow and possibly never come back. Because he was so sexually attractive he would have a full life with one partner or many. She couldn't even guess his age but felt whatever it was, it was less than hers. She'd let herself literally 'be joined' to a man who had not given her the slightest idea of his intentions towards her. Hours of screwing couldn't do anything like as much harm. And her heart was where?

'We've just come out of the sky,' he said and looked back at Parliament Hill.

· *Twelve* ·

He came with Kay to the mental hospital. As she was going in, he pulled at her silk scarf and pointed at her basket of foods. 'You remind me of this woman in Paris. She tried to poison her husband but wiped out her entire family. The husband lived.'

'Did you know her?' Kay was disconcerted.

'This was in the sixteenth century. The woman wanted to go off with her lover but needed her husband's money. She tried to concoct a poison that was undetectable. In one of her experiments she introduced the poison into a hamper of food and went to a charity hospital to dispense it in the ward. She waited to see the way the poison worked; if she had used enough, too much . . . What kind of death it provoked. It wouldn't be suspicious in a ward of very sick people.'

'And I remind you of her? Thanks!'

He fingered the crusty rolls. 'Not in those. Pâté would be good – nice texture, strong taste. A spicy country pâté, or a rice pudding.'

'Even an omelette,' she said.

'They all thought this Frenchwoman was so good and charitable.'

'What happened to her?'

'She made a perfect killing dish for the husband but he had a sudden liver attack so gave his meal to the woman's brother who died in agony. In the meantime her lover was using poison to kill adoring older women for their money. Then the lover was killed. Nothing to do with her. Some accident. But in his effects a letter was found; he didn't trust her. He said that if anything happened to him she was responsible. And he listed her crimes. She was arrested and accused of two dozen poisonings.'

'Who was she?'

He couldn't remember her name or what had happened to her. He sat under a tree opposite the main door and took a slim book from his pocket. He started to read immediately, totally engrossed. She asked the title but he didn't answer. It was a book on the history of London. She kicked his leg lightly and he looked up. 'Are you coming in?'

'They might not let me out again. You go.'

She was going up the steps when he said, 'Kay. Don't forget. Fire purifies.'

Sarah Prince looked thinner and her eyes were smudged, yet strangely still. Kay thought it might be the drugs they were giving her.

'My daughter came to see me. It was a terrible visit. They shut me away after that. She said that if I get out she will start a criminal prosecution against me for attempted murder, and he, the boyfriend, will back her up. The facts are on her side, aren't they?'

'Perhaps if you don't react and stay calm they'll have to see you're all right,' said Kay quietly.

'But they're going to extend the Section Two. I'll never get out.' She was gasping with panic. Kay held her, stroked her hair.

'I don't want the money. She can have it, money to burn. I'll move right away from Kentish Town. She can keep the house in Lady Margaret Road.'

Kay knew that road. Alexis the singer had lived there.

Sarah Prince clasped her hands tight together, the knuckles white. 'If I stay here I will end up – will end up . . .' She pulled away from Kay. She wasn't sure about physical affection. 'The more I tell them it's her, the more they say it's me. They don't even believe about the trust fund. They've never heard of that sort of thing here. I've got my lawyers onto it. I've written to them. Will you help me? Do you believe me?'

As vehemently as she could, Kay said, 'I will help you. Have I your permission to see your daughter if necessary?'

'That's up to you. You'll have to be prepared to listen to lies.'

That suggestion had disappointed Sarah and she turned away, her eyes not as still as they had been.

'I may have to involve her,' said Kay. 'After all, I am doing this for you.'

Sarah shrugged as though the whole visit was a great strain. She moved away like an actress coming off stage after an exhausting performance.

The administrator again allowed Kay a quick interview. From his window she could see Angel half lying under the tree. He turned the pages of the book quickly. He read as though he had no time to spare, devouring knowledge. Again the administrator listened to Kay's argument that keeping Sarah could only make her more disturbed. 'Put me in. Try it,' she said.

'So you want her to be released?' He was holding a letter about Kay's intervention from the GP.

'I'll be responsible,' Kay said.

'Why?'

'I think her story is terrible. I believe it's a miscarriage of justice. I'd go and see her lawyers, talk to people who knew her, go through the right channels, but quickly.'

'It's a risk, Mrs Craven, a big one. She may leave the hospital and set fire to a department store. She's a severely disturbed woman and she stays in our care, not yours.'

'But her story's so plausible. Have you talked to her?'

He didn't answer.

'I'll fight for her,' said Kay, her voice shaking.

'That's your privilege.'

When she got outside Angel said, 'Why are you doing this?' He looked at Kay's strained face.

'Because I'm always writing about it. I need to *do* it for once.'

Instead of staying in Camden Town he drove south. He handled Kay's car as though he used it every day of his life. It had no mysteries for him. He touched the gears lightly and got the best from it.

She was nervous. Did he want to take her to a room and sleep with her? As though knowing her thoughts he said, 'Playing with fire? Scared?'

'I prefer sitting by the hearth with the fireguard on.'

'Of course you do. A safe fire, one you can control.'

'Why not?'

'Well this one won't burn you up, my darling Kay. You're going to have a Spanish meal in a restaurant owned by a friend of mine. You're going to make a fuss about the paella. I told him to prepare callos – that's tripe. You may not like that either. So you see, my best beloved, you're safe. And yet if you leave your hearth you're up to your neck in bad taste.'

She was relieved. Also disappointed.

That afternoon he talked to her. Looking back, it was all immediate stuff, things of the moment, ideas. Life passed through him and he tried to express it, make sense of it, make it better, but he didn't tell her anything about himself. Before he went to the theatre for one of his last performances he said, 'I'll come for you early, so be up. I will make you a speciality of Andalusia. If you can eat tripe you will eat this.'

She smiled, didn't reply.

'You are one of the few women whose early morning make-up doesn't just sit on their face. What you put on looks like skin.'

'It is my skin. I don't wear make-up during the day.'

He appeared almost shocked that she was so beautiful.

The next morning she didn't eat the Andalusian speciality because he didn't come.

Sarah Prince's daughter would not see Kay. She was quite defiant about it. She, too, had a nice voice, like her mother's, a boy's voice full of energy.

Liz sitting at the kitchen table said, 'Face it. Sarah's off the wall. It's obvious, because she only writes to important people.'

'Because they're the only ones who can help her get out.'

Kay phoned the hospital ward and Sarah Prince was brought to the phone. Liz sighed loudly and opened a bottle of wine.

'I've got good news, Sarah. I'm contacting an independent psychiatrist today.'

'So you believe me?'

'Yes I do. Of course I do.' Kay put all her force and warmth into the assurance.

Sarah Prince said, 'So does the Queen of England.'

Liz opened a second bottle of wine and poured Kay another huge drink.

'I nearly fell for it. She was so convincing. I was about to get a shrink in, the lawyers. She never put a foot wrong with me . . .'

Liz thought it was very funny.

'She could have been let out and torched half London! She would have been busier than Guy Fawkes! The daughter said it's the money; she can't bear the idea of family money, can't tolerate the thought of receiving it. It's dirty money.'

'Money's neutral,' said Liz. 'It's the owner that gives it its shading.'

'Her family owned mills in the north. Apparently the thought of her family having a lot and other people having not enough upset her as a child. Then it must have turned into something else.'

Liz laughed, a sort of laugh. 'Well you have – more than other people.'

It was two o'clock. Angel still hadn't come and Kay didn't feel like eating. Liz said, 'Come on. What you need is a real drink,' and she opened the Spanish liqueur with its forty-one herbs.

'You know you said I had a soul mate, Liz? And he wasn't with me so I was only half alive. What is a soul mate?'

She poached a chicken with a green caper sauce. Sophie toyed with her homework and watched her mother furtively. There she was again, cleaning the consommé with eggshells.

'Mum, that soup is a lot of work.'

'A good consommé is worth it. But there are no short cuts.'

'I don't like it. What's for pudding?'

'Spotted dick.'

'Dad likes that. What's for me and when is Angel coming again?'

'Do you like him?'

'Life's more exciting when he's around.'

Kay mashed apples and hung them to drip through jelly bags. She opened the wine to let it breathe.

Sophie said, 'Mum, what is adultery?'

'Why? Who's mentioned it?' Kay was immediately defensive.

'It's in Shakespeare, that's why. What does it mean?'

Kay told her.

'Oh, screwing around! Oh that!' Sophie was disappointed. 'What do you think of adultery, Mum?'

'They all seem to tumble into it around here. I think it's a mistake.'

'So you should stay with the man you've married. What if you're bored?'

Kay sounded sarcastic and cold. 'Get on with what life gives you.'

'What if it's not enough?'

'Make do with what you've got.' Kay, on the verge of anger, nearly forgot the dumplings.

'So you're not bored with Dad?'

'Joel is a friend as much as a husband and I would never be disloyal.' The force of the words blew out the match she'd just struck. 'Nothing could topple our marriage.' She struck another match. The cigarette was lit. The Booker prize winner and her publisher were coming to dinner. And the arts minister and his Greek wife. Roly said he'd come over for coffee. Joel was in New York.

'So you'll never leave Dad?'

'Never,' Kay whispered.

And then the gypsy was in the room and her life suddenly made sense.

· *Thirteen* ·

Like those women with a swelling stomach and nausea, who rush to the doctor thinking they have a terminal illness, Kay believed she was experiencing a near-religious revelation. Just as it never occurred to the women they could be pregnant neither did it occur to Kay that she was in love.

The gypsy sat with Sophie trying to help her with the homework although she was more interested in talking about music. He gave her a cassette of his latest recording. 'They tell me it's going into the charts, so perhaps you should have my autograph too?'

'Are you a popstar?' Sophie was suspicious.

Kay loved the way he explained things to her daughter. He could get close to her, show warmth, be playful. It's the women over twelve he has trouble with, thought Kay. She asked him to stay for dinner.

'I can't. I have a performance. I came in to say I'll see you later. Don't eat too much, then you can have dinner with me.' He got up, pulled himself up tall, in touch with all his muscles, breathing, reflexes. Then he stretched and smiled at Kay and it seemed so intimate, as though they were in bed. He was what had originally been promised to her. She'd been waiting for this all her life. There were two obstacles: she was married with two children; and he might not want her.

There was no chance she could meet him, her evening was filled. The following night too. He said he would give her tickets for his last performance as he drank a glass of wine quickly. 'It's a shame you're so busy because I wanted to talk to you.'

Her face felt hot. It wasn't just the stove. She asked what about.

'Alexis Scott. There's so much I need to know.' He frowned. 'I can't stop thinking about her, you know.'

He left. Kay's cheeks had cooled down considerably.

'You know, Mum, he's really famous! There's posters of him all over the tube stations.'

Halfway through dinner Kay left. She hadn't been paying attention anyway. Nothing anyone said got past her one continuing thought: the way he had got up, stretched and smiled at her. She told the guests something silly. 'I have to go to Roly's house.'

'But he's coming here,' said the arts minister.

'So I'll go and get him.' And she left her own dinner party. It was the first time she'd ever done such a thing.

Her car was parked at the top of the road near the garage. She opened the door, then paused; she needed to calm down. Her heart was all over the place, beating, not beating. She thought she had caught a virus. They happened so suddenly. Between one minute and the next she believed you felt you had literally been stung, like a wasp stinging. She had heard these viruses came from outer space. So she'd been stung by an astral wasp. He would be starting the second act. How she longed to hear him sing, see him move. 'Phenomenal,' Roly had said after seeing the show. That meant it was beyond Roly's descriptive range. She got into the car and started the engine. Then she remembered to shut the door. She slumped forward, head on the wheel. How she longed for help, protection. Where was the crucifix Joel had found in the house? If she could just hold that. She'd forgotten how to pray. Her prayers were awful bribes to God.

I have choice, freewill. I do not have to see the man dance. That's all it is – seeing something out of the ordinary, that's fantastic. Turning on, being high.

She got out of the car thinking, I'll stay low and peaceful. A drunk watched her from the corner. He sniggered.

She ran into Roly's house and found Liz embroidering a

blouse. The scene looked too demure. 'What's happened?' said Liz, alarmed.

'I need a drink.' Liz got up and poured a brandy. She gave it to Kay and kept her hand on her shoulder, kept in touch with her as though she'd slip away.

'Has he insulted you?'

Kay blinked.

'That prat. The arts minister.'

Kay shook her head.

'He insults everybody else.'

'I came to get Roly.'

'But he's at your house.'

Kay looked again at the embroidery. Even *she* could see it was a front. Was there a man hiding naked in the cupboard? Why so demure?

She stood up and the colour came back into her face.

Thinking about Kay's strange behaviour later, Liz decided she was pregnant.

Kay went back to see Sarah Prince. If her method of escape was part of her illness why drop her? She'd seen other people with easier illnesses. Sarah sounded just the same until Kay offered her money.

'Money?'

'You might need some. For the coffee machine, cigarettes . . .'

'Money's shit.' Her eyes swivelled round and Kay could see their pain; they looked as though they were made up of bits of broken glass. Kay was reminded of the broken windows in York Way, the sun shining on the jagged glass and the gypsy saying, 'It has a madhouse atmosphere here.'

Sarah didn't look too steady. It could go either way. Kay drew away from her, prepared to go. 'If there's anything you need, you ring me.'

Sarah said, 'You could send me a box of matches. Swan Vesta.' She sounded sarcastic.

Kay didn't know how to respond. They were no longer in the same world.

Sarah walked with her visitor along the passageway, down the stairs. Kay said, 'Don't you think you should go back?'

'You *will* get me out? You do believe me?'

'Yes I do,' said Kay.

'You're the only two. You and the Queen. You help me and she'll hear of it. You might even get an OBE. I've got influence. Her Majesty will appreciate it. So just now when you asked what you could do for me – really it's what I can do for you.'

On her way out the ragged man, who worried about winning the football pools, asked Kay for a cigarette. He pointed up at Sarah Prince. 'You want to treat her right. She's in at the Palace. One of them.'

Another man said, 'They call her fire dragon because she sets fire to things with her breath. You wouldn't have a cigarette would you, lady?'

Kay went to see Sarah Prince's daughter in Lady Margaret Road. The first floor of the house was still blackened from the fire, the windows boarded up. The daughter, wearing dungarees and the latest, most fashionable sports shoes that Sophie had been raving about for days, took Kay into the extensive kitchen, which also showed signs of fire. Part of one wall was congealed – that was the chip pan incident. The daughter had a gamin face, cropped hair, no make-up, a lovely skin and kind innocent eyes. Kay accepted a coffee and sat on a stool. The garden was strewn with charred furniture.

'I wanted to help her and I would still like to do something,' Kay said. 'I'd feel better about it if you'd agree.'

'Help her how?' The girl had the same boyish voice as her mother but the eyes were quite different. The girl's were very blue and showed she was sensitive, could be hurt, could love deeply. In her, there was no charm and no underlying anger.

'I could visit or – ' She wanted to commit to how often but didn't know suddenly what her life might become. 'I could

certainly write to her and send some food. I cook all the time.'
Kay felt awkward. There was something she hadn't understood;
it was there in the atmosphere of the kitchen, in the way the girl
looked. She felt on unsure ground.

'But why?' said the girl. 'What has she to do with you?'

'She asked me for help.'

'She writes to lots of people. She sends telegrams to herself
signed Elizabeth R. She bestows all kinds of honours on herself.
Elizabeth R has given her an OBE by telegram. She photocopies
the good news and sends it all over the place. You'll get that next.'

'Is she fixated on the Queen?'

'Only when she's sick. It's a power thing. Also, perhaps, the
Queen is the one person who doesn't ever handle money. My
mother hates money. She hates this house because her father
owned it. She loathed her father, what he stood for, the money he
made. She can't bear her family blood, in her or me. She thinks
by burning everything she will get rid of the guilt, atone for what
her family did – '

'What did they do?'

'Made money. It was always money talk when I was young. My
grandfather was on about it all the time. He hated banks. He used
to say a bank is like an umbrella, they hold it over you when it's
sunny, when it rains they take it away.'

The girl's eyes were cornflower blue and stricken with pain.

'The mad thoughts began when she was very young, when she
used to see the women who worked at the mills get ill. Many had a
lung complaint, something that irritated the lining of the chest.
She couldn't bear it, when they fought for breath. Sometimes
she's fine. The royal telegrams are a sign of it all beginning.
There's nothing you can do, Miss Craven, I wouldn't get
involved. The causes happened a long time ago. It's all lost in
sickness now.'

'Don't you want to help her?' asked Kay.

'I can't. And the fire thing is terrifying.'

'Will *you* take the money then?' Kay asked softly. In spite of
herself she was looking at the girl's arms for tracks.

The girl didn't answer.

'Has she any friends?'

'She did have a friend, up the road in the corner house. She was a singer: Alexis Scott. You might have heard of her. She sensed it long before I saw it, the thing about fire. They used to go to the pubs together and the clubs. They were close but not everyday close. My mother believes fire is the only way to get rid of things.'

'Alexis Scott died?'

'Yes.' The girl took a deep breath. 'She had reason.' She locked the back door. 'There have been quite a few fires that the police would like to know about. In some ways it's lucky Mum's where she is.'

Kay felt it was time to go, but she wanted to know what had happened to the money. The girl washed the cups, smiling gently. 'I have to go to work.'

'Can I give you a lift?' Kay sounded polite.

'I've got a motorbike, thankyou.'

Kay asked what she did.

'Social work.'

There was a pause, Kay was about to ask what she specialised in. The girl said, 'I'm kept busy. I look after drug addicts.'

'Well I hope you and your boyfriend will be happy and – '

The girl laughed rudely. 'Boyfriend?'

'Your mother said – '

'That fantasy is about as real as her friendship with the Queen. She thinks he's a big black pusher. I don't have a boyfriend.'

'Well I hope you will,' said Kay, ready to leave.

'I don't.'

Kay realised what it was about the girl she'd half perceived, not understood.

They walked to the front door and Kay wondered how many more mistakes she was going to make. She didn't listen to her intuition. 'Will you keep this place?'

'I'm thinking of turning it into a halfway house for kids who have got off drugs but aren't ready to go back into the ratrace.

That's where the money will go. I'm sure you're curious. Well it's natural, after all you've heard.'

Kay said that was a very nice thing to do, and out of bad some good might come.

'You don't support gays, do you?'

Kay tried to be honest. She accepted the idea of it – it didn't offend her. But it wasn't a state she understood.

The girl said, 'You never support the gay scene in your column.'

Kay sensed she was going to be asked to. She was always being used. But she had the ability to see it coming, at least her instincts didn't let her down there. Quite fast she started towards her car, then stopped to let a very pregnant girl pass. The girl had a pale, composed face and long hair. She looked 'otherworld', like a Madonna. Sarah Prince's daughter reacted quite violently. She shook as though electrified but whether by desire or dislike Kay couldn't tell. The girl went into the house on the corner. It was the one where Alexis had lived.

Then Kay saw the gypsy quite casually cross the road and go in after her. She was almost sure it was him, who else had his style, his way of walking? She sat in the car for several minutes but he didn't reappear.

Then she drove back to her world.

· *Fourteen* ·

Kay made kedgeree for his breakfast because she was sure that was one dish he'd never tasted. He sat reading Joel's books on London and in spite of the noise in the kitchen, the phone, the cleaner Hoovering, Sophie shouting, his concentration did not waver. Once he looked up directly into Kay's eyes and smiled, and she turned away thinking, I never imagined life could be so good. Exultant, the feel of his eyes still on her, she went into the garden. Happiness made her beneficent and she wanted to share it. She wanted to fill her house with the impoverished and lost. And she thought of Alexis. Why had she cut short her life? By doing so she'd cut off the happy communal past outside the school when the kids had been young. Obviously memory had been no match for a distressing present. What had been her last thought as she fell in front of the train? What was the last thing she saw? Kay rubbed her arms, chilled, and went back into the kitchen.

'I've got you "Firechild",' Sophie told Angel, and she opened her school case and passed over a cassette.

Kay said, 'Did you find the Darby house, by the way?'

He shook his head casually and went on reading.

'You don't want to go there,' said Sophie. 'Rick's got all her songs. He's the one to deal with. If you go to her husband you'll have to pay.'

'Pay?' said Kay.

'Of course he will,' said Sophie rudely. 'If he wants to record her stuff.'

'Do you?' said Kay. She was concerned because he hadn't told her.

· 82 ·

'Who knows? Or, as they say in Spain, *qué sera?*' He looked at Kay with a kind of challenge. He didn't like too much being known unless he chose to reveal it.

Kay reached for her daughter. 'Come here, your hair's tangled,' and she pulled the girl into the downstairs lavatory. 'Come on. Otherwise it will only hurt when you finally have to brush it.' In the lavatory, with the door shut, she said, 'What is he doing with these songs?'

'Listening to them. What else?'

'Is he going to record them? Is he looking for more of them? Has he seen the family?'

'Am I his recording manager? You're in such a state, Mum, anyone would think *you'd* written them. No, he hasn't said he wants to record them although Rick thought that's what it's about. No, he hasn't seen the family that I know of. And yes, I think he'd like to see more songs. You want to stop investigating these people in the mental hospital; you're going crazy yourself.' She ran out of the lavatory to answer the doorbell. Liz's youngest daughter was calling for Sophie. She had a chubby face but was trying to look grown-up. She'd just turned ten. Sophie was taking her shopping and the child said, 'I'm so pleased you're letting me go with you, Soph. If I behave babyishly, kick me.'

Sophie flung back her hair with the arrogance of the grown-up and they left for Woolworths.

Saturday – the gypsy's last day at the theatre. He went on reading intently. He'd been quiet for hours. The phone rang and the cleaner shuffled out of the storeroom to answer it. Her swollen toe would ensure a short working day. Sophie rushed back in asking for more money. 'What can I get for £1.50? What could *you* get?'

Kay reached for her purse.

'Don't give in to her,' said the cleaner and handed Kay the receiver. 'Sky television.'

They wanted to come and interview Kay at home. 'But I never give interviews,' she said, 'especially at home. I'm sorry.' They were insistent, she became cool. 'My private life's my own.' She hung up.

'All that publicity you could have got, Mum,' said Sophie, outraged. 'Certain people I know would give their eyelashes for just the chance. Think of the newspapers you'd sell.'

'Let Mr Grab Everything sell his newspapers. I only write the stuff.'

Sophie turned to Angel proudly. 'Everyone wants to meet my Mum. They're always asking me what she's like.'

He'd been reading but he hadn't missed a thing. He certainly didn't look impressed by Kay's TV offer. It was obvious he was trying to be as nice as he could when he said, 'She must find very interesting subjects.'

'Not really,' said Sophie. 'It's the way she writes about the subject.'

Kay gave her daughter another pound. 'Not make-up, d'you hear?' Then it occurred to Kay the gypsy might be jealous.

An apple in her mouth, Sophie grabbed her jacket and sped out of the house.

The cleaner was eyeing Angel. 'Has he been here all night?'

'Of course not,' said Kay.

'He looks as though he has. He hasn't slept.'

Kay shook her head, exasperated.

The cleaner wiped the Aga, giving Angel sharp little looks. She hadn't made up her mind about him. Again he smiled at Kay, a deep smile. His eyes stayed on her face. The cleaner's eyes stayed on him.

'You will be there tonight won't you, Kay?' he said.

'Of course,' she said.

'Because I have made a song about that street, York Way, and I want you to hear it.'

'Why?' said the cleaner.

'To see if Kay approves. I need her approval.' He sounded very soft and very seductive as he crossed to the stove, almost touched her as he bent to smell the consommé. Finally it was prepared.

'My son Tom comes tomorrow for Sunday lunch, so I like to give him something special.' Her voice was shaky.

'If you like I will make you some tapas. Our food is mainly fish and yours meat.'

'Traditionally,' she said.

'Why don't I make you a paella? It comes from the north but we eat it in Andalusia. The Catalans aren't all bad.' Beneath the words another conversation was happening. She wanted him to know all the real things about herself, she wanted to know she could go on seeing him, every day of her life. Touch me, said her blood. Her lips said, 'So you'll make a paella?'

'He's been in some bad places,' muttered the cleaner. 'He's got bad road on that face.'

Kay had never seen a performance like Angel's last one at the Festival Hall. He went beyond the usual definition of performing. The rapturous audience took the gypsies higher and further until the next step must be off the edge of consciousness. When Angel sang she knew what they meant about his grandfather; he drew out souls. His feet clattered out the secret gypsy language, his body held tight as a bullfighter, his head high, and the audience were on their feet shouting. She, sweating profusely, thought, He's mine, mine! And watching his body she could only think of how he would be in bed. For a while, that's all she thought. She went outside to cool down and powder her face. She kept telling herself, I'm all right, it's all under control, nothing has happened. Nothing fatal. She reassured herself as though she were terminally ill.

Backstage contained not a soulmate waiting eagerly for her but five hundred delirious fans. They wanted his autograph, his body, his life. One of the gypsies recognised Kay and two bodyguards pushed through and rescued her. She was escorted to a dressing room way off in the administrative building where Angel, stipped to the waist and glistening with sweat, was being wiped down by a beautiful girl. He nodded at Kay quite casually. She, overwhelmed by what she'd seen, tried to find words to do it justice but he'd heard them all before. 'You're too kind,' he murmured, as though to a sponsor.

'And that song about London! Oh God, it was marvellous!' She burst into tears.

Angel tried not to laugh and the gypsy girl bit her lip. Her eyes were hard and assessing. She snapped out something fast in Spanish.

'What was that?' said Kay.

'She asks if you want some water.'

'What was that!' Kay said again.

Angel laughed. 'She wants to know if you're going to immortalise me in print.'

Kay felt suddenly cold. She sat down speedily. Everyone had a point of view they'd like in print. 'Is that what you want?'

'Kay I don't know how you write. Everyone says you're marvellous, but I haven't seen one word yet. Let's look in Sunday's paper, then we will decide.' His voice was cold and spoilt.

She got up, flung herself out of the door, every move untidy, as she clattered up the empty corridor. The gypsy girl followed her, took her arm. With difficulty she said, 'Angel, *siempre malo*, bad – afterwards.'

Angel, standing in the doorway, said, 'By afterwards she means after a performance.' He gestured with his head, quite cool. 'Come on, don't be so dramatic. I am the one who should be crying. I've just done a billion volt show.'

As they walked along the river he sang gypsy songs for her in English.

'Take my red scarf and dry my wounds.
For if you don't cure them my life will fade away.

'When I loved you in the long dawn of that short night,
I thought, as with all things, it would pass, be forgotten.
I did not forsee I would be bound for eternity to love you.

· 86 ·

'I cannot share the magic of the hour before darkness.
I can only think of you. Nothing in this life approaches the ecstasy
I knew.

 Darkness covers the town fully.
It's now a time of unquiet.
Ghosts walk, without the necessity of sound, they call for you.
You are with me. I share with you my blood, my breath.'

The sky was ice blue in patches amongst the night clouds. It was a clear, new-born blue. Angel looked at the moon and sang about its power: the *femme fatale* of the sky. The perfume that was so definitely his permeated his clothes, even the leather of his jacket.

'They were very impressed you came to the show. My company, my family – '

'Why?'

'Because you are a media star. I told them about you. And they could see you are a woman of quality. You have grace. You're kind, and blessed.'

None of it sounded complimentary. She said, 'What do you think?'

'You remind me of something I read.

'Have I not seen the loveliest woman born
Out of the mouth of Plenty's horn
Because of her opinionated mind
Barter that horn and every good
By quiet nature's understood,
For an old bellow's full of angry wind.
It's certain that fine women eat
A crazy salad with their meat
Whereby the Horn of Plenty is undone.'

She said coldly, 'You certainly know the English language.'

'I like languages, I learn them fast. What do you expect – a shabby foreigner?'

· 87 ·

She thought he was laughing at her. His eyes were bright and feverish.

'That's what your husband expects.'

'I love Yeats, Angel, but the poem was a put down.'

He gave a generous shrug. 'When I first saw you, so harmonious and respected, with all those men idolising you, in that little group, that's so rare, I thought; men showing a woman respect. I was touched, Kay. Then I looked at the men.' He shivered dramatically.

He sang in English, challenging her. 'If I were to die would I lose you? I would come back, the shiver in the hot night. Sensing me you'd turn from your new lover and turn to ice. Join me, my love, in the labyrinth where all is not forsaken, before the fires of hell begin.'

He said, 'No point worrying about death. People spend their lives worrying on the subject: cancer, assault, aircrash. Then they go out for a breath of air between worrying and a slate falls off a roof and hits them.' Then he sang about Alexis. 'Death didn't worry her,' he said.

Kay asked him about the earlier song, 'Join me, my love, in the labyrinth where all is not forsaken. Who was that for? Alexis?'

'It's a saraband. Seventeenth century. Probably came from the Orient. How can it be for her? She is the one who's not here, so let her sing it for me.'

And then he changed his mood, prepared to be entirely Kay's. 'I feel so at home with you.' He put his jacket over her and the perfume was strong. She asked what it was but he didn't know. He smelt the leather.

'It's a lovely smell,' she said, 'it will always remind me of you.'

He had no answer for it. He occasionally used eau de Cologne on his face and hair. Nothing else. 'Perhaps it's the smell of my skin mixed with the leather of the jacket.'

Kay made sure she kept the jacket. It hung in her cupboard and often she held it against her face. The perfumed smell didn't go away or even fade.

· *Fifteen* ·

Sophie woke her, screaming, 'He's in!'

'In?' Kay lay naked across the width of the bed – was he in the house?

'In at number three. I told you, Mum – he's incredible.'

Kay tried to go back to sleep. Since knowing Angel she hadn't slept more than four hours a night – if she slept. She lay bunching Joel's pillow against her breasts. Her heart beat fast. 'It's all right,' she said aloud, 'I haven't done anything. Nothing's been said.'

She thought about the walk along the riverbank the previous night. When he had touched her she'd felt blessed. He brought joy with him. He was unlike anyone else. He made her alive. She was seeing all the old things as if for the first time. It was like the night he'd first arrived in her house; how she'd noticed the moon and trees against the bedroom window.

Because he obviously wanted to be with her she felt valued. The vividness with which she had first noticed the moon was now her way of seeing, more like that of an artist or gypsy.

When she got downstairs he was already working on the hors d'oeuvres for Sunday lunch. His song was on the radio again and Sophie turned the volume up. Afterwards Kay asked what it was about.

'A poor waiter in a second-class brasserie near the Gare St Lazarre in Paris. He dreams of taking the train to Dieppe and flying free across the ocean on one of those surfboards. Flying to freedom.'

'Is that *your* story?'

A short caustic laugh took care of that.

She made a traditional Yorkshire pudding, cooked under the meat so it caught the drops of juice, with real herb jelly. For pudding, jam rolypoly, the custard made with eggs, cream and a vanilla pod and served from a jug. They worked together, saying little. One look at the guests and Angel dropped paella from the menu. For this sort of people he made a quick, simple speciality of his region which they could ignore without giving offence. It tasted like a garlic mayonnaise. Kay let him do the vegetables and he used oil, not butter, and plenty of herbs. The guests approved and it occurred to Kay that he was as good a cook as she.

They sat around the table, friends she'd known for years, but now Kay felt divided, tense, not sure of them. Not sure of herself. She noticed that only Sophie spoke to Angel. The others spoke politely but only as a form of introduction. Then they talked amongst themselves as they always did: gossip, clever ideas, politics, all of it one-upmanship, all of it making him feel left out. Sophie knew what that felt like and throughout the lunch turned her dark eyes to his, serious and compassionate. They were conspirators in a soulless place where no music played.

For a while Tom, Kay's son, was the centre of attention and talked about his school, about trends and politics; he sounded like his father. After lunch Angel backed away onto the sofa and read a book. Then, when Kay was making coffee, she noticed he was gone.

'Where is he?' she said to Sophie.

'Kentish Town I expect. At least people talk to him there.'

Kay explained her guests had not been rude to him. Performers, to them, didn't mean a thing. They'd treat any outsider the same.

Sophie said, 'He's gone to see where Alexis Scott killed herself.'

She found him by the railway bridge. One of his posters was on the wall opposite the place where Alexis had jumped. Contrary to what the Irish cleaner had predicted, there was no new safety precaution and it looked as if Angel could be the next one over. He stood very still and thoughtful and as Kay approached he moved, almost irritated, as though disturbed at a grave.

'Why did you come here?' she asked.

'Don't you worry yourself, Kay. You've got peace of mind. It's hard to find that these days. That's why they all gather in your house. It's not because you're a celebrity.' He started to move away, back to the road.

She saw a few white flowers poked through the rails. Some had fallen onto the line.

'I wonder who brought those,' she said.

'I did. I wanted to honour the place where Alexis died.'

'She must have meant a lot to you,' Kay said, without thinking.

He looked cold, almost arrogant. 'Of course.'

'But you didn't know her,' she replied, stung.

'Oh but I do.'

'How?'

'Through her songs.' He walked on fast and once again she was obliged to keep up, to put herself out to match his pace. She stopped. Then she walked on at her own pace. If she lost him, too bad – he also lost her.

He was waiting by her car. 'Shall I drive?'

His fingers touched hers as she was about to toss the keys across the bonnet and the touch stung all the way up her arm. She thought, oh no, pal. You won't have me. He was looking into her eyes, looking for something he couldn't find: complicity. Then he laughed.

'So jealous. Even of the dead.'

Furious, she stamped her foot, not unlike Sophie. 'I'm a married woman and I intend to stay that way. You probably don't meet many of those.'

He laughed, highly amused. 'You're just like your daughter. Get in.' He got into the car on his side and left her to get in on her side.

'I don't like your manners,' she said.

'Nor I yours. You're spoilt. I meant you were jealous of her achievements. I wasn't referring to your personal life.' Instead of driving her home, he went towards York Way.

He looked out at the walls, the chimneys, the factories, the expanse of sky. 'This is where she wrote "Inner City Blue". I am sure of it.'

Kay said, 'I have guests back at home. I'm afraid I'll have to go.'

She would never sleep with him. She thought, You can write that on my tombstone. But she couldn't understand why he didn't even try and kiss her.

The next morning she was busy with an urgent piece on the NHS cuts. She interviewed two doctors at the local hospital and Sarah Prince's GP. When she got back her cleaner said Angel had sat in the kitchen waiting for over two hours.

'He doesn't say much, just sits and reads. He asked me what a word meant, but I didn't know.'

.Keeping the agitation out of her voice, Kay said, 'So when will he come back?' The cleaner didn't know.

Kay read the titles of the books he'd been reading. History interested him, poetry he loved. He was more like a scholar than a performer.

The cleaner said, 'The press all make mistakes about him; they think he's after women. He may have them but he's puritanical at heart, he is.'

Kay could see him, over in Roly's house. She called to him as he left, even went out into the street. He came towards her and the feeling between them – it was so dynamic that the whole street must see. His hello was a caress. His, I thought about you a lot last night, burned her blood.

Roly came out and it looked as though they were off together. Kay said quickly, 'If you want to know about Alexis Scott I'll take you to the people who knew her. I'm sure you've already been, Angel, but they won't talk to you – you're a stranger.'

'And a gypsy.'

'They'll talk to me.'

'Because you're a well-known person.'

'It's one way to open a door.'

Angel cancelled his arrangement with Roly and they drove to Lady Margaret Road. On the way Kay said, 'I know you *did* go to that house, I saw you going in. You went in just behind a pregnant girl. Why deny it?'

'Why not? Do I have to tell you everything I do? Are you my keeper?' He flicked her hair. 'Come on. A joke. Well, it isn't, but it should be. I hate it if people challenge me about what I do.'

'Why?'

'Because women – there's no women's lib where I come from.'

'The woman who cleans for me says you're puritanical.'

'She's safe in my hands. She's right.'

He stopped the car in a sidestreet by the house but didn't get out. 'I'll do this your way because you're my friend, my true friend, Kay. My spiritual love. But I tell you, if one day you came to me in Seville you would get the same treatment as I do. My people wouldn't talk to a stranger there either.'

William Darby was too attractive and he used it to get his own way. Kay saw that at a glance. It was odd he hadn't done better; a teaching post at the local poly didn't fit in with his obvious sophistication, intellect, class, education. He thought fast and could handle five things at once. She thought he must have wonderful stamina and the low pulse marathon runners yearn for. Everyday life for William Darby presented no problems. She thought it probably got tricky in the emotional arena. She'd expected an untidy intellectual with neurotic movements but this man was effective. He was more like a high-powered lawyer than an academic. Looking at him, she thought of sex. He probably had it three times a day. It was apparent as soon as you saw him; his sexuality was as obvious and strong as cheap scent. She tried to think of other things: his bereavement, the motherless children. He came from an intellectual Oxford family who had money. He hadn't done quite as well as they'd have liked. He didn't have money. His mouth was firm, hard and sexually greedy and he drew heavily on a cigarette. She could see the students would be mad about him and one was possibly standing in the doorway. It turned out to be a local girl who cleaned the house.

'So what do you want to know, Mrs Craven?' His voice was modulated and nice to listen to. She explained about the songs, how she'd like to see them because she wanted to write a piece on Alexis. She felt the gypsy stand in silence beside her.

William Darby made some kind of refusal which Kay missed. He said it again. 'It's a bit late isn't it? For obituaries. Alexis died two months ago.'

'Do you object?' asked Kay.

'I don't object. This is a street of disasters. I'm sure you could find plenty to write about here.' He was cynical and disapproving, letting her know she'd crossed the tracks to the wrong side for material. 'And how's your husband? Joel, isn't it? I was up at Cambridge with him.'

She spent the briefest time on Joel.

William Darby said, 'I'm glad he's doing so well.'

'Are there any notebooks containing songs or – '

'There may be.' He got up to let a cat into the garden. It had a sad, gaunt face. 'I haven't gone through my late wife's things. I can't face it at the moment.'

Kay said she understood. Then she asked if there were any songs just lying around.

'I've already told *him* that.' He indicated Angel. 'I've been through it all already. Bringing you along does not alter my view, however ardently this performer feels about my late wife's musical output – '

Angel stood up and touched her arm. 'Let's go.' He started towards the door.

Kay said, 'If you do find anything would you call me?' She gave Darby her phone number. 'Would your sons know of – '

'I shouldn't think so.' His voice was abrupt, eyes icy. He reminded her of silver; opaque, shimmering and mysterious like the moon. He said the right things, but who knew what he thought?

Kay said, 'It could be a tribute to your wife if we produced her songs.'

William Darby gestured his agreement.

As they got to the front door she said, 'I'm very sorry for your loss. I'm sorry for the boys.'

'Yes, they're shattered. Thankyou.' He couldn't wait to shut the door on her.

When they got into the wide street she could breathe again. He'd seemed bereft enough but she knew she was listening to lies or half truths. He was angry more than bereft.

Angel didn't say anything as he opened the car door.

'I'll go back there,' she said. 'I'll get something.' She felt a fool.

'Why should you crawl to him? He hasn't an idea in his head about who his wife was. He has no idea as to the songs' worth. But he'll keep his hands on them and be – '

'Bloody minded,' she said.

They could see the pregnant girl sunning herself on the first-floor balcony. It was nearly midsummer.

'Is that his daughter?' Then she remembered he only had sons. 'Perhaps one of the sons' wives or girlfriends.'

'Perhaps,' said Angel.

· *Sixteen* ·

The day was beautiful and he headed straight towards the motorway. She asked where he was going.

'Let's just go.'

She wound down the roof and he overtook everything on the road. He drove casually, one hand on the wheel, the other arm resting on the opened window. Driving gave him pleasure. He felt about cars the way some people did about horses. They went to the sea. Sometimes he sang. He told her about his journeys in America, the tribulations of being a flamenco gypsy around people who didn't know where Spain was. 'They thought it was somewhere in Mexico. Some of those people I met are less educated than many gypsies I know.'

'Do gypsies generally travel?'

'Never. We stay in the houses in which we were born. We see the same people and don't try to change things; we know what works for us. *El Cante* comes from our roots, a collective atmosphere. It can't be taught, it comes from our mothers. It's our birthright. In our blood. We are born knowing how to do flamenco. It belongs to us gypsies and no one else.' He smacked the wheel. Then he said how rich they were and how much they got for a performance.

'But I thought you said a fiesta could break out in the street between one minute and the next? Didn't you say one person would start singing and it would catch on like wildfire? The people would come out into the street and dance all night for the joy of it, you said.'

'That was in the old days, the days of my grandfather. Now I earn 40,000 dollars a week and my cousin – you saw her in the dressing room – 15,000 dollars.'

Kay shuddered. 'It's all so commercial.'

'Kay, we miss those times, but we can't go back to the old ways – dancing for the joy of it.'

'Why not?'

'We've made too much money and money is a hard thing to give up.' He told her that pure flamenco came from Seville, Jerez, Cadiz, his village Utrera, and Labriza. There were many traditional forms – Siguiriyas, Bulerias, Fandangos, Tangos, Alegrias, Tarantas. The gypsies came originally from India, not Egypt; they'd passed through Central Asia into North Africa and crossed to Andalusia in the fifteenth century. In spite of persecution they'd stayed ever since.

'Some of my songs are sarabands – old Spanish sixteenth century. I believe they came from the Orient. Our families were infiltrated to some extent by the transient people of Southern Spain, the Arabs and Jews. The Spanish have always looked down on us but we are more aristocratic than they. I'm proud to be gypsy.'

'You've done very well. Your family must be proud of you.'

He didn't answer.

'But you've travelled a great deal. You know French, your English is excellent. You moved around before you became a star performer, surely?'

'Why do you say that?' He sounded antagonistic.

'Because your languages are so perfect. I can't believe you picked them up in a Berlitz school in Malaga.'

He still didn't answer.

'Come on, Angel! You don't learn languages when you're performing – you don't have time. That happened before you became famous. Why make a secret of it.'

'Yes, I did take journeys.'

'So that is unusual for a gypsy?'

He shrugged.

'So what did your family think?'

'Obviously they didn't like it. You've realised that. They don't like you leaving your *corral* – that's a yard. We don't trust the outside world.'

'So why did you do it?'

He almost told her a lie. She could see that. He preferred not to speak. She laughed. 'Angel, you're like my daughter. She flicks her eyes around like you do and tells me some serious story and I pretend to believe it and give her some money or let her off school.'

'Perhaps I wanted to see the world.'

'Perhaps you had to leave.'

He didn't answer. She liked that idea. A fight to the death or a girl with his child and he wouldn't marry her. Something passionate, on a Shakespearean scale. And he had stolen like a thief into the night, and had to get by until they let him back. She knew now he was older than he had first seemed.

'Perhaps you went off to university?' she said.

'The university of life. Yes, let's leave it at that.'

She asked what city he liked best.

'New York, of course. The first time I saw that city I thought it was a space station belonging to another planet. A metal concrete jungle. How did it get there? Did anyone see it being built? I was high from the moment I saw that bridge crossing into Manhattan and everyone speeding and shouting and radios blaring. As I looked at the city all the lights came on and I saw that as a welcome. I was high and I never came down until I got to the Mid West. You can come down easily in the Mid West,' he said sarcastically. 'I love the city though.'

'Where did you stay?'

'In New York. In the Spanish quarter. My company didn't have any language problems. On that bridge, I think it was Queensboro', I took a deep breath and I could smell the city. It was just about the time of evening when all the crimes hang in the air, waiting for the right victim, and the dreams were cooking. I could smell the violence, despair, new ideas being born. All those gurus on the forty-ninth floor in Brooks Brothers suits, dispensing power and law and protection and ways to save your life while losing your mind. And all they want in return is your soul. I inhaled it all like St Semilian grass.'

'Do you take drugs?'

'Of course.'

'But I thought gypsies – '

'We're not innocent, Kay. We've got all the same sins as you have – perhaps a few more graces. Don't romanticise, it's dangerous.'

'Fantasise?' she suggested.

'I don't have time.' He turned and looked at her. It was the first overtly sexual look she'd seen from him. They sat without speaking. When he did make a move she'd block it immediately. She knew exactly what she'd say. But he did not make a move.

'So who are the forty-ninth floor gurus?'

'Your people: lawyers, agents, doctors, promoters, impresarios, PR consultants . . .'

'You don't trust them?'

'I won't have them near me. I do all my own deals.'

They ran along the sand at the edge of the sea. He turned and watched her running towards him, caught her, held her tight. 'You run fast for a woman. You're strong. I like that. I expect you give birth easily.'

'D'you think I should do it again?'

'If you want to.' He made it sound as though he'd have nothing to do with it.

'I'm getting too old,' she said.

'Oh I expect you've got a couple more waiting up there inside you.'

She laughed and ran away from him. She knew as she ran that he did not like talking of birth. The idea of it appalled him. Spirits trapped in flesh. She knew it as surely as she knew she loved babies, having them.

They played pinball on the pier, ate fish and chips, went to an afternoon tea dance. And she thanked God because she was truly happy. The way he held her as they danced, with the out-of-work and the old, would never be forgotten. He said, 'You dance very well. You surprise me.'

'You speak very well. You surprise *me*.'

'I will buy you ribbons to adorn your hair and perfumes from the East to – ' He stopped suddenly.

'Are you stopping because gifts are meant for a young girl?'

'I'm stopping because I forgot what came next.'

Most of the afternoon was spent laughing. He said what a wonderful time he was having; he thought he should bring tea dances to Seville. And she thought, He doesn't look at other women. He isn't arrogant or starry. He doesn't seem materialistic. He lives in the moment, wants a life on the move.

He talked about his desire to sing from his heart, with phrases that could only come from the heart. 'People still talk about my grandfather's songs. They say he was in touch with unseen things.' He'd sing and tap his stick on the floor – '

'Accentuating the rhythm?' Kay said.

'Setting it free. If I could sing from that inner place like he did then I would die happy.'

'What about your father?'

He waved a hand dismissively. 'Money money. *Dinero*.' He mimicked his father. '*Quiero solamente una cosa*. Applause is cheap. Fame is more fleeting than a woman's – beauty. Love has a price, and never forget it. Money never lets you down. It's your best friend. I heard it all my childhood and he was more vulgar even than that. I've cleaned it up.'

It was dark as they reached London. She said, 'What did you think of Paris?'

'Paris?' He was cautious.

'Well, that's a city. You never mention it. You obviously know France because of that story you told me – the French poisoner.'

'I don't know France.' Quite taut, unfriendly.

'Haven't you performed there?'

'On occasion.'

'So how do you know that story?'

· 100 ·

'Well I could have read it in a book. Books go everywhere, Kay.'

Outside her house he stayed sitting at the wheel. 'Do you want to come in?' she asked.

He shook his head. 'I want to thank you for a marvellous day.' He took her hand, kissed it.

'Oh come in,' she said recklessly. The truth was she couldn't bear to let him go. 'I'll make you a hot meal. Lamb chops, grilled tomatoes, mushrooms. And you can make that mysterious caramel pudding.'

He smiled, almost tenderly, shaking his head, wanting to protect her.

'And we can put on some music and do those incredible steps – Tango. And we'll open champagne and celebrate the fact we're happy.'

He squeezed her hand, almost until it hurt. He wanted her to listen. 'Is that what you really want. Is it?'

She nodded, not looking at him.

'OK,' he said, his voice tight. He was sexually involved now, tense, quite changed. They got out of the car. He said, 'Providing you don't steal my heart, Kay, everything else is yours.'

As they passed the hedge – almost awkwardly – and turned onto the front path she felt her body tug with expectation. It was going to happen. She longed, burned for him to touch her, just once. It wouldn't make any difference. Who would know?

The lights were on. Sophie was supposed to be with Liz. She decided dinner would be quick, if at all, and the dancing quicker. Time would be given to what followed.

Joel was sitting at the table. He'd come back a day early. Around him sat his executive friends, two professors, Roly and some women.

Joel said, 'There you are, darling. What about some dinner?'

· *Seventeen* ·

Three days passed and Kay still hadn't heard from him. She blamed it on that last fatal dinner. She'd had to whisk up some quick dishes for Joel's gang of friends, so wasn't aware of what was going on at the table. Angel had been asked to join them for a drink. But the men were snobbish and superior. One of the women drunkenly challenged Angel to take her to bed. 'Let's see if you are different from other men. Let's see if you're as good as they say you are.'

The harm was already done by the time Kay smacked the food onto the table. She had slopped some sauce onto the woman's lap. During the first course the atmosphere was discordant; during the second, cruel. By the end of dinner she thought different social elements should never come together except perhaps to die. Snobbery? Eating? Never again in her house.

Angel didn't wait for dessert. Without saying goodbye to the guests he stalked to the back door. Kay saw him from the kitchen and he waved to her. Quickly she joined him and began to apologise. He seemed like a stranger. She started to say, 'Take my car and – '

He didn't wait to hear the end of it.

And now, on the fourth day, she thought, What if he's ill? An accident? The way he drives. Panicking, she phoned Liz.

Liz reassured her without calming her. 'He's fine. He's been doing a recording session and working with Roly. They're preparing a film about Andalusia.'

Kay thought of how skilful he was in the kitchen, his movements superb. She'd fallen in love with his movements and then with him. She was caught at her own stove, the scene of so many of her culinary triumphs. She had been filled with an elation quite foreign to her; like a priest of life he'd made the everyday vibrant, precious. He'd examined her for happiness and was satisfied. His hand had touched hers as they'd shared a tortilla. His touch scorched and didn't fade. Kay admitted that she did not know the rules of the game and was dealing with an expert. He'd been aware of every nuance of her mood and could measure how he'd affected her. He'd understood her possibilities of passion.

Part one of his game had been to treat her with respect, part two to disappear and make her suffer. That, of course, had only happened once she was hooked.

He was sure of me when he left that last night, he must have seen it in my face as I ran to the back door, offering him my car. Isn't life cruel? You can't show your love to the one you love. It isn't done. It isn't English or even Spanish. The trick is to play games. Life likes those.

Thank God I didn't sleep with him! And then that was all she could think about – sleeping with him.

She believed she hadn't fallen for him immediately. She thought the walking in the park at night, looking at the sky, had been loving life. Now she saw she had loved him from the first. Only her natural arrogance allowed her to think she had a choice over it.

The questions she asked produced what should be comforting answers: he had not gone off with any English women or girls, Roly would have known. So he wanted me, she thought. Yet she ended up hurt and abandoned.

Liz came in and caught her talking to herself. 'Are you going on *After Dark*?'

Kay didn't quite sneer. She didn't have a sneer left in her.

'I thought that's what you were doing – rehearsing a little anecdote. That's what Roly does.'

'How's the embroidery?'

'I've sewn my fingers to the bone.' Liz collapsed into a chair.

'What's the embroidery for, exactly?'

'I know you think I'm all over the place. And I'm trying to find – '

'Yourself?' Kay didn't see handycrafts as quite the answer.

'A man.'

Kay was amused.

'What's that?' said Liz, 'A laugh! I haven't heard you do that for days. So I want to appeal to a man. It can't be in the kitchen because you've claimed that role. Anyway I can't cook. But I can sew prettily – '

'Which man?' Kay sounded almost frightened.

'A rich man. I could do with a little TLC too.'

'What about the gypsy?'

'Oh no! Can I have something to eat. Have you got one of your coconut cakes?'

Kay fetched the cake tin.

'I'm thinking of going for re-birthing,' said Liz. 'It might just be the answer. The only answer. I need to start again in every way, and you're my ideal mother.'

Kay gave Liz another cake; she responded to compliments, even ridiculous ones. Then she spent a great deal of time skirting around the subject of Roly's world until she arrived finally at the gypsy.

'Why don't you like him?' Kay asked.

'Frankly, he's common. I can't see much in him. And all those languages – swank!'

'Do others? See much in him?'

'I don't know. Roly might. He spends enough time with him.'

'Has he got someone?'

'They only go with their own kind.' Liz spoke carelessly and didn't see the pain in Kay's face. She was more interested in the cake.

'He must have someone, surely?' said Kay.

Liz shrugged. She thought about it but had nothing to say. Kay talked a little about the flamenco film of which Liz knew even less. Then she said, 'Did he mention me, by any chance?'

'Oh yes. He's on about you all the time. Roly said it's – obsessive.'

Kay's heart soared. She grabbed a second cake tin. Another slice was on offer. 'So what did he say?'

'The general feeling is you're his perfect woman. You've got kindness and patience, you're a good companion, and when Roly said, Isn't Joel lucky? Angel replied, Too lucky. His ears prick up when you come into the conversation and he did sort of ask how famous you were.'

'Perhaps that's what he's after,' Kay suggested.

'No, I think he's intrigued by you. Come on – a lot of people are. However open you think you are, you're still mysterious.' Liz ate the cake, drank the coffee. 'What do you mean "after"? Has he been hanging around?'

'Only when invited.' Kay's voice was enigmatic.

'You're obviously picking over him to write something. That's what Roly said.'

'Of course. What else?'

'Roly did say he reads a lot. He's quiet for hours. And he has a good opinion of himself. Roly thinks he wants to be as good as the next person. That's why he knows so many languages, so he can be an equal. Also he can cure animals by the laying on of hands. He got rid of Roly's migraine so those animals must feel good. Roly, as you know, doesn't believe in that sort of thing. So it was very hard for him to accept that his headache disappeared with the touch of a dancer's hands. Apparently he draws the person's pain into himself. That's why they feel better. D'you want to see him again?'

'Of course not. You haven't left home, I see.'

'My kids sense it. There's never been so much trouble; letters from the school, so I am trying to stay for their sake. Note the "trying".'

When Liz had gone Kay tried to locate the peace in her house, to fold the silence like a shawl around her. It didn't work. It was just a house and she not alone but lonely.

She threw herself into the business of cooking and her entertainments bordered on the fantastical. She wanted to fill her house with celebrities. She gave them food they would never forget. Neighbours looked on with envy as she became a professional hostess. She spent whole days shopping, cooking, entertaining. She bought herself lavish clothes. Her newspaper articles were mere slivers, like new moons.

The cleaner said, 'It's funny. Now that guitar player's gone you've changed. You've gone back to what you really like best – feeding people.'

'He's hardly a guitar player. He's one of the greatest flamenco artists in the world.'

'Yeah,' said the cleaner.

'What does "yeah" mean?' Kay was ready to sack her.

'It means yeah. I've met some of the greatest criminals.'

Day eleven and Kay asked Sophie about the Darby family. She wanted to get hold of some secret information about the singer; then she'd have a reason to contact Angel.

Sophie said, 'It's no good talking to them. He's a horrible person, the dad, he's why she topped herself. And he's moved his girlfriend in right under Rick's nose. That's why Rick's gone. And the others have gone. She's one of his students, Paula Strong, and she's having his baby and Alexis knew about it. He's put her in his wife's house. Rick told his father that even an animal never brings a new mate to its old lair.'

Kay thought Rick sounded as though he had his head screwed on. 'Would the other boys know about the mother's songs or – '

'They're on scag. They'd get money off you and tell you nothing, then they'd buy scag.'

'Where do the older boys live?'

'Here and there. They all hate the old man, but then they all blame each other for her death.'

'And Paula Strong?'

'I don't know, Mum. She definitely wants to marry him. But then she's having his baby.'

'What's she like?'

'How do *I* know? She won't speak to me, I'm too young.' Sophie disliked fast questions. She could easily slip up in her answers and reveal absences from school, outings to clubs.

Kay shouted at her. 'Just tell me what was so special about Alexis Scott!'

Kay lay beside her husband. Again she hadn't been able to do it. In the end she'd given him a quick wrist job. He expected her to be involved enough at least to spice it up with salacious talk, but she'd remained silent.

'It's all these dinner parties, they're wearing you out. Who do you think you are, Mrs Trump?'

'I thought that's what you wanted.'

'Kay, I want you.' And he wanted a few family meals like the old days. There was no chance of that.

She lay wide awake, watching the moon. So what that it was unlucky to see it through glass. Could she be any more unlucky? She knew he was thinking about her. She could feel his eyes watching her. It was as though he were in the room. No, he was closer. She tried to remember the song about the labyrinth and death: if I were to die would I lose you? I would come back, the shiver in the hot night. Sensing me you'd turn from your new lover, turn to ice –

Joel said, 'I've started to dread coming home; all those ill assorted people, that food. Every meal is a banquet. How do you do it? The sight that sums up the full horror of it for me is that huge pastry fish with one dead eye gleaming.'

'It's a black olive. I poach the salmon in a fish kettle, roll out the pastry, put the salmon on top and more pastry on top of the salmon. Then I fold the fish in, completely surround it, and pull and pinch the pastry into the shape of a fish. I mark fish scales – '

'Oh no, I don't want to know!' Joel covered his head with a pillow.

'Then I give it its false eye. An olive and a caper will do. I glaze the sides with beaten egg yolk and put it in the oven for twenty minutes.' I think I'm going fucking mad.

· 107 ·

· *Eighteen* ·

Kay called Liz the next day and asked where he was. She said she wanted to do a piece on him with photographs. He should like the coverage.

Liz said she would find his address.

'No, Liz, let's be clever. Let's photograph him unawares. Find out where he does his shopping.'

'He always wears the same things.'

'Food. He'll buy food.'

Liz said she would try. She added that Kay was looking strange. 'I see all the smart cars pull up but I think, underneath it's a different story.'

Kay laughed drily. 'When I start getting telegrams from the Queen, start worrying!'

She'd been all right as long as she had been in control and able to choose whether to have him or not. Now he was gone. There was no choice. She wanted him, could think of nothing else. She thought he was probably a go-getting little shit, only wanting her patronage. How she hoped he knew about her parties and felt left out.

Liz called within the hour. 'He lives in a flat with the gypsy company in Westbourne Grove.' She had the address of a shop which sold Spanish food; he did all the cooking for the group. He was finishing recording some new songs, his single was now number two and his LP in the top twenty. He was going to New York, then Paris.

'You didn't tell him about me?'

'Kay, I didn't speak to him. Roly's assistant, that Sloane temptress, is in love with him – '

Kay jerked as though electrocuted.

'At least it means she's not sleeping with Roly. I'm off, Kay, any day.'

'And the kids?'

'I take Baby and he takes the rest. After all, they go to school. There is a time to quit and I'm on overtime.'

The phone rang as Kay was leaving. The cleaner couldn't fail to notice the way she jumped. What a reaction for someone who got a hundred calls a day. A Polish woman was asking Kay to help her. 'I was in a nervous breakdown house and I shouldn't have been there.'

'That's what they all think,' said Kay to the cleaner.

As she drove to the shop where he bought his Spanish groceries – nearly always at the same time, after the recording session – she thought about Liz; she would never win. Roly had too many smart lawyers, had witnessed Liz's unfortunate sexual indiscretion in the kitchen with the whipped cream and the French count. Whatever he got up to, it was out of reach of Liz and her lawyer. When a relationship had gone so wrong it was wise to treat your partner as an enemy, thought Kay. No half measures, sloppy compromises. Get in first. Go for the jugular. And get out fast. For the first time she thought about Joel. Would he exchange her for a new model and insist on keeping the house and assets? Could he become that sour? People were nice only according to the circumstances of their lives. A gypsy at the door, a bad time in bed and who knew what Joel would do?

'I am still safe,' she said, 'I've done nothing. Except in my thoughts. I'm just going to straighten out whatever the problem is with Angel and that will be the end of it. I'm still Joel's wife.'

When she arrived at the store she wanted to turn back for home and run into Joel's arms, cling to him and stay safe.

The gypsy came in during her second visit, thirty minutes later. She was buying some continental delicacies and it could have looked like a chance meeting. He saw through her move immediately but pretended surprise. She waited for him to buy some long-grain rice, olives, peppers, squid, chorizo. 'I am making paella. Would you like to eat with me?'

She knew her appearance in the store was too plotted-looking. When they got outside she said, 'I didn't think I'd have to buy a half-kilo of beans and some torrone just to speak to you. Go on, you have them.' She tried to give the packages to him. 'You don't call or phone so I decided I'd offended you. As I wouldn't dream of offending a friend,' – she accentuated the 'friend' – 'please tell me what's upset you.' Being candid was her second choice; a 'surprise' encounter over the squid tins would have been better.

'Oh I don't know, Kay.' His face looked thinner, sharper. It would appear he was having an off day. 'I thought we were seeing each other too much.'

'I thought the dinner party upset you.'

'Why should it?' He put his arm through hers. 'Come on, I'll cook you something. My temporary home isn't as atmospheric as yours.' He turned the corner and stopped at a Victorian terraced house.

She held back and said, 'Those people that my husband knows are – '

'Just business. Kay, you don't have to explain them.'

He opened the front door and they climbed wide, carpeted stairs to the first floor. Being with him, just knowing he was in the world, soothed her, took away the pain. Then he pushed open the unlocked door: twenty, maybe thirty people filled the two rooms. She recognised a popstar and one of Andy Warhol's friends. Angel took Kay straight to the kitchen. In Spanish he told the hard-eyed gypsy girl to open a crate of wine. They seemed intimate together. Kay asked who she was.

'I told you. My cousin Conchita.' He started work at the stove.

Conchita gave Kay hard curious looks, not those of a cousin. Kay decided not to be passive in that atmosphere and got up to prepare a salad. She cut up the torrone into squares and they carried the food into the largest of the two rooms.

There may have been a large group of people in the apartment but by the time the meal was finished, she felt there were only two. The electricity between them hadn't gone. When he looked at her his eyes changed. He looked happy and he didn't look at other people or things in that way. After coffee he got his guitar and sang. 'This is for Kay. I am dedicating it to her.' It was the song about York Way.

The gypsies played cards. He sat a little to one side, didn't quite hold Kay's hand. He seemed intimate, perhaps in love with her. There was a definite attraction – she wasn't deluded.

He suggested they leave and his cousin gave him a long look. Complicity, anger, Kay wasn't sure. Westbourne Grove was crowded and he stood on the corner by the big store, identifying people: pushers, underground police, working girls, their flics, thieves, office workers, writers, the homeless. She was sure, absolutely sure, he'd make a move which she decided to rebuff. She'd play hard to get. Being soft had been her downfall, let him do the running.

Surprisingly he made no move. He made little hints that he was glad she was happy. Happily married. There was so little of that about. Then he took her back to her car and drove her home. At the door he pressed her hand warmly, said a soft goodnight and disappeared. She went into the kitchen and wanted to smash everything in sight.

She heard the song dedicated to her on the radio the next day. It was in Spanish but she recognised York Way and fabulous woman: *'Mujer fabulosa'*. Her, or Alexis Scott? She got Sophie to go and buy it and a neighbour to translate it. It was all about standing in a forlorn street in the early morning with the walls of the madhouse to the east and the smell of the slaughterhouse to the west; the buildings were condemned, and the fabulous woman gave the morning warmth; her eyes were full of sorrows for the sins of others, but she was the woman who had everything.

Kay said, 'The woman who had everything. Meaning?'

The neighbour said it was the best translation he could do. Angel sang in dialect. 'Perhaps he means wealth used well, to enhance the lives of others?'

· III ·

'Does it sound – uh – '

'It sounds jealous.'

Jealous. So he is *jealous* of me because I have too much. Is that why he wants to humiliate and make me suffer?

She agreed to be on everything they offered: TV, radio, at parties where she'd be photographed. For all the good it did she may as well have stayed at home.

· Nineteen ·

Every time the phone rang she thought it was him, every creak of the back door – he was coming in. He was making her wait. It might cause her pain but he suffered too. She would wait. No more excursions to strange grocery stores.

'That gypsy got to number one,' said the cleaner. 'So now he doesn't bother to come round.'

For some reason the malice of that stung Kay. It was illogical. What had the charts to do with making things together and being happy?'

'He's in Paris,' she snapped.

'No he's not,' said Sophie. 'I've just seen him.'

Kay turned with unusual speed. Was Sophie lying? 'Where?'

'He's up at Rick's going through all those songs Alexis wrote. Rick's had them all the time, but he's letting Angel record them because he rates him. He won't even take any money. I think he loved his mum.'

'What's he doing exactly at Rick's?'

Sophie, surprised by the savage note in her mother's voice, looked up and took care how she replied. 'He's looking through notebooks. And there's some diary. But Rick won't let him read it. And he's talking about Alexis, like he knew her. He's saying she'd look at a wall in a certain way and see its colours. The pattern of shadows the sun makes on the bricks is a language and she could read it. He said Alexis had definitely gone beyond the ordinary pain we suffer from, so Rick ought to be reassured.'

'Was he with – '

'*With*? Himself.'

'Does he – has he mentioned me?'

Then the Irish cleaner understood. She knew Kay hated people suffering, loved doing good, loved her husband and children. She went into the storeroom and crossed herself.

Sophie didn't like answering Kay but thought she should stick to the truth; her mother looked very dodgy. 'Did he mention you? No.'

Kay nodded as though it was what she wanted to hear. Then she went back to her article on the new Sainsburys in contrast to the corner shop. She included Angel's Westbourne Grove grocer with malice, then crossed through it and closed her eyes, wishing she could cry. The cleaner put a cup of tea in front of her and gently touched her shoulder.

'I'm all right,' said Kay. 'I just wish I could sleep.'

'God puts things in front of us, Kay. They're tests, that's all. So just laugh and pass.'

Liz brought her an embroidered scarf. It was beautiful and had taken her hours to sew. All those empty evenings had not gone to waste. 'Well you're always giving other people things, so let me give you something.' And she hugged Kay. 'You're so valuable. You're the only thing Roly and I have in common. Our love for you. And I'll miss you.'

'But you haven't gone.'

'I will. I was talking to Angel last night.'

'Last night?' Kay's voice belonged to a ghost.

'They've started the film. Angel said the reason I hadn't left Roly was because I hadn't found the right place. He said his uncle has a house in Cadiz and I could rent it. He said it was the right kind of neighbourhood for my kind of flight. He's told me how much everything costs and how I could let part of the house, and I could get a girl to look after Baby. He's very practical. He's put off New York at the last minute – the impresario's furious. So Angel's doubled his price. *And* he'll get it. Then when he gets to the States he'll double it again. Typical gypsy.'

'I'd be careful he doesn't double the rent.'

'I can look after myself, don't worry. When's that piece coming out on him?'

Kay didn't know what she was talking about.

'The grocer's shop. Candid photographs.'

Kay just looked at her. She looked into Liz's face as though the whole structure would fall apart. She couldn't bear to think that this face had been near his, the eyes had seen him, mouth spoken to him, the cheeks even touched him in the polite goodnight Mediterranean kiss. And she, Kay, was banished because she was the woman who had too much.

She made Joel spaghetti for dinner.

'Oh no, *please*,' he cried, 'it's the sort of thing Liz cooks.'

She lifted a strand from the boiling water and tested it. 'We'll have it *al dente*.' Showtime was over. No more showing off with parties. It didn't make the phone ring. She smiled sweetly at Joel as she stirred the tomato sauce, which he saw with relief was at least homemade, and grated Parmesan cheese into a dish. There was a frightening ordinariness about the meal.

'I thought we had a tacit agreement, Kay, that we only ate the best. And surely that's traditional English food, isn't it?'

She strained the spaghetti and added some oil, then dumped it onto two plates.

'I thought we were going to have kidneys and rice – '

One glance at her expression and he decided to shut up about the meal he should have had. He asked what was wrong.

'Wrong?' She gave an overdone shrug, her eyes hostile.

'I think you should tell me. After all, I'm part of what you write.'

She thought she was having an hallucination. Strain could bring those on. Was he trying to take the credit for her work?

He changed the subject to something safe. 'She hasn't gone after all – Liz. All that talk of flight funds, exotic places. She's having an affair, that's why.'

'An affair?'

'Yes, one of those.' He stabbed his fork into the spaghetti.

'With that gypsy.' He threw his fork down. 'Kay, I can't eat this. I get this in hotels, for God's sake!'

'Who told you?' Her eyes pierced his, not a nice sensation. He reconsidered his tantrum with the spaghetti and took up his fork.

'Don't worry about her. She doesn't get involved. It's just physical for her. I know her type. He's very – well . . .' A shake of his head dismissed the gypsy and he went on eating.

An affair. Her heart sped and lurched and rolled like a wounded beast. Her feet tapping on the floor were almost a flamenco dance. She couldn't wait for Joel to go upstairs and watch TV. Perhaps Liz was giving the gypsy the whipped-cream treatment right now?

As soon as Joel left the kitchen, she sped across to Roly's house. Their eldest boy let her in. She found Liz in the bedroom looking at a map of Spain.

'Well I know why you haven't left.' Kay's voice shook. 'You're making a terrible mistake. They're not like us – '

Liz laughed. 'Suddenly so racist, Kay! I wonder why?' The way Kay looked discouraged any more teasing. 'Perhaps it's your aristocratic background showing through at last. You know that Angel's family were horse traders? They all lived in one house: grandfather, mother, kids in a Seville slum. Then they started making money and bought properties and land. His uncle's home is in the Santa Maria district of Cadiz. That's where the gypsies live.'

Kay wanted to kill her, not listen to a travelogue. 'You're sleeping with him, aren't you?'

Liz, not liking the tone of her voice, turned round. 'I must have been blind. I just didn't see it. Oh Kay.' She sat behind the map as though the Spanish peninsular would defend her, her hands twisted emotionally. 'Are you? You are, aren't you?'

Kay looked pale, almost floury, like an undercooked meringue. Liz thought it was funny how comparisons with food immediately came to mind when dealing with Kay, even in the gravest situations. She thought Kay might really have flipped and considered calling Roly, but Roly of course was out, supposedly taping a show. Liz said the first thing that came into her head. 'I swear on my baby's head I'm not sleeping with Angel. It's never entered my mind, I swear.'

How often as a child Liz had had to swear to other children. She was always in trouble. Greed was usually the cause. And she'd always been provocative. 'Kay, I'll help you, just tell me what you want.'

Kay left the bedroom. The eldest boy was standing on the stairs and the whiteness of her face alarmed him. For a moment he thought he was seeing a ghost.

· Twenty ·

Kay was surprised to find Joel in the house at 10.00 am. He was changing the lock on the back door. 'They've had their television and video stolen next door, so let's keep this bolted from now on. It's the gypsies.'

She was insulted. 'What gypsies?'

He meant the caravans of the homeless parked illegally between the sedate crescent and the squalor of Camden High Street.

'They're not gypsies.' She was furious. 'They're out-of-work, homeless, mainly Irish. They've as much to do with gypsies as you have – '

'So defensive, darling! I didn't realise there were so many categories of gypsy. I'm sure your visitor, being in work, would hardly steal from our neighbours.'

'Fuck you, Joel.'

'Come on, Kay. Gypsies have a bad name and they commit petty crime.'

She thought she'd be committing murder if he went on. She felt so angry she left the house.

That night Joel came to bed with some books. 'I've been reading about gypsies and how they had to keep moving because no one would allow them to settle. They don't fit in with society. That goes with your friend the guitar player. It's a mutual distrust and has been going on for centuries. They just settle on a site and steal and beg and generally destroy the wellbeing of the resident community.'

'Not in Seville. Not in Triana.' Her voice was shaking.

'Really?' He opened a book. 'Do you know what Richard Ford, the English traveller writing in the 1840's thought about Triana, the gypsy neighbourhood of Seville. He says, "Never is there wanting some venerable gypsy hag who will get up a *función*. These festivals must be paid for since the gitanesque race, according to Cervantes, were only sent into this world as fish hooks for purses . . . The scene of the ball is generally placed in the suburb of Triana, home of bullfighters, smugglers, picturesque rogues and Egyptians (gypsies). Here they dance the *romalis* and sing *al caña*." '

He shut the book. 'They seem to set out to destroy, by any means, the status quo.'

For the first time the editor of the Sunday paper rejected one of Kay Craven's articles. He wasn't interested in Sainsburys for heaven's sake! Or corner shops. Kay was supposed to write about compelling issues from her own point of view, so she wrote instead about Angel finding the unknown singer's work. She went back to the Darby house and asked for photographs.

William Darby said, 'You won't say too much about the suicide?'

'I don't know too much.'

'It'll only hurt the children.'

'Aren't they already hurt?' She too was hurt. Wasn't everybody?

His hands reached out to reclaim the photographs.

'I can go to Rick,' she said.

'If you mention my private life, Mrs Craven, I'll come after you and the newspaper.' He sounded almost seductive, as though suggesting a sensual pleasure. His eyes were cold and he kept the photographs out of her reach.

'Why did she do it?'

He didn't answer.

'Perhaps if between us we make a really good article and her songs are released and successful that will put something to rest. It's what she wanted isn't it? Success?'

'So you're writing her epitaph?'

'Better it's me. Because when the flamenco singer releases "Firechild" they'll all be at the door.'

'I've heard that sort of thing before. From the press.'

She explained she wasn't 'the press'. She was a highly acclaimed original writer who happened to concentrate on contemporary trends.

'I know you've been invited to Washington to represent the London women's view.' He put on a kettle.

Quickly she looked at the photographs. She was amazed at just how beautiful Alexis had been. In some she looked like a street urchin, in others like a moviestar. Kay thought what a waste her death was. 'Did she leave a note?'

'Would you, Mrs Craven – leave a note?'

'Couldn't you have got her to a doctor? Surely you could have seen it coming? I used to know her at one time when the children were young. We used to wait outside the primary school and – '

'I remember you. You had a friend.' He tried to recall her name.

'Liz.'

He nodded.

'Liz remembers you. She said you've got big eyes,' Kay rolled hers around, 'always looking at women.'

He half laughed.

'And that's why she did it. Jumped. You could say it was because the kids were on smack. Or because she wasn't getting anywhere. The modelling contract on TV cancelled . . .'

'You know, Mrs Craven, you're too lucky. I wouldn't like to be too lucky.' He made a hot Ribena and put it on a tray.

'You and Paula Strong broke her heart,' said Kay.

William Darby looked at her as though she were an executioner. Was there anything this woman didn't know? How he regretted letting her into the house, but it was better he deal with her than she go to Rick's. She was a grim bitch. 'So you liked my wife?'

'Yes I did. And I think she's going to be posthumously famous;

nothing like death for public relations. So you'd better get rid of any loose ends.'

'How about illness? As you say you like her I will tell you she'd recently had a hysterectomy. Apparently that can cause depression.'

A good-looking boy with ragged hair and torn jeans sped into the kitchen. He was barefoot and around his ankle he wore a chain. 'If you want me to visit grandmother you'd better give me some money.' He was well-spoken.

William felt in his pockets.

'And give me the car keys.'

'You're not taking that. There's a fast train to Oxford every hour.' He gave the boy two ten pound notes, then the tray of Ribena. 'Give it to Paula.'

As the boy took the tray he looked at the gold ring on his father's little finger, then at his eyes. Kay saw it, the jealousy. The boy was jealous of his father's sophistication and sexual success. And he was cut off from any kind of love. William Darby's son knew the mistress got that. Kay had been given plenty of reasons for Alexis' death. They were bad enough. But something else had driven her to kill herself, Kay was sure, when she saw him make the Ribena. It was something about the way he put the cup on the tray and said, 'Take it to Paula.' Had he taken care of his wife? Cups on trays when she didn't feel good? You can just come to the end of yourself, she thought. From the pure exhaustion of having to carry on for an unspecified amount of time in an adverse world.

'Was that your eldest son?' She knew he was the worst.

William Darby nodded.

Kay doubted if the twenty pounds would get him to Oxford. Grandma would be waiting a long time for that visit.

'I expect *your* son goes to Eton. That's where Joel went,' said Darby. 'So I tell you what you want to know and you write a conclusive piece, securing loose ends, about Alexis' death. No thankyou, Mrs Craven. I'll take my chances with the tabloids.'

He let her have two photographs. She knew if she'd been in

better shape she would have got him to talk to her, but she was so sad herself. As she left he was feeding the cat. She said, 'I hope you'll be happy.'

He looked up. 'I wish you the same. I pity the ones the sun shines on. When they have bad luck they haven't a clue what's hit them.'

Kay took the same route to the railway bridge that Alexis Scott had taken that morning in early spring. Perhaps she should look less – opulent?

She decided to write a piece on the mothers outside the primary school. How gentle that time had been. As she stood on the bridge she suddenly remembered Alexis clearly. One of the boys' mothers had died; she'd been depressed and taken an overdose. The woman had seemed like a little mouse as she described being on antidepressants and how they didn't work and the doctor had said it would take three weeks. How did you get through the three weeks? She had not. And it was Alexis Scott who had taken her son in. She had shown such warmth and kindness. She had had the courage to actually embrace the father, to share his bereavement. She had not been afraid of other people's grief. She didn't mind being physical and loving even if it allowed them to break down and sob and release their sadness. Her behaviour had not been typically English, and her kindness didn't go with the filmstar looks exactly.

Kay would definitely put all that in her article: it would be about her kindness as much as her talent and songs. The gypsy wouldn't get a look in.

The bridge was empty. She almost expected to see him arrive. Then she saw further along, fresh white flowers poked through the bars. Some had fallen onto the line, and she realised Angel had been there only minutes before her because trains passed frequently yet none had crushed the flowers.

Kay could see Liz and the cleaner had been having a good gossip; as she came in Liz was saying, 'I thought she was pregnant. She's been so unlike herself.'

'What's she want another one for when she's got a career?' said the cleaner.

Although Kay was now in the room the cleaner went on talking. 'Women nowadays may be able to do everything, but there's one thing you can be sure of: they might get their fella into an apron but he'll never have a baby.'

'Is that an Irish proverb?' asked Kay.

'You've been funny ever since that woman killed herself – that singer,' retorted the cleaner.

'Funny?' said Kay, sounding hostile.

'If I had to pinpoint the day when you changed it was that morning we heard about her tragedy.'

'But I didn't even know her,' said Kay.

'That's what's funny about it: a woman dies, you don't even know her, yet you change. And that's why *he* came around.' She mimed strumming a guitar. 'To find out about *her*.'

'So what's the significance then?' said Kay.

'I don't know,' said the cleaner. 'Just the way it works out, I suppose.' She said all the usual things before leaving; complaints about tiredness, waiting for transport. She was never too exhausted however to reach up to the second shelf for her money.

Kay threw her bag onto the table and wished Liz would go. She had to start cooking and the thought of it suddenly exhausted her. She could feel the frown-line between her eyebrows deepening into a headache and thought, I must stop frowning. It'll be plastic surgery next.

'I wish you'd go, Liz.'

Liz stayed where she was.

'You just come over when you want, take me for granted.'

Liz tried to laugh. 'Don't think for a minute that I'll let your fame get in the way of our friendship, of the way I feel for you. I'm the last one of the old crowd. Fame can be isolating and you're too nice for that to happen to. Which neighbours just pop in? They used to.'

'So it's for my benefit you keep crossing the road. You're sure it isn't to be part of what goes on here?'

'Kay, I have what goes on here over there.' She indicated her own house. 'OK, Roly and I aren't quite such a team. I am determined not to lose you, you're too valuable. I'm going to keep you as a friend, whatever you say. Now let's drink to that.' She poured some Spanish liqueur into two glasses. 'I have to protect you, don't you see that?' And in a world of change Kay saw she had one friend. Liz put her arms around her, embraced her warmly, and Kay thought, That's what he's doing of course: protecting me. That's why he doesn't see me. It was the first flutter. Obsession had set in.

· Twenty-One ·

In the morning Kay's thoughts were depressed before she even woke up. She came to in a black, unbearable place. It was like toothache in the deepest, most vital part of her. Her body, so heavy, like a bag of wet sand, her legs off somewhere, stranded and bloodless, on their own; numbed hands, eyes baggy, depressed, toxic; everything about her felt bad.

Her GP said it could be the menopause. That was a condition Kay had never thought of. Neither did she want to.

'Would antidepressants help?' Kay thought of the mothers outside the primary school; they hadn't helped the little mouse mother. And Alexis Darby came yet again into her thoughts. She remembered Alexis saying how much sadness children had. She'd worn a yellow jacket and her hair was dyed white, fluffy and clean.

But Kay wasn't a victim. She was valued.

The GP said, 'I am not sure you are depressed, Kay.'

'No, I'm not depressed.' She laughed. 'I'm desperate.'

How could Angel simply forget that day at the sea? Did gypsies have some magic that made them forget even glorious days? Unless someone else was making his life more euphoric, some young blonde model. Her mind settled on that and she started to imagine him taking the girl's clothes off her, having her. She had to drop that train of thought – too agonising. She took a drink and made a few business phone calls. When she'd calmed down she saw that one person did not replace another. However many blonde models he was ecstatic with, he would not forget the hours they'd shared, any more than she would. She wasn't mad, she knew how his eyes brightened when he looked at her, the way his breathing changed when he was close to her. Why put herself down? It was obvious he was protecting her so she could keep her marriage and what he called 'harmony'. That was perhaps his best gift of love.

In her worst moments she had no resources to turn to. She couldn't assume things would get better. They were already as good as they'd get. She'd seen that in the doctor's surgery. People loved her, needed her. She was admired, fêted, even spoilt. But she didn't have the recourse the Darby family had in adversity: they could think, Someone will come along and love me, value me, take care of me and all this will be better. Again she counted her blessings.

Every phone call was him calling until she found out it wasn't. Every post contained some message explaining his absence from her life. Except the letter didn't come. She blamed herself for playing hard to get – she should have let him sleep with her. Maybe he needed encouragement. How she regretted not seducing him. Perhaps he needed some kind of tacit permission to take another man's wife? Marriage, she was sure, meant more to him than to the average Anglo Saxon. Gypsies owned things: animals, women, land. For what she wanted him to do, he could be stabbed, banished. She thought it odd she was so obsessed considering she hadn't slept with him. One touch meant more than the full act of love with another man.

Was it so good with Joel these days? When they did make love, the only way she got through it was to think of Angel. She couldn't bear Joel to speak.

Then she thought he was waiting for her, willing her to contact him. She would not be the one to give in. She went through the obsessive's alphabet of hope.

Liz said he had simply dropped out of sight. That, too, added fuel to the obsession. He'd stopped performing because he was getting over his passion for her, Kay was almost sure of it. For a while she blamed herself for killing off a career. She wouldn't talk about him, not to the cleaner or Liz. She did ask Sophie if he still went to Rick's.

'He's done the album. Why should he go back to Kentish Town? Mum, you don't understand. He's the Mick Jagger of the flamenco world. He'll be travelling all the time. He meets a hundred new people a week.'

Thanks, she thought. It took a child to see it clearly.

Roly came over that evening. She thought it was to have a 'discussion'. Liz had obviously told him about the gypsy and he was going to do the right thing by Joel and the English middle class as a whole. She waited for the well-meaning lecture to begin. She'd tell him to bugger off. He opened his mouth. 'I don't know how to say this – '

'Don't try, Roly.'

'But you're the only one I can talk to. I'm so unhappy,' and he put his head on the table, like a tired child. He asked her for some ice cream. Did she have any of the mint flavour?

'I've always had a fantasy. Let's call her Miss Right. A certain kind of girl, almost Oriental in her ways, and she'd fit me like a glove. Obviously it isn't Liz I'm talking about. I thought success would give me that perfect woman. It's given me the opportunity to look and not find, so in some ways I'd have been better off unknown. I wouldn't have had to challenge the fantasy.'

She'd never heard him deliver so many sentences without a single touch of obscurity.

'So you see, I'm empty and stuck. I look, she isn't there. I can't get anything out of Liz; she belongs in my past. We're like two comfortable old armchairs together, domestically intimate; she'll never leave me . . .' He paused. He wasn't entirely fooled. 'Well, let's say she's capable of – look, she fooled around with a French guest on the show. Not a pretty sight. It involved food.' He stopped eating his ice cream as he remembered what he'd seen. His face was sad and sagged. 'All right, she's kinky. But I'm leaving that to my lawyers. I wish I could say the same – that I'd never leave her. Kay, I'd be off tomorrow. But I can't find Miss Right and I can't settle for less.'

'So why don't you live alone?' Kay cut in.

He blinked, frightened. 'I'm trapped in my own ideal of what I want. I think I should have it because I have everything else. I want you to look after Liz. That is, when I do go. That is, if I find what I'm looking for. Because you're strong and capable of supporting her.'

Kay almost laughed in his face. How Liz would love this! How wrong could Roly get? 'If you can't face being alone why don't you go and look in Japan, Roly? Or Thailand?'

'I thought you'd understand.' He sounded angry. 'It's not a question of taking a plane to Tokyo. I have a sense of my true wife, and life will produce it or it won't.' He finished the ice cream and crunched some ginger biscuits. 'I can't just take up with five or six exotic Eastern girls – I have a sense of commitment to what I feel is meant for me. Do you see?'

She saw that having your face on the box night after night did not necessarily guarantee a hundred per cent audience rating: Miss Right hadn't seen the show.

Roly asked for some homemade cake. While she was getting it he lifted the saucepan lids and smelt the soup deeply, the lentils spiced with garlic. He even had a quick snoop in the fridge. 'I often have fantasies about sex and food. D'you know what I mean?'

'No,' she said very quickly. She saw the French count was not on his own.

'I want you to know, Kay, that I respect you. So do most men. More – idolise you. It's rare these days to feel that way about a woman, so please don't change. I feel much brighter and more at ease now that I've spoken to you.'

He jogged off across the street like a giraffe, with his long neck drooping down and big sad eyes. She couldn't imagine his fantasy woman at his side. That woman seemed to belong to another kind of man altogether.

She told Joel about the visit. They had little to talk about these days.

'He's spoilt.' said Joel. 'What he wants to do is get his hands on an Eastern girl and introduce her to the West, make her totally dependent on him, choose her dresses, her food, teach her about sex. She'll speak no English except what he chooses to teach her. She'll be his adoring sex slave – '

'Most women wouldn't go for that. Even Eastern ones.'

'I'm not talking about women as such. She'll be about fourteen.'

'Is that his fantasy or yours?'

'Most men's.' Joel tipped her under the chin with just a touch of mockery. He got into bed and lay on his side away from her. It wasn't going to be a sexy night. Maybe now she didn't keep him satisfied his fantasies had had a chance to surface. She thought he would do a lot better than Roly.

· *Twenty-two* ·

The article on Alexis and her life came out in late July. It was beautifully written, sincerely expressed, sad and nostalgic. Alexis Scott was presented to the world as a complex figure; it had taken death to release her talent. She was also a sensitive person who cared for others, a good mother. The article coincided with the release of 'Firechild'. Angel Lupez did what Alexis could never do: he got her songs to the top of the charts. His English, perfect in ordinary life, had a coating of accent and Kay suspected this was more appealing to his fans.

Quite early that Sunday morning William Darby phoned. 'I found the piece about my wife very moving and I'd like to talk to you. I think I owe it to you.'

They met in a pub on the Kentish Town road. He said, 'I didn't see it coming. For a long time there were so many problems, just getting through the day was hard. Quite often, dreadful. The boys just broke her heart. It wasn't one incident so much as an accumulation of horror and strain. One after another they went onto drugs, the older one is an addict – you saw him. We both went through a hell on earth. The younger boys are both off now. Then she was ill, not surprising after what she'd gone through. She had several haemorrhages and had to have an operation. That must have depressed her. And every day she believed she'd finally make it, that she'd be recognised, that her songs would be hits. She began to understand that wasn't going to happen, yet lesser people did well. And she was worried about looking old. She was replaced on the commercial. And I did my share. Everything was fine between us until I met Paula and started to need that kind of sex. I couldn't live without it. Then Paula was pregnant. At the time I didn't know she had even guessed about Paula. After her death I learned differently. Rick didn't waste any time telling me. And Alexis' friends. I kept wishing she would meet somebody. And then – '

'And then?' repeated Kay, knowing what was coming next.

'That gypsy appeared.' He laughed. 'Ironically, he would have been just right for my wife, I'm absolutely sure of it. But he turned up too late.'

Kay had learned to keep herself together. She never showed pain. She had plenty of practice these days.

'She could have done it on any day. Why that day? She'd been in the middle of washing up and just left everything and left the house. A cup was still on the draining board covered in suds, the scourer inside it. It's odd because Paula won't wash up at all. Not a cup. She washes my clothes and irons them but won't do housework, so we have a girl come in to do it.'

'Did she leave a note? Really?'

'Not that I saw. But I found her diaries.' He shrugged. 'She sometimes found life unbearable, always hard, and she escaped into her songs. She thought a lot of things were so dreadful they had to be funny and she saw the funny side in a very dry way. But there was no mention of taking her life. She writes a lot about the area and the people, and Paula. And, of course, betrayal. So I couldn't have known or done anything to prevent it. The impulse must have occurred in the middle of washing up because she never left a job unfinished. It irritated her unbearably if she didn't finish cleaning the stairs or cutting the hedge.'

Then he said he'd been very much in love with his wife. His students had sometimes had crushes on him, but he'd never taken advantage of that situation because he didn't need to. Only Paula – he couldn't get enough of her.'

Kay was dying to know what kind of sex she provided.

'After Alexis' death I hated Paula, and she left for a while. Then I found I couldn't do without her and she was a solace.'

'Is it just sexual?'

'Predominantly. But I like to have her around. Just? That's a surprising word. Isn't sex what keeps everything going?' He looked at her then, really looked at her, and she could see he was attractive. She added 'fatally'. When he had stopped looking at her he said, 'Your daughter Sophie sees a lot of my son Rick. She's mature for her age. Very bright.'

'We all start off bright. We're inclined to lose it as life educates us.'

'Wordsworth longed for where he had come from because he did not see where he was going. I'm inclined to think we get brighter the longer we're here.'

'What did Alexis think?'

'She thought God would look after her.'

'Perhaps he has.'

As she left she thought, Get those diaries, then you get him back. He'd do anything to see those. So she asked about them and William Darby said they were safe. He didn't want the kids knowing about them. It wouldn't do any good.

The following day Paula Strong gave birth to a boy, but William Darby still wouldn't marry her.

Joel said he remembered William Darby at university being quite privileged, from a good family, with style, looks, intelligence. So Kay asked how he ended up at the local poly. Joel said, 'Luck. Some people have it. And others? Darby just didn't get the breaks.'

She was sure Angel would see the Sunday paper, or someone would show him. She waited in for the phone call which never came. She kept thinking of the tea dancing by the sea, how they'd laughed; you could kick love out, but surely not laughter? If someone really made you laugh you never let them go.

She made several enquiries as to his whereabouts. He'd cancelled his New York performances and the Paris concerts. His recording manager reckoned he was in Spain.

A week later she was booking their summer holiday. The cleaner had put a hot drink by the phone. 'You're too pale, Kay. You're not looking your best.'

Sophie glanced briefly at her mother, then went back to the theatre school prospectus she was reading. She wanted to be a performer but the first thing in the way was her father. The second, she'd have to leave Rick. He had another year to do at the comprehensive.

Kay arranged to fly to Bermuda with Sophie during the third week of August, then they'd go on to San Francisco and Mexico. She had friends in all these places and by this route she'd avoid jetlag. Joel would fly to Mexico directly from London at the end of August and continue into South America on business. He didn't allow himself holidays. They were used to keep him in good shape and he'd have preferred walking and climbing in the Swiss Alps or the Dolomites. He had allowed only four days in Mexico.

As usual Kay would write a batch of articles to cover the holiday period. She realised she hadn't thought about the gypsy for a whole morning, and possibly not the night before. It was as if by planning to go away she was releasing her obsession. Hours had been spent waiting, imagining, hoping, suffering, inventing his dialogue, his side of the duet and she'd lost a lot in the process: her sex life with Joel, her sociability, her pleasure in life, her peace of mind. But she had not given in. She had not gone rushing between a day and a night to Andalusia. He could make her wait, as she could him, so it wasn't a love affair as much as some kind of contest. But why?

As she cooked the fish and chips for Sophie's lunch she thought how much he liked them. How he would cover the chips in salt, the fish in vinegar. Her cleaner said, 'I know why you're pale. You never go out. That's what it is.'

'Firechild' was playing on the radio and Kay switched it off. Going away would be a new start. While she was gone she'd have the kitchen painted. She'd get a barbecue; food cooked on charcoal tasted better. She lifted a pan onto the stove to fast fry some vegetables.

The door opened and the gypsy came back into the kitchen; the colour came back into Kay's face.

The first one to react was Sophie. She yelled, 'Oh no! Not him, oh no!' and she got up and stamped her feet. Then she pushed him. Kay shouted at her to stop. The cleaner grabbed a broom and held it as though to fend off a wild beast while Sophie tried to knee him. He laughed as she ran from the room shouting more curses than he'd probably heard in his entire gypsy life. The cleaner was so thrilled she wanted to stay on, polishing things but Kay told her to go. Since when did she dally into the afternoon?

'I'm sorry Sophie was so rude.' The child's outburst had destroyed all chance of delivering one of the greetings Kay had rehearsed to use if ever she saw him again. To attack him now for not visiting could only be an anti-climax. But he didn't seem upset. He opened the French windows into the garden. 'It's so sunny, why aren't you outside?' He leaned back gracefully against the wall, at one with the day, with life. Looking at him she noted everything was in place, all his well-loved features. There would be nothing new to see, she already knew every little thing about him. His being there in front of her was almost a religious experience. and her eyes filled with tears. She was so happy life had been given back to her.

The cleaner said, 'Give him some money and send him on his way.'

For the first time Kay nearly burned some food. She caught the fish just in time.

'Let's go out,' he said. He wanted to be in the sun. They left the kitchen and the fish and chips cooled in their oil, which in turn congealed. Looking at it later she thought it had a sacrificial aspect.

They went to a grove of trees on the other side of Parliament Hill. Her cleaner, Liz and most people she knew would not approve of this, he was bad for her. And yet he made her happy. She thought this was how junkies must feel when they got a fix. She realised that a lot of life's trouble came from the fact that what you needed was provided by the wrong person: a father's love came not from Daddy but a lover so the affair was doomed; craving a baby, which alas was never going to be conceived, made a woman turn an ageing husband into an infant. 'They've got it wrong,' she said aloud. God should be giving her this happiness which the gypsy was handing out.

She had so many things to tell him, but instead she stayed thoughtful against the trunk of a birch tree. Being too happy was not necessarily a wise thing. The resulting trough of pain she'd sink into when he'd left her was not to be recommended. She kept silent. He stood close to her, chewing on a stalk of grass, his beautiful eyes intent on her face as though examining it for any change.

'Seeing you're such a star these days I thought you'd have more to say, Kay.'

'I save that for my column,' she said swiftly.

'You don't speak the way you write.'

'No I don't,' she agreed immediately, 'It's a different voice altogether. We decided on that some time ago.' She was determined to keep a dignified control.

'You're a stinging nettle, Kay. You only *seem* nice.' His eyes were teasing.

'I wasn't aware that you read my articles. Last time we spoke it seemed you didn't.'

'I don't. But somebody showed me what you had to say about Alexis Scott.'

She thought he was lying. She was sure he read every article, looking for some mention of himself. 'Why don't you read what I write, incidentally?'

'Because I hate that middle-class "clever" stuff written from the unchanging stuffiness of your Habitat life.'

'Liberty's, darling.'

'You've been put together like a Habitat catalogue: a bit of chintz, a half clever kitchen arrangement, old English tea cups, a cook book.'

'Oh that is unfair. And so wrong. I come from a very old

English family if you must know and we don't depend on Habitat for our ideas.'

'An aristocrat?' he said lightly. 'Yet you have a whore's mouth.'

She rapped him hard across the face and his mouth started to bleed. She said, 'I'd rather get laid and get paid for it than be a cheap trick like you. You'd go with anyone for nothing, just for the degradation. You can't sink fast enough into the dirt you come from. If you didn't prostitute yourself by selling your grandfather's songs you'd be a diseased nothing with your arse hanging out, your looks gone, standing on any corner in Seville. And you wouldn't get that much.' She snapped her fingers. 'At least I'm beautiful.'

He laughed. 'Stinging nettle. I told you.' How he enjoyed her loss of control and how distraught she felt. He spat out some blood and laughing said, 'Come on, tell me your menu for lunch today.'

Suspicious, she looked at him. Then she started angrily away from the tree. She was going home. He swept an arm up, imprisoning her against the tree trunk. 'As you're more beautiful than me and would get paid for action, you start.'

'You're cruel aren't you, Angel?'

'I won't let you go until you do what I want. I'm stronger than you.' He waited.

'What do you mean? Tell you the menu?' Her voice was icy.

'Of course.'

'Strawberry soup, spinach roulade with fluffed rice and pears in red wine.' She said it without hesitation. She was forcing herself not to cry.

'Tapas, paella, bacaloa, which is a fish of the region; a sweet cheese with honey and nuts and an apple always to finish the meal. Then a peppermint tisane. I win.' He'd spoken quickly, in a burst, like machine gun fire. 'Don't you want to know why?'

She shrugged.

He said, 'Because I am a better cook than you. I could make *your* menu better than you.'

My God he's spoilt, and so full of himself. Did I actually long for this? She couldn't wait to leave.

In a different tone he said, 'I don't think you got Alexis right at all.'

She could smell the perfume on his clothes, his hair and it produced in her a very definite and unwanted excitement. Dismissively she replied. 'Oh I don't know. I did meet her, after all, and I talked to her husband. He told me a lot of things.'

'The dead can say anything. How do I know what I read is right? Because that husband said she said it? I don't think so, Kay.' He didn't look as though he was being insulting.

Very calmly she said, 'William Darby told me the reason she died.'

'Whatever he said, that isn't it. He wouldn't see the reason if it was pinned on the pregnant stomach of his mistress.'

She was taken aback by just how bitter he sounded. His eyes closed and he reached for her hand, held it, really held it. She said, 'I don't want to stay here with you. You insult me, my work –' She tried to get him to release her hand.

'Oh no, my friend, I haven't insulted you. If I had even approached an insult, you wouldn't be standing here dry-eyed and smug.'

She tried to hit him again, but he held the other hand. Both of hers in one of his. She realised the man she'd been pining for was a recipe of her own making: a bit of the gypsy, a lot of her imagination.

'You're smug, like the cat that takes the cream. You know that about yourself, surely you do? Life is good to you in a fashion and you're pleased about it. You enjoy being Kay Craven. It pleases you.'

'So what! I'm not smug. I think for once, one of your English words has let you down. Don't you mean content?'

'With me you wouldn't be smug.' He looked at her calculatingly as though he were going to take her there, against the tree. She turned away to hide her reaction. He was on to that and asked what was wrong.

'It's too hot.'

'That's right. It's lucky the day's cool.'

He sauntered away into the grass and took off his shirt. His body was beautifully toned, the skin light brown like silk. There was a thin scar across his left ribs. She thought he had been knifed. He kicked off his moccasins, pulled down his trousers and gestured for her to join him. 'Get some sun, Kay.' He was wearing another chain with a small stone in it. He lay back on the grass and closed his eyes. She could see how strong his legs were and she thought, That body sees a lot of action. She could so easily see it in bedrooms, in all sorts of company.

Disturbed, she said, 'I wrote the truth about Alexis Scott.'

'I don't think so, Kay. I thought you were on the wrong track.'

Inflamed, she replied, 'I *did* have the advantage of knowing her. And I did have her diaries, my sweet.'

He opened his eyes and sat up, suspicious, sensing the life.

'So I think I do know what she's talking about.'

'You know her intimate thoughts? They certainly don't appear in your article.'

'I know why she died.'

'Not a chance.'

She saw they were fighting over a woman neither of them knew and now never would.

He said, 'You don't understand that sort of person at all.'

'And you do?'

'Of course. That's why I recorded her songs. I know her very well.' He turned onto his stomach, away from her.

She sat in the shade, deliberately leaving a noticeable space between them. She would leave, only when she found out what this man was and what he wanted.

'I'm on her side too, don't forget,' she said. There was a silence for a while then she said, 'It's terrible that she died. She had such a marvellous voice.'

'Is that any reason to live.' Angel pulled at her dress. 'Take it off. The sun is delicious.'

Kay wasn't shy, she just did not want to show her body to him. Her breasts were too obvious in the fragile brassière under the silk of her dress. She felt him looking at her body, assessing it for pleasure.

'So you don't need protection.' he said. 'You're not wearing the chain I gave you.'

'How can I explain it? I'm married.'

'The stone has been in my family for years. It's a lodestone that gives protection from danger. It's not intended to cause rivalry.'

'Why are you with me?'

'Perhaps I'm your guardian angel.'

'What do you want?'

'You are one of those straight, English, middle-class people who hate being criticised. Yet you won't even fight. I insult you and you absorb it like a sponge. What are you? A sponge full of hurts and insults? I tell you I'm a better cook than you, you accept. A Spanish woman would hurl a pan at my head. Fight for yourself.'

'I'm the way I am and it's worked so far. You seemed interested in changing it.' She smiled provocatively. 'I wonder why. Why do people want to change others?'

He looked slightly ill at ease.

'You're spoilt,' she said.

'I know.'

'How was Paris?' Her voice was very steady now.

'Paris?'

'Didn't you go?'

'No, why should I?' He was very defensive. 'Why do you ask?' She shrugged.

'No, come on.'

Too lightly she said, 'I thought you were booked for some concerts there. But I see the subject of Paris worries you.'

'Oh that!' He was noticeably relieved. 'I didn't want to go. I thought it better to work on Alexis' songs.' At a disadvantage now, he didn't look at her.

'Did you like Paris?' Now *she* had the control. 'In general I mean.'

'Like?' His tone suggested indifference.

She sensed there had been plenty wrong with Paris. 'So where were you?'

'Kentish Town.'

'*All this time?*' Her voice shook. She couldn't disguise it. All that suffering and he had been no more than a mile away.

'Did you miss me?' He sounded like a schoolboy poking at her with a stick to see if she'd cry.

'Where did you stay?'

'Here and there. Sometimes with the youngest boy, Rick. He's bright. And I met the other two. There's quite a scene going on there.'

'So you stayed with Rick?'

'On and off.'

She would discuss this with Sophie when she got home.

Very seriously he said, 'As I did the recordings I became very involved with Alexis.' He talked as though she were living.

Kay, pained, said, 'I thought we were friends. You don't treat a friend like that. You stay in touch.'

'Sometimes people do just disappear. They get too close and so they go.'

'Why?'

'Perhaps because they don't like being too close.'

She had no more idea of him than she had had when it all started. She was trying openly to define their relationship and called it friendly, but he wasn't fooled. Would she be so pained about another woman, even a dead one, if they were just friends?

'I'm calling Alexis' album, "Songs and Mysteries of the City at Sunset". Do you like it? Alexis would. I was in touch with her through her songs, and that's how I knew what made her end it all. I would have done the same.'

Kay said sharply, 'It's as though you're in love with her. You would have been, wouldn't you?'

'I am,' he said quite simply, 'in love with her. Light me a cigarette, Kay.'

The way he said it was devastating. She wanted to throw herself on top of him, kiss him, savage him, kill him. 'Men usually light mine.' She got up. 'If you write a song about me, call it "Just

Friends".' She hurried across the yellowing grass to the path. The heat was murderous, her thoughts seemed to melt. One survived, cold as ice. 'I've done it. I've been strong enough to walk away. I've won.'

· Twenty-three ·

Liz said, 'He is interesting on the subject of Paris, I agree. Mention even the Eiffel Tower and there's a rebuke in the air. We were in a French restaurant the other night and he ordered in rather good French, with a real understanding of the menu. Roly commented on it – Angel had obviously lived there to speak French that well. Yet he denied it and behaved as though he was insulted. It's his Achilles heel. If you ask me, he's been in some dark alleys in his time and they had French names.'

'Do you like him, Liz?'

'He's got too good an opinion of himself.' She lifted a South American blanket and showed Kay a silver tin chest. 'That's all I'm taking, just my best things. I've got enough money for a new start.' She looked at the chest admiringly. 'Discreet, isn't it? All packed right under his nose!' She replaced the blanket.

'So when exactly are you off?'

'As soon as I'm sure that Angel's uncle's house is all right. I've made enquiries and I want to see some photographs. I've got to think about Baby: schools, doctors, children to play with.'

Baby was four and looked as though he were going to grow into someone who would need a lot of attention. Already he was trouble.

'And the others can come out during the holidays. I've got to be absolutely sure because I can only go once, I can't come back.' Liz sprawled across the cold, silken bedcover. 'I've tried to stay for the kids, but it's no good. As I know the settlement will be lousy I'm taking a very big whack from our joint account. In fact, all of it. He won't do anything because I know too much about him. He'd hate all that to come out in public: little embarrassing details about TV's Mr Number One. I wouldn't do it, of course, but he doesn't know that. And, Kay, you're to come out as often as you like. Promise?'

Kay was thinking, Why does he keep challenging me? Why try to change me? Because he wants power. After leaving him she had thought she had freedom. She had the same freedom as a slow-witted donkey who believes because the rope is slack, he can go anywhere. The rope might be long but the end was still tethered to a stake. As though to confirm that view, the gypsy was the first thing she saw as she left Liz's house.

He was immediately opposite, sitting on her wall. 'You look cool,' he said. He made it sound like a compliment. 'I like the "Just Friends", but it's too American for me. You did mean it as an album title? How about "Saving Face"? That's good.' He flicked her hair so she might think it was a joke. 'You know why your menu wasn't as good as mine? Your strawberry soup – you don't eat chilled food on a very hot day. And you make the mistake of thinking you should eat little because of the heat; you need to be fortified against it. You must have protein or you could collapse, and salt. Where's your protein? Spinach has iron. You would serve coffee – bad for the liver. You drink a camomile or peppermint tea.' Without changing even his expression he said, 'You can come with me, Kay, I'll take you across the desert. Sand, like fire, is purifying. But no preconceived ideas. You just come, and trust me.'

She didn't answer. She didn't know from one minute to the next what he would do. Prepare a trip, insult her, excite her, cook a meal, leave her. She stayed absolutely still. Then she said, 'I'm onto you.'

He stared at her challengingly. 'Be careful, Kay. You can't have power *and* love. You have to choose.'

'You want to destroy me,' said Kay.

He leapt up from the wall as though accused of a crime.

'That's how I end up, Angel.'

He shook his head as though she were mad.

· 143 ·

She started towards the door. She did not want him to come in. 'I don't know why you do it.'

'Perhaps I do discourage the parts of you that are not worthy. That article, for instance, on Alexis. It's the same as that woman you saw in the hospital. You did it for your own advantage, to get a story. And then you got it wrong.'

'You couldn't be more wrong.' She was so furious she was shaking. 'I wouldn't think of writing about Sarah Prince, I only wanted to help her. And I hear you've been helping my friend, Liz. I hope it is "help" and you know what you're doing.'

'You went back to the mental hospital not to see her but because you couldn't believe you might be wrong that's all.'

'I won't get it wrong when I write about you. Never fear!'

'Blackmail. So what? Readers will think you are just one more fascinated fan.'

She spat at him.

He laughed. 'Oh, Kay, let me hold you and make it better.' He held out his arms.

'Get out of my life,' and she meant it.

'But we belong together,' he said simply.

'Just go!' She reached the door, but he followed her.

'I would leave but I don't know which voice to believe. You have so many. Promise me you'll write with your true one. Because I sing with my true voice, I can tell you that.'

In spite of everything she was listening to him. She sensed he knew things she hadn't dreamed of. How could she have all these voices?

'There's the Kay married to the chemical executive – I don't smell any love there; the sweet cook who likes to appear beneficent, yet at the same time mysterious. Why? So, we come back to power.' He tapped her chest. 'You like power. You like to captivate them. Then there's the stinging nettle: as long as your story is entertaining, who cares about the truth? Then there's the other voice. Which is the one that you want to use. But you're sulking. It's the voice that belongs in the desert; it's the voice of the girl you were before you sat on this silly Hampstead throne, kowtowing to critics, fading bores, listening to them and then, my God, writing about them. Did you think you could mix with them and remain the same?'

He waited but she didn't answer. How she hated criticism. Of course she liked acclaim. Usually she made it impossible for someone to criticise her to her face but he'd sort of slipped it in, in the heat of the day.

'You'll be quite safe in the desert. You'll be with me. I can see, Kay, that stinging nettles sell – I can see why you do it. But there's a better way to deal with the inexpressible. I do it with songs.'

If he compares me with Alexis I'll kill him, she thought.

He went on talking to her, his eyes sombre, not wanting to hurt her. He would hurt only if he had to, until she saw what he saw and accepted it. At the end she still thought he wanted power. He wants me in his power for some reason. I'd better watch my step or he'll break my heart. He offers me an experience which could change my very soul. If he leaves, I'll regret it for the rest of my life. So he'll have to come in. I'll have to chance it.

Sophie took her mother to one side and told her to get him out. 'Now, Mum.'

Automatically, Kay put the kettle on; a hot drink always reassured her. Angel walked towards them and Sophie widened her eyes dramatically. 'Get him out!' she hissed.

'Did you ever see Alexis perform?' he asked Sophie.

Still defending her mother, she turned her head away as rudely as possible.

'You go to all those clubs, you must have seen her. Come on. I see twelve-year-olds pretending they're sixteen at the door of the Starlight.'

'Fuck you,' and Sophie ran away.

Kay made some kind of apology; it sounded false.

'She echoes the unspoken in this house,' Angel said.

'She's bad,' said Kay. In all truth she didn't mind her daughter's tantrums, quite enjoyed them; Kay didn't mind trouble.

'She's the only good one,' he said. 'All those detestable people around her, no wonder she's angry.'

'They're all part of getting there. Haven't you ambitions?'

'Of course not. I have everything.'

He began to cook a hot spicy spaghetti. 'She wants to be a performer, your daughter. You should let her. I think she's fabulous.'

'My son's fabulous.'

'Sophie's the only real one.'

'Is "real" being impolite?'

'She's angry, that's natural. She's got things to be angry about. Your son's already in trouble.'

She sighed, furious. 'I suppose I'm going to have to ask why.'

'He's like your husband.' He put the food on the table and told her to sit down. He even cut the bread. At last it was dark and the air was bearable. All the doors and windows were open.

'Are you good or bad? I must know,' she said.

He reached across and took her hands. 'It takes a stranger to see it. We're born into this world blind and we have to open our eyes before we die.'

'Is that a gypsy saying?'

'Alexis wrote it on the back of one of her shopping lists. On another shopping list she wrote, "Catfood, cat litter (the cheapest), cleansing milk, biro, notebook, baked beans, cut loaf, respect, loyalty and some tender care." She gave the list to her husband. She was sick at the time. She didn't eat like we do; she ate convenience foods, shopped at Sainsburys. she didn't have money. The family never ate together, they just opened a tin.'

'I'm sure you'd have dealt with the malnutrition in the Darby household.' She sounded frosty.

His hold on her hands tightened, his eyes brightened and as he laughed the mood was quite changed. He went from dark to joyous without a word spoken.

They drank a lot, put on music and danced, and ended up lying on her bed, side by side on their backs, laughing. They laughed helplessly. Sophie got out of bed and looked through the half-opened door. The laughter dwindled and then started again and their bodies shook, eyes streaming with tears. Their laughter was like the sea coming in and going out, growing in strength, then fading.

Sophie said, 'Mum, are you on something?' They lay not touching, completely separate, like bodies in coffins.

As he was leaving he pointed to the string of garlic hanging in the kitchen. 'You should hang your garlic over your front door.'

'Is that a gypsy custom?'

'Anyone's custom,' he said reprovingly. 'You're too happy.'

She was taken aback.

'If you're too happy you should protect yourself, no?' It was obvious to him.

'Are you?' she said sharply.

'I tell you I've been through so much I think I have exhausted all possibilities of ever being happy. For me, happiness is fleeting. No more than those few seconds of oblivion an orgasm gives. The days for me are hard, all of them. Sometimes I can't tell one from the other. How much longer do I go on? How do I get out?'

She thought how like Alexis he sounded.

Then she wondered with whom he had these fleeting orgasms? He was intent on leaving, although it was the middle of the night and the spare room comfortable. 'You won't get a taxi.'

He knew the main road was bristling with nothing but. 'Do you really want me to stay?' He looked at her with perhaps the slightest possibility of sexual invitation. She swallowed nervously. She was in the same predicament as so many women who wrote to her: if she didn't sleep with him she'd lose him. If she did sleep with him she'd lose him.

He's done this thousands of times, said her wise head. Don't be used. 'You go and find a taxi, Angel,' she said firmly. 'If you can't, use the spare room.' Relieved, she shut the back door and locked it.

She stood beside her sleeping daughter and confessed how

much she felt for the gypsy. The light of fidelity went out in the
only remaining solid family house in the street.

· Twenty-four ·

He didn't come back. Again Kay waited. She didn't even go out because she knew his plan to take her to the desert had been genuine. After two days she just could not believe it: so all he'd done was come back, inflame her more, give her an injection of longing. She noticed his visit coincided with her beginning to get over him; she had been on the point of recovering, off on holiday. So his gypsy mind had sensed she was slipping away. She went over all his words, scraping their sense for hidden meaning. 'Sometimes people do just disappear. They get very close and so they go. Perhaps because they don't like being that close.' That was, 'I love you', in any language.

She tried to make light of it; the whole thing was a joke by fate. She rewrote the script of the passion, cast him as a life-enhancing spiritual friend who had made her rethink her character. She was getting sloppy – too many compliments, too much praise. She didn't need a trip to the desert, she just needed a life spring-clean.

She tried to see herself as a collaborator in bringing Alexis' music to the world. All she really saw was his body naked, except for brief underpants, on the heath; the way he took off his clothes; the way his eyes lit up; the evening when he had danced. It all came down to sex. She imagined him on top of her, shuddering with excitement. He would be a good lover. He'd keep it going, take them both to near euphoria. Sweating, she wiped her face and tried to stop thinking about it. It all came down to the bedroom.

She was so obsessed she even considered sending the cleaner

to Rick's house to see if the gypsy was there. She said to Liz, 'He's obviously sleeping with someone.'

The intent with which he left her house on the last night had suggested a woman waiting.

Liz said, 'I don't think it matters that much. In that way he's rather like me, out for a good time. He's not on the look out. He'll get someone when he needs them. Like me – over with quickly and onto the next. In my case, rich, kind and taking care. In his, practical and hard. I'm sure he likes hard people.'

'Why?'

'Because he can't fuck them up. He hates guilt. He likes a woman who's independent, a good mother who'll be there if he's lonely.'

'What about love?'

'What about it?' said Liz.

On the fourth day of waiting Kay went to see William Darby. She'd get hold of those diaries and that would bring the gypsy back. They were standing ready to go out, William and Paula, with the baby in its pram. The sun shone deep into the hallway. How solid it was; moulded Victorian ceilings with original rosettes, a wide oak staircase with smooth wooden banisters, cool to the touch. Original stained-glass windows, original marble fireplaces, a Victorian lamp pulled down by weights, decorated doorhandles, and panels, and tiled floors. It was a solid, admirable house. William Darby agreed they knew how to build things in 1860. He said regretfully that they were on their way out, there was no time to speak. It was obvious that the last thing he wanted was Kay let loose on his mistress. He stood between them quite overtly. So Kay asked outright if she could see the diaries. She said how much Alexis was beginning to mean to her. She could have added, more than he would ever know. His refusal was quick and dignified. As she left she saw Paula looking at her with a certain speculation.

Liz tried to get Kay to go swimming, to the country. She suggested a quick walk in the park. 'You can't go on like this.' Telling Kay off took courage – 'You've got to get on with your life. What do you do all day? The column takes what – a morning? You can't keep turning down things, especially TV. There will come a time when they'll give up. Don't you see, Kay, he's at least ten years younger than you?'

Kay reeled as though she'd been slapped.

'And he's narcissitic. You're a catch: sought after, beautiful, classy, and frankly he's the opposite. He's screwing you around, and it's cruel. He swans in, gives you a fix, and off he goes without a care in the world. Show him you don't care.'

Kay tried denying her love for the gypsy.

'It's not love, Kay. It's becoming an obsession. You're bright enough to stop it now.'

'Where is he?'

Liz gave up. 'How do I know? He's supposed to be calling me about the house. His uncle called but I couldn't understand a word.'

As a parting shot Liz said, 'Joel's very attractive you know. I'd watch it there.'

Kay knew Liz was right. But she also knew there was attraction between her and Angel which he wouldn't want to disappear, anymore than she.

Joel watched Kay frying the steaks, her heart wasn't in it, he could see that. He thought he was having an hallucination when he saw a tin being opened; tinned food in Kay's kitchen? It was unthinkable! Mercifully it was only sweetcorn.

The steak was not as it should be. The Irish cleaner had bought it.

Joel said, 'I hear you don't shop or go out. Why's that?'

'Because I prefer to stay in.' An ambulance rushed past. It made Kay feel uneasy. Then the wind started up. Within minutes it was a gale. The world couldn't be trusted. She cleared the plates.

'You're angry with me?' asked Joel.

'Of course not.'

'You've drawn away from me. It's because I'm not managing director yet. That's what you wanted. The idea of power turned you on. But I will be. It's all taking longer than I thought.'

Listlessly she washed the plates. She'd forgotten about dessert. He watched her and it seemed as though she was listening for some sound, something that would give her pleasure.

'I haven't told you what's been happening within the company because you don't seem interested anymore.'

'Oh but I am. Of course I am interested.'

'We've decided the best way to get the chief out is a vote of no confidence in his leadership. And the threat that one of the rival conglomerates will go for a takeover. We need a strong person to succeed him – '

'You.' She smiled sweetly.

'The move has to be right. Timing is everything.' He didn't like her smile. The house no longer felt hospitable. 'Also, we'll go to the stockholders if he – '

The house didn't even feel like his. 'One of the deciding factors – he's allocated fifteen million dollars for drugs trials that could be spent on health improvement schemes: better health controls; diagnostic research; immune system build-up. Fifteen million on a new tranquilliser! No wonder drugs companies are unpopular.'

Kay smiled again. He thought better of demanding a pudding and left.

She sat at the table and laughed and laughed. It was crazy, shaking laughter. When she stopped she wiped her eyes and drank some water then started washing up. She thought, If I was watching this on film everyone would come rushing to the laughing woman, concerned, trying to help her. The next scene would be the hospital and the woman propped up in bed with men in white coats trying to coax her to eat. And her neighbours and family and her lover would gather around, docile and

· 152 ·

worried. She'd stay in the comfortable bed for weeks. In real life you stop being hysterical and you wash up.

The next day she cancelled her holiday arrangements and told Sophie it was pressure of work. She didn't tell Joel anything.

Liz called by on the way to the gym. 'He just phoned. He's in Paris. I only know that because he was calling from a bar. The house in Spain is fixed. He sounded very nice and persuasive, as though he really understood my problems. It was as though he took them on himself. Afterwards I felt better.'

'He was nice and persuasive, Liz, because he knew you'd tell me.'

Liz hadn't thought of that. She agreed it was possible. 'But I do have some life apart from you.'

'Well go and live it. Go! Let's see how nice and persuasive he is when you're on his doorstep. Don't forget there's a sea between you at the moment. He can be charming without obligation.'

Liz saw she couldn't have said worse things to an obsessed woman. She tried to put it right, but it was clear Kay wanted her to leave. Liz was very surprised to see instant coffee in the kitchen. Normally Kay ground her own.

Kay said, 'My cleaner does the shopping.'

'Why?'

Kay shrugged. 'Why not?' It was obvious she didn't care anymore. She sat very still, completely absorbed in some private world, full of secret ecstasies. Liz thought it could be day-dreaming; she hoped that's what it was. 'I've got last-minute things to do with my lawyer. Angel told me exactly what to do.'

'I'm sure he's had practice, so listen to him.' Kay showed her to the door sternly, like a disgraced guest.

Then she kicked a rubbish bin the entire length of the house. Sophie, hearing the noise, ran down from her room.

'Is everything all right, Mum?'

'I'm beginning to realise that life is quite difficult.'

A top American journalist came to interview Kay at four o'clock. She'd forgotten all about the appointment, the sort she never normally accepted. She had made the minimal effort with her appearance when the ghastly day had begun; she was wearing the dress she did her housework in, the stuff the cleaner wouldn't touch. Some of her hair was up in a chignon, the rest hung down. It said a lot for Kay's style that the journalist found her one of the few mesmerising women he'd seen. She was a lovely woman, needing no artifice. She raved about her husband and the happiness they shared; it was meant for only one reader. He couldn't fail to see such a prestigious interview. The journalist concluded his piece with, 'She's comfortable with herself and the world and people gather around her as though to a fire.'

Not everyone, thought Kay when she read the piece.

When she was alone she played his songs. The most well-known was about a man who was trapped in Paris, longing for the sea, longing to fly away across the water to freedom. She thought a lot about that. His dark side belonged in Paris, Liz was right about that.

Joel wanted sex. He wanted it there in the kitchen. Maddened with frustration, he unzipped his trousers and shoved his erect penis into a carton of cream. Kay thought the French count had set a fashion. He wanted her to rub it, lick it, but she wouldn't do it right. He pulled his trousers half down, sat back in a chair and pulled her on top of him. He lifted her skirt and pulled her underclothes to one side and shoved his penis up her hard so she cried out, not with pleasure. He tore her dress, trying to get hold of her breasts. Then he pushed her up and down on top of him. Unexpectedly the excitement flooded her body and for once she got as far as a climax. But all she saw was the gypsy. Joel didn't take her pleasure personally and without speaking wiped himself on a roll of kitchen paper and pulled up his trousers. She stayed on the chair. What she shared with the gypsy went beyond the bounds of normal convention. Her pride had vanished, she'd crawl to him if necessary. Joel left the room. The very civility of the door closing gently was hostile, more threatening than any shout or blow.

Kay crossed to Liz's house and woke her up. Roly was out, apparently night shooting. 'I'm going to come with you to Andalusia. I want to be sure what you're doing is right.'

Liz, still half asleep, said, 'But Angel will be there – it's fiesta.'

'I love you, Liz, you're a very special person. You've been loyal. The thing is, when we get in the fast lane, Roly and I, we pass everything we can and there's you standing still on the spot we've left. You remind us of our past and we don't like that, but that's our problem. You're true to yourself. I just want to see the house in Spain is all right.'

As she left Kay thought, Am I true to myself?

Kay couldn't cook any more or even eat. She opened tins for Sophie and Joel. Why, if Angel was in love with her, did he do nothing? Was it because he felt beneath her socially? Was she forced to take the active role? He wants power over me but I can see through his game. So she did nothing. Nor did he.

She made a quick visit to Sarah Prince, took her toilet water and face creams but no food. Sarah said, 'You look terrible.'

Kay thought, Then I *must* look terrible.

When she got home Joel was there unexpectedly. He'd left the London office hours before his usual time. For a moment she thought something had happened to the children.

He said, 'Do you want to see a psychiatrist?'

Automatically she replied, 'Do you? For dinner? What do they eat?'

He said, 'This can't go on, Kay.'

She made a funny little gesture of agreement, then went to pack for Andalusia. She took the minimum. He found her in the bedroom and immediately got the wrong idea about the travelling bag.

'That's not the answer. Can't we even talk about it?'

They could but she thought it would only make it worse. She would have left him standing there in the bedroom but he pulled at her arm. 'Oh no.' He forced her onto the bed. She resisted. 'I don't want to hurt you, or fuck you, so relax, Kay.' He forced her to sit down and kept his hands on her. 'We were happy together. And now you've changed. You're going to have to talk about it or you won't leave this house. I'm stronger than you and that's a good enough reason.' He looked cold and tough.

'I'm not some chemical deal going down, so don't pressurise me. I'll tell you when I've got something to say. If I was sick you wouldn't behave like this.'

'No, I wouldn't.'

'Then I'm sick.' She tried to stand up but he pushed her back down.

'It's all right, Kay, I'm not going to force you to have sex with me. Whatever it is that preoccupies you, sort it out. Because you've got three people who love you very worried. You're just not here any more.'

'OK, I'll sort it out.' Again she tried to stand up.

'Is it – '

'No it isn't.'

'Your work will start to suffer next. I was talking to the editor – '

'God, I wish you wouldn't.' She was furious.

'And he says there's a loss of colour in your writing. It's all black and white. I said – '

'You're driving me mad.' He let her get away from him. She threw a book at his head.

He shoved a finger in her face. 'I've made you, Kay. Remember that. You started writing because you were happy with me – '

'Don't you ever patronise me again.' Savagely she left the room.

'See a psychiatrist, darling,' he shouted.

Considering she came from such an over-refined family, she was quite strong. She wasn't like her snobbish, silly mother or weak, degenerate father. Her brothers were fops but she didn't resemble any of them in character or even looks. Joel often wondered how someone could be born into such a family yet bear absolutely no resemblance to its members. Roly had said the gypsy was like that, apparently; nothing like his family in looks or intelligence. And whereas they were typical of one's idea of gypsies, Angel was educated. He was well-read and spoke several languages. Joel thought it didn't make sense.

· *Twenty-five* ·

Kay collected Liz and Baby and they took the plane to Malaga. The silver tin trunk stayed behind because this was only an exploratory visit, but Roly looked distressed. He still hadn't found a replacement and now even the original was looking unstable.

On the plane, Kay asked, 'What is a soulmate? You remember you once told me mine was absent. You never did explain it.'

'A person you've known before. They come from the same energy and evolvement as you.'

'What does *that* mean?'

'You know each other in a deep way, you're similar. It sounds romantic but they're not necessarily good for you.'

They took a taxi to the gypsy's uncle's house in the Santa Maria district of Cadiz. So this was Angel's territory. Looking at the houses surrounding the courtyard, where the gypsies occasionally danced, Kay thought, If I don't see him I'll die. The longing and the separation will be the end of me. She was so sure of death she thought she would write a will leaving her few possessions to Sophie and her money to Tom.

Angel's uncle showed them the house which had plenty of atmosphere and bad furniture. There was a patio on the roof and they could see across to Africa. They couldn't understand a word he said, in any language. He didn't look like Angel.

Kay said, 'Is Angel here?' He broke into excited dialect and called his wife and children; this was the famous English lady writer, Angel's friend. They found a guitarist Kay had met before, who spoke English.

'Angel isn't here. He may have gone to the villages near Seville. There are many fiestas now.' He spoke slowly with care. Down below in the square a dozen dogs ran in a fast circle.

'Do they always do that?' she asked.

'They run in a pack,' he shrugged.

'Who looks after them?'

He shrugged again. 'The butcher I should think.' He saw it as dogs running in a circle, but Kay saw it as a sign.

In a small darkened room they drank sherry; a branch of the family lived in Jerez.

'Jerez, a village, means sherry.' The uncle gestured 'much money' and gave Liz a slow cheap wink. Liz took a handful of nuts and made the most of her bosom as she did so.

'They're very rich, these people,' she said to Kay. 'I can smell it.'

Kay asked about their charms and potions. Could they make one to bring your lover back? Could you capture the one you want? Could you cast a spell and make someone rich?

The women laughed and talked amongst themselves. She heard Angel's name mentioned. The uncle showed her signs and the guitarist said, 'They're for protection. He is showing you the green pyramid, the green triangle, the green letter three, all to protect you from danger.' He said they'd come originally from Egypt. The gypsies had brought them to Andalusia in the sixteenth century.

'What do you think of the house?' Liz asked.

Kay didn't think anything. The same went for Andalusia; it was as though she didn't see it. She passed through shade, light, day, night, white buildings, mosaic floors, all of it an hallucination. She needed him to appear so it could all be real and she could see.

Kay hired a car and they drove out to the villages near Seville. Liz wasn't at all surprised; the purpose of Kay's visit had not been to see the house. In the three days she was there, Kay met many gypsies, was entertained by their public fiestas, curious about their way of life, interested in their cooking. Angel wasn't there but everywhere she thought she saw his face smiling and it brightened her day. He did enhance life. She'd made the mistake of thinking it was just love.

She drove across to Jerez, then up to Carmona and across to Utrera where his family lived. The trip was a dream, it had no solidity. She was in it, trapped, unable to escape until she woke up. The images, the smells, the sounds were not of her world. But they all added up to one conclusion – Angel Lupez. In the cries of the birds she heard his songs.

In Utrera, Angel's cousins and nephews gathered to meet her: this was the English lady they'd heard about. One of the women warned, 'Be careful of Angel. He has *duende*.'

Kay asked what that was.

'Magic. The ability to touch the soul of another.'

The women gathered in the biggest house and prepared a meal. In no way could Angel have accused them of not honouring his friends. Yet neither Kay nor Liz were shown respect; they were considered to be his well-heeled groupies. It was obvious they were really looking for him. Renting a house? Subterfuge. Only Baby was accepted. Like all the Spanish, they approved of children.

Young boys on horses came to see Kay. They told her Angel Lupez was their hero, their dream was to be like him.

The rest of the family were not so starry-eyed. She could sense that. His uncle, a butcher, had plenty of complaints but Kay could only understand one world – *Payo* – non-gypsy.

The hard and beautiful cousin who earned 15,000 dollars a performance said, 'His family say Angel doesn't know whether he's a *payo* or a gypsy. That's his trouble.'

'Perhaps he's Parisian,' said the English-speaking guitarist. 'He spent enough time there.'

Kay was intrigued.

'He went off before he was famous and they didn't like that here. Who knows what ideas he brings back? They say he's no longer one of them. He doesn't know who he is, that's his trouble.

He's a scholar. We don't read books, we have life. He forgets that.'

'Why did he go to Paris?' Kay asked.

'Fame I expect. But he had to come back here to get it.'

After a dinner of beans and rabbit they went in a group to visit a very old woman who lived at the edge of the village. Apparently she had taught Angel to read fortunes in the flames of the fire, although he preferred to 'see' in the patterns of sand; he had always loved the desert.

When they moved, Angel's family clinked with jewellery and money. Their shoes made noise. The noisier they were, the richer. They showed their teeth, plenty of gold there, and swung their fans open contemptuously. They lived well. They were hospitable, but only because the English lady was famous and his friend, and the other, less of a lady but very rich. What they really thought was, He's taken them for a ride. Not even in their oldest songs did a woman leave her home and husband to follow a gypsy.

Again Kay couldn't sleep. With relief she got up off the scented mattress which was stuffed with some dried, unrestful grass. She drove for miles along an unlighted road that curved into a stretch of sand until she could go no further. Was this the beginning of the desert? Mountains were not quite hidden by a night completely without light and smelling of trees and highly scented flowers. She sat on a rock, her bare feet in the sand. Certain birds of the night hovered, then flew on, their wings huge and strong. She sat still and her mind became calm for the first time in weeks. A little wind started up and lifted the sand, stars were now visible and the sky changed to blue-black. She became aware of what she supposed was the truth; it was inside her, tangled up with her everyday life. Wasn't that where it was supposed to be?

Angel knew he'd captured her, the elusive Kay, the woman no one else could get near. That was enough for him. He knew his absence would make her suffer because the memory of his presence still lingered, like his perfume. His gypsy mind knew this. He was sought after, indulgent, and he clearly possessed charisma. But she had something, some quality better than his; Kay had grace. And she was at peace. Her admirers said she was divine, out of reach, a Madonna. One touch from him and she fell, shattered, into sexual disharmony. Angel loved and hated women. Compulsively he betrayed every woman he took, she was sure of that. He was jealous of Kay, jealous of her indisputably superior and female character.

She knew he would marry a hard Andalusian gypsy from the family in the next village, a second cousin, rich, fertile. And she'd cook and clean and have his children and dance and laugh and do all the things he was familiar with. He wouldn't hate her or love her either. He loved playing games with society women, teasing, tantalising, leaving them hungry. When he did sleep with them they'd spend their lives getting over him. They'd remember him at their hour of death. That was all he wanted.

Kay understood this because she'd gathered information from the villages, from the eyes of the gypsies, the way they had changed when they spoke of him. He was a bad bird who'd left the flock. He'd lived in strange lands and when he came back could carry bad habits, ideas destructive to the flock. Automatically he'd be kept out, left to die.

It was as though he spoke to her across the sand, told her the truth. It was his best gift to her. The sky lightened and she thought she had experienced a revelation. She wrote his name in the sand, then her own. Then the wind blew everything back to order again.

On the way back to the village she saw a riderless horse in the sand and she took this to be a sign.

Angel's family said a formal goodbye and gave the women and Baby presents. 'Don't forget – be careful. He has *duende*.'

Kay replied, 'So do I.'

Going to the airport Liz said, 'So what do you think?'

'About what?'

'The house. You didn't see it, did you?'

'No, I really only saw him. It was as though he was everywhere.

And yet I couldn't find him.' Kay paused. 'I'm sure he was there.'

On the plane she said to Liz, 'They have their own ways. They don't like foreigners. They don't like non-gypsies, even if they're Spanish. So where do you fit in?'

'He was right. The house does suit me, and it had another angle to it, that area. I even felt like singing. I haven't sung in my life and they're very good to children. They liked Baby. Yes, I felt right there.'

Kay was disapproving. Liz said, 'I see it differently to you. But then I'm free.'

· *Twenty-six* ·

Kay was hardly inside the door when Angel arrived with a hamper of French food. He had flown in from Paris especially to see her. He threw her latest Sunday column across the table; he was flattered by the way she'd described him. But if she thought flattery in print was the way to his heart she was wrong. His attitude showed her that.

'So where have you been, Kay?'

'Nowhere.'

He nodded, as though believing her. 'I phoned several times but you weren't here.'

'Why are *you* here?' She began to unpack her travel bag. 'You look flustered. Was it a journey of impulse? Perhaps you have an unexpected TV appearance?'

'I came to see you.' He told her the truth and expected the truth in return. Her phone rang: Joel was on his way. Should he bring food? She looked at Angel's hamper. 'No.'

'I've been feeding Sophie frozen stuff from the supermarket.' It sounded like an accusation. The rubbish bin, unemptied, was full of packets and slim boxes. He'd left it there as a reproach.

She replaced the receiver and smiled at Angel. Then she unpacked the hamper.

'Perhaps you were in Andalusia,' he said. 'Does that qualify as nowhere?'

'Perhaps I was in the desert. Well, I had to find one – you said I should.' She was firmly on her feet, in her own space, he could see that. Was she still needful of him?

'So what did you learn in my country?' With a quick elaborate gesture he lifted his hand to examine his nails. His eyes lifted over his hand, piercing eyes. It was similar to the gesture the women in Spain made with their fans.

'Were you there?' she asked lightly.

'Kay, I was in Paris. They told me you'd been to my home.' Suddenly angry he said, 'Why didn't you ask me? How dare you go to my village, talk to my family in Utrera. How could you!' He was very angry, becoming violent. 'What business is it of yours, my life?' He smashed a hand down on the table and various French delicacies fell off. She knew now he had something to hide. For once he was vulnerable. He wanted to know what she'd seen, heard, found out.

She simply smiled. He stopped shouting, stared at her. 'How could you speak to my family? Who interpreted for you?'

'I told you, my sweet, I was nowhere.'

A taxi pulled up and Joel got out. The gypsy said, 'Shit!'

Kay said, 'Better have a drink, darling.'

Angel took every opportunity to question her. He wanted to know what they had said, what she had found out. Obviously something, because she was acting so superior. The only thing she could think of that would worry him was that perhaps he'd impregnated his sister. Or that he'd been gay, or screwed goats. In fact she could think of several things. Some of them made her laugh.

Now she had power, how she enjoyed it. She told him nothing. She did say she'd seen a riderless horse in the sand at dawn and what did it mean?

'It means a chance to go. If you see it three times you must go.' He flapped angels' wings.

'You made that up,' she said.

'So what did you see?'

'I didn't see anything.' It was the truth.

When he'd gone, Liz ran in, barefoot, excited. 'My God he's in a state. Absolutely furious! Where did we go? Who did we see? What did they say? Who spoke English?'

Kay stood thoughtfully for some moments. What was his Achilles heel? He was proud, successful, clever and not afraid of showing it. 'You know, Liz, he's ashamed.'

'Of the way they live?'

'But it was so middle-class,' said Kay.

The feeling of power did not last long. Liz said, 'He's been in Paris for over two weeks. Roly said he's living with that beautiful French film star. She's part Arab and very young.' Liz couldn't think of her name. 'He's been "escorting" her, if that's what it's called. They're in all the French papers. When he lives it up, he certainly lives it up. Roly said he's doing it to look good, she's that sort. But why does he need to?'

Paula Strong called the next morning. She simply came to the back door looking cool and pale and said, 'I really need to talk to you, Mrs Craven, because I think you've got the wrong idea.'

To which of my many wrong ideas is she referring? thought Kay. Her appearance on the step looked impertinent but Kay let her in. She watched the girl as she came towards her into the kitchen. Her presence was heavy, her movements sustained, in the style of a religious procession. Her saintly face, pale and matt, gave nothing away. She looked around the kitchen. Was her glance proprietorial? It seemed she liked nice things. She sat on the chair impassively and didn't speak.

Finally Kay said, 'Yes?'

'I don't want you to think I'm to blame for Alexis' death.'

'What do you do?'

'*Do?* I look after my baby.'

'What *did* you do?'

'I've just done my degree course at the poly. I got a first.'

'Is that where you met William Darby?'

'Well I didn't meet him in the Camden Palace.'

It seemed she could be rude without apology. It happened from time to time, followed by normal conversation. After some to-ing and fro-ing and a few drinks, it came out that Paula Strong fancied herself as a journalist. She knew Kay was powerful, and she didn't want to start off with a handicap.

'So I'm telling you that when she did it I was as gutted as they were. The boys blame me. You know that because your daughter is always round at Rick's.'

Kay made a mental promise to put a stop to the 'always'.

'Rick's got quite a thing going; he's only fifteen and he's got his own place and the Kentish Town kids think he's a very cool guy and look up to him. He's drumming for a pop group, and he's friendly with that flamenco dancer, who's fabulous. I'd love to meet him.'

In spite of her pallor and lack of make-up she had a sexuality that was as obvious as Woolworths scent. Hold your nose and what was there? Ruthlessness, thought Kay. She got off the subject of the fabulous flamenco dancer and back to Alexis Scott.

'Of course I knew her. I was his student. She was always very nice to me and I respected her. Frankly, Kay, she had a lot of trouble with those boys. That older one! He's born for sin, he'll end up inside. Or dead. I've told Will.'

'What about the other one?'

'He does furniture-making. City and Guilds. He's motivated so he'll kick the Kentish Town scene. I thought to prove that I'm not the cause of a woman taking her life, you should see Alexis' diaries.'

Kay's eyes were solemn as she considered Paula Strong and all her attributes, including the gift of the diaries, which weren't hers. Paula didn't like the way Kay looked at her. 'It's up to you. I'm just out to clear my name.'

Kay almost laughed.

'They've got all her ideas for songs in them. The big bad city certainly turned her on.'

'What do you want then, Paula?'

'I told you – a clean slate.'

Paula's idea of a clean slate was to arrive one Sunday lunchtime, when several media guests were visiting, dressed up beyond recognition, the modest look quite gone. Several pairs of male eyes brightened as Paula chucked five notebooks of various sizes insolently onto the table. Joel, looking at her intently, poured her a drink, and she gave him a full smile, mainly in the eyes. Paula liked what she saw. He kept his reaction to himself.

'I'm Paula.'

'Stay to lunch,' he said.

Kay had laughed at the gypsy's frustration, the ways he tried to get her to talk. How angry he was when she wouldn't! How she'd laughed! But she wasn't laughing at the Sunday lunch when she saw, in the reflection of a saucepan of boiling beans, the way he was looking at Paula Strong. The surge of jealousy made Kay feel faint. She realised during that terrible Sunday lunch that she couldn't live without him. Her cooking was terrible, the meat burnt.

As Joel removed a few assorted tough potatoes from his plate he realised his marriage was over.

Angel talked to Paula Strong about audiences, airports, fans, the life of a star. Every time he looked at her she wriggled like an eel. Her body was dying for him. Everyone else in the room saw it, so he must have, thought Kay. All Kay could think was, She's so young. How can she come in here and take what's mine?

Joel helped Kay make the coffee. 'D'you want to put some cinnamon in it?'

She shook her head. 'Just as it is.'

His hand, so clever and well shaped, slipped over hers. 'Stay.'

For a moment she wasn't sure she had heard it. So he'd sensed she was off, had decided to leave to try and catch her happiness. It was the worst moment of her life. Her mind seethed, her face looked old. Joel's hand was still over hers. Behind them at the table, Paula asked Angel why so many people ran after him. What was his secret? Was it gypsy magic? He laughed and, looking at Kay, said, 'No, I prepare potions taught to me by my great grandmother. They go into your loved one's blood and she is yours forever. The potions cure or kill.' In that moment he gave

Kay her idea for revenge. She slid her hand away from Joel's. He went into the back garden.

Paula got the gypsy doing something he never did; singing socially. Unaccompanied, he sang songs expressing the pain of love, all the while watching his prey. 'How beautiful is my love,' he sang to Kay. 'The more exciting to take and destroy.'

And she saw the riderless horse fully saddled in the dawn, and images of Andalusia that she hadn't noticed at the time came into her thoughts and stayed like holiday snapshots: the thrilling light; yellow wasn't the same thing at all over there, nor red, gold or mauve. It was a vibrant yellow, a pulsing red. The trees were dry and against them the women's hair was gleaming and lustrous.

He left suddenly – the song ended and so did his good humour. Up and off, he ran up the back steps. Kay sped after him. He stopped by his luxury car, long and silver. 'If you come with me, Kay, be careful. You have a lot of blackness in you and it's dangerous. You see, I will activate it.'

'Blackness?'

'You will end up cursing me and in turn you will be harmed. I bring out your destructiveness and it will rebound on you.' He got into the car.

She hung onto the door, now desperate. Behind her, the pavement was filling up with people. 'Blackness?'

'My family saw it. It's in you. Don't play with the gypsies.' He drove off fast; her hands, where the car had lurched away, were deeply marked.

Liz was beside Kay and she put an arm around her. Indicating Joel standing in the crowd by the gate, she whispered, 'You've got a lot to lose.' She led Kay back, saying, 'These flamenco performers have terrible mood swings. Even Kay can't placate him. Roly has had such trouble.' She got her friend into the kitchen and wrapped a napkin around the hand, which was starting to bleed.

Kay woke up, her head in the dirty plates scattered across the table. Depression had made her sleep. The Spanish liqueur had

had something to do with it too. Still tight, she went to the sink and drank from the tap. Joel was standing in the back garden and close to him, Paula Strong. She was a little unsteady. She had a satisfied smile and very ripe luscious lips. There was something full and complete about Paula; her eyes were those of a happy snake. Joel said, 'You're a lovely girl.' He corrected himself. 'Lovely to look at.'

He's got that right at least, thought Kay.

Then she saw Joel's eyes close and he grimaced with unbearable pleasure. Kay peered forward and saw that Paula Strong had thrust her hand on his trousers and was gripping his penis hard. Her shapely rich lips opened and she told him what she'd do.

'Oh don't,' he said. 'I'll come. I haven't for so long.' With a tremendous effort he got hold of her hand and removed it.

'So why don't you jerk off over me? Go on, I love it. And I'll pinch your nipples and your balls and – ' She licked his ear and bit it. Her tight skirt needed some lifting. She wore no knickers.

Kay was transfixed. She'd never seen her husband in sexual activity with someone else. She was too amazed even to act. Again he discouraged the girl but it took a lot of effort. 'Paula, Paula, don't.' Now she had his trousers opened and was giving him some very effective caresses. Kay was beginning to see what William Darby couldn't resist. She was coaxing Joel to fuck her. Suddenly he shook her off and walked away. She followed. One shoe fell off as he ran up the stairs – however drunk, he could always run. Paula slumped down against the back door.

He's brought this into my house, all this evil. I will repay him, the fallen Angel. Kay's pulse slowed, her mind was clear, her heart cold. She started to wash up.

· *Twenty-Seven* ·

Kay read the notebooks. Alexis had used hope to get her through the suffering. She had thought she would get her husband back, that she'd be successful as a performer. She described the boys' terrible behaviour so well Kay couldn't think of anything else. That kitchen in the Victorian house had been the jousting place between modern discomfort and hell. No mention was made of the liaison between Paula Strong and her husband. Her songs were merely things she wrote to keep sane. They were the bit of her that was hers. She wrote about her longing to go to another land, sensuous and loud, that would free her. Andalusia fitted the description. She was waiting for a gap in the horror of her life she could escape through.

About Sarah Prince, Alexis wrote, 'She is odd about money. Says she doesn't want it. Who wouldn't want money? It's the first time she's played games. She wants me to say I want her money and it's a test. Isn't everything! She wanted to burn Mr Cheap's clothes, said it would cleanse me of his sins. I can see fire excites her. Then Mr Cheap's car caught fire right outside the house and I thought naturally of Sarah. The other day she told me to get rid of all my associations with him, put them in the garden; the dress I was married in, letters, presents, photographs, and she'd burn the lot. It's the only way, she said. If I give them to Oxfam some other poor schmuck gets my bad deals. I'm so unlucky that I think she may be right. Mr Cheap must spend plenty in his love nest but says he hasn't got enough for Marks and Spencers' food. I'll have to go back to Sainsburys. She's not two-faced – seven-faced doesn't describe that one. Sarah asked if I was happy, but I've gone beyond happy, unhappy. It's all somewhere else now. Let's say I know the purgatorial path.'

It was obvious from the notebook she had loved Rick, the youngest boy. She loved him in a quiet way, didn't dare make a thing of it in case it all went wrong. She split from Darby, Rick was on drugs again, she didn't trust life anymore.

Kay went to see Rick because his mother had loved him so and because Sophie was spending too much time in his company. The house was a squat in a sidestreet directly behind Rick's father's big house on the corner. It was full of musicians, a Scots artist, kids in temporary work, on the dole, on the run. A bright technology student was fixing the electric meter so it ran backwards; he'd already fixed the phone. Rick was small and good-looking and very energetic. He cleaned the house, cooked for everyone and looked after them. He was a surrogate mother to the down-and-out neighbourhood kids.

'Angel just came by,' he said. 'He's giving me a cut of the royalties from my mother's songs. Wants me to start a pop group.'

'Will you?' said Kay.

'I've got to look after my brother first. He's badly into smack and he'll have to do the cure. Private. That'll cost. But there's so much money. Angel said he'll get my mum's songs to the top. "Firechild" has been number one for three weeks. I'm all for starting a pop group but I want to get out of London for a while first, go to Jamaica maybe and hear some sounds. I just can't get over what happened in April. You know about my mum?' His voice shook and Kay wanted to reach out and touch him. But he pulled around quickly. It was obvious he was near to cracking several times a day. He sped through his domestic duties. Kay was dying to say, 'What was your mother really like? But it was inappropriate. Unknown to the gypsy she did value other people and their lives were not just column-fillers.

'Where is your brother now?'

'With the social worker, Nan Prince. Her mother's in the bin. It's been a bad year for mothers.'

Yes, thought Kay. You can say that again.

'I expect you're round here because you're worried about Soph?'

'Not at all. I was passing and wanted to meet you. Did Angel just leave?'

'Five minutes ago. He picked some white flowers off the hedge opposite. Sophie's a great kid, you're lucky.'

This time as Kay saw him her heart beat, but not with love. Hate made her cool. As she walked towards him the planks of the bridge shook. He seemed deep in thought and as she approached he said, 'I'm leaving London. I won't be back.'

'So you're settling your debts?'

'Only the ones that matter.'

In spite of herself she said, 'Where are you going?'

'Andalusia for the last of the fiestas. Roly's coming to film me. I want to do something about Alexis. I want Roly to film this part of London.'

Kay thought, What was so special about Alexis that the man I love thinks only of her? 'I've got her diaries.'

'Maybe you have.'

'They're sad.'

Scathingly he said, 'She had something in spite of her bad luck and bad life that you will never have, in spite of your success and good looks. She was just in the wrong place. All gypsies are if they step out of their territory. I leave Andalusia and I'm up to my neck in shit.'

'So now she's a gypsy,' Kay's voice shook with bitterness, 'on top of everything else.'

'There's no doubt.'

'I sometimes wonder why you see me, Angel.'

'You have a kind heart.'

I don't, she thought. Not anymore.

He appeared carrying his belongings in a large canvas sack over one shoulder. Not for him, the trappings of stardom. His bad mood of the railway bridge was quite gone.

'I said I would take you to the desert.' He looked her straight in the eyes, challenging.

Sophie ran down the stairs already demanding things; money, attention. Then she saw Angel. She looked at him with fury.

Kay was stunned. If he'd come a month ago, a week ago, it would have been so different. 'It's too late.' She said it too loudly.

He laughed. He didn't believe it.

Sophie shouted, 'Don't talk to him! Shut the door on him!'

'You can't expect people to jump when you say so. I can't just leave my house, my life.'

'Kay, you were supposed to drop all that. Just leave with me. None of the old fears, none of the old persuasive fears that stop you being really alive. It's all remembered fear. How can you know what the future is? Just bring your passport and come.'

He picked up his bag and started to leave.

'Where are you going and with what?'

'Oh ho, all the worries already beginning: where will we sleep? Will it rain? What if we don't get the boat? You're worrying about life before you live it.'

'I like to plan – '

'Plan!'

She knew she was making herself appear ordinary in his eyes. She was putting forward the worst arguments. She knew exactly what he meant; to go into life without fear, trusting it, letting every moment be new. He wasn't the only one who knew about that. And yet she had responsibilities. She thought about them: Sophie could go to Liz; the Sunday article could be written from anywhere. It was herself she had to be responsible for. She needed a blueprint and time to prepare. And, anyway, it was too late.

Sophie raged at him. 'I used to think you were really special but now I hate you for changing my mum.' She ran into the street yelling for Liz.

'I can't go.' She pointed at her daughter.

'A very good excuse, Kay. Come on. You know I know what I'm doing.'

'So how long are you going for?' Another boring question.

'One night. Or forever.'

'But why me, Angel? You don't seem to approve of me. What's wrong with the French movie star – '

'More defences. My God, you'll use your husband next!' He pointed at her chest. 'I'm talking to *you*. You want to come away with me, to the desert. You know it will be marvellous – '

'But I no longer trust you. You come into my life when it suits you. I'm sure your absences are deliberate – '

'I have my own life too.' He sounded reproachful.

'I'm not coming. I never was.' And that was the end of it.

Seeing him walk to the gate, turn into the street, almost broke her heart. Not for the loss of him but for the loss of the person she could have been.

She went into the kitchen, put bones in a saucepan to start a chicken broth, then turned it all off; her heart wasn't in it. Fate had decided she would be with Angel. But life in the meantime had been dealing with things, and life was messy.

· Twenty-eight ·

When she came back from her delayed holiday with Sophie and Tom she decided to paint the kitchen. In spite of her jetlag she immediately moved everything into the storeroom or garden and started preparing the walls.

Tom was amazed. 'Why, Mum?'

'I need to have a clean start.'

'What shall I do with the garlic?' said Sophie.

'Throw it out.'

'Why don't you get some people in to do it?' Tom sounded just like his father.

'Go to bed,' said Kay. 'We've got to get you ready to go back to school. Tomorrow's a shopping day.'

She washed walls, filled in cracks, started painting. She had no idea of the time although she could see it was night. She wondered if Liz had made her escape. The cleaner had stacked the mail on the dresser and a card poking out intrigued her. She got down off the table and pulled it from the pile. It was a picture of a desert. On the back, scrawled, 'You didn't come, so I send it to you. Thinking of you with love.' Signed 'Angel'.

Had Joel seen it? It was postmarked Spain. She couldn't read the town. She held the card and thought of him, saw him clearly. She could see him riding a horse, and she felt alive for the first time in weeks. She got back on the table and went on painting the ceiling. That kind of alive was not for her.

She was surprised when Roly came in, followed by Liz. Roly took off his sweater, grabbed a brush and started on the door; Liz got a roller and went to work on the walls. After a while, Roly started talking about life.

'What are you on about now?' said Liz.

He explained he was trying to make some meaning out of his life. 'I have to, to stay sane.'

'You don't have to bore everyone to death in the meantime.' Liz asked about the American holiday and Kay said something about Mexico. It was obvious she hadn't really been there. She'd passed through it all, the holiday, and now it was over. Why go on about it?

'And Joel?' Liz sounded cautious.

'He's coming back in about a week.' Kay was surprised to hear it was three o'clock. They made some coffee and continued painting. They got faster and the atmosphere lighter. They started telling anecdotes and laughing and it got sillier and funnier and turned into a good time. By daylight the kitchen was finished and Liz made breakfast. Kay prepared to go shopping with Tom. She thought, 'I'm doing all right.'

Angel had brought Alexis Scott into the limelight. The papers were full of her, she was a posthumous star. 'Firechild', as sung by Angel Lupez, was still in the charts. Alexis' friends said how happy she'd been, what a wonderful person, how her husband was devastated with grief. Even Paula Strong had come out in print. Nothing like unavailability to make you famous, thought Kay. And no price or impresario got around death. In 'Firechild' Alexis sang of the city, of its horrors; good would win, God held the world on merciful scales, evil was just good embarrassed, left out, angry.

Kay thought of the revenge she would deliver to the gypsy. It was still inside her. So was the – was it love? She had nearly got herself over it, she was almost well. Her cooking wasn't as it had been and she'd been a superb cook. But although she'd put the tin-opener away, she served plain meals, with little decoration. A sprig of parsley, a lonely olive, took the place of the icing, the pastry sculpting, the mousse motifs. She went to bed with Joel in the same way as she cooked: adequate but no embellishments. By now she could get through anything, but she couldn't look at a night sky or trees against the moon. She didn't want to smell sweet night air and was glad there was so little of it in the city. She longed for winter. Once, off guard, she did look at the garden trees at night and it was as though a thorn had pierced her chest. She almost cried out. She could smell his perfume as though he were in the room. Her family and friends kept saying how happy Kay seemed. They said it so much, though they'd never even mentioned it before.

She met Sarah Prince's daughter in the street and heard about the programme she'd started with her mother's trust money. The girl's description of drug addicts' behaviour sounded very like Kay's own: how they could come off for a month and be high with the relief of it, how that was dangerous and was the slippery slide down into the black and further addiction. Watch the highs, keep level.

The girl – Kay could never remember her name – was wearing a cross and chain. How wrong her mother had been about her. Where was the black pusher boyfriend, the criminal fires? Did her mother's view of her change with her illness?

The cross and chain made Kay think of protection. What better, than from God? She went into the church in Lady Margaret Road and knelt stiffly in prayer. She lit a candle and mouthed another prayer for help, for release from all-consuming love. She did feel better and lighter leaving the church. God's hands must be full up with people's burdens. Why couldn't they carry their own?

The phone was ringing, she could hear it from the street. The latest Sunday paper was offering her a fantastic fee if she'd go over to them. She didn't have to go into church for help with that one; her answer was negative because she knew new papers had a habit of folding.

She answered the phone whilst lighting a cigarette. Angel's husky voice said, 'Kay. I'm in New York. I'm going to sing all Alexis' songs tonight. Send me good thoughts.'

'Good luck then.' Her heart was leaping around like a bad child eager to get to him.

'Come to me here and bring me luck. Why not? You could make me marvellous just knowing you're here.' He seduced her into joining him with words.

'But you don't say you love me,' she said, hating herself for her weakness.

'You say it.'

She hung up. Was God mad? Sophie trailed into the kitchen. She had a bad period and wanted comfort. Kay held her and promised her soothing things. Sophie said, 'He's been calling you all day long.'

From her window Liz could see Kay sitting at her table, just staring into space. She knew that look. She called to Kay to come outside for a walk but the invitation went unheard. Liz, heart sinking, entered the kitchen. 'He's been on again hasn't he? You know he's not worthy of you.'

Kay said, 'Have you unpacked the tin trunk or what?'

'Maybe knowing I can go makes it possible for me to stay. Roly senses I'm independent, he doesn't take me so much for granted. And I'd miss the kids. I should have just gone.'

Kay agreed. But she knew Liz was solid about her children.

Liz said, 'It makes me wonder how Alexis Scott did it. She must have thought of those kids, surely?'

'I think Andalusia is a little different, Liz.'

'I went back for five days while they were filming. Kay, he's a tatty gypsy, he's got a lot of talent and a thrilling voice, but I don't like him and he doesn't belong in your world.'

'Does he want to – belong in my world?'

'He's got an awful lot of – well, pretensions. All right he's read a few books. And he can make two and two add up, and does he let you know it! He's crazy about history and culture and myth. You are in a way, too. Aspects of life absorb you. But you don't push them.'

'All I want to know is, does he love me?'

'Don't you know?'

Kay shook her head. 'Sometimes I think, Yes, he does very much. But he wants to protect me so I don't lose Joel and my family and my peace of mind.'

'Kay, you've got everything he's ever wanted. He will never have peace of mind or respect, or choice. And he said something that made me think: Roly said that men adore you but it's hard for you to have women friends because they're so envious. And the gypsy said, "Yes, it's easy to be envious around Kay." So Roly replied, "How lucky, Angel, that you're not a woman." He replied, "But I have a woman's soul. I am the moon, I only reflect the sun".'

Kay thought, He's seen me surrounded by admiring people. I would appear to him to lap at a saucer full of the cream of life. If he didn't love me, but was envious and wanted to destroy, what better way than seduction? He wants to have his prey, pin it down, screw it, destroy. Hadn't he sung about that in the kitchen on that dreadful day when Paula Strong came to lunch?

Kay saw they were well matched. Who would win? She who could sit it out patiently or he who needed to conquer.

Kay went to New York. She had to know one way or the other whether it was love or destruction they were sharing. By going, she gave him the chance to love her and her mind to heal of revengeful thoughts.

· *Twenty-nine* ·

He was waiting at Kennedy Airport. She carried only an overnight bag which confused the customs people. She hadn't seen Angel for six weeks and he looked hard-faced, almost brittle. They had a drink and then drove into Manhattan.

At the hotel he ordered club sandwiches, coffee, a bottle of wine. He'd filled the suite with flowers. His hand was near hers against the wall and she longed for him to touch her. He moved his hand away. 'If we do that – what you want – then we're no longer free. What we have together then becomes predictable and needing. I can have you but it would be a downward fall for both of us. You slide from the possibility of the divine into sexuality, then lower.'

'Would it be a downward step?' The speech certainly surprised her.

'Of course. We'd be imprisoned in that act which is not nearly as fascinating as laughing together, dancing, crossing a desert. Sexuality is depressing because it can only go downhill. By its very nature it would destroy what we have.'

'Why?'

'It would lead to jealousy, habit. Everything would relate to that act. We'd be trapped in our fleeting desires, without choice, when we could fly.'

'Fly?'

'I've always wanted to fly. Over water. Just to take off across a sea and go upwards to freedom.'

'But surely you want me to fall from grace? Isn't that why I'm here?'

He ate a sandwich and bits dropped onto the floor. 'I could have you. I know everything about that. But I've done it so often. What you'd get you'd be sharing with hundreds of others before you. Whereas what we have together is quite unique. I think love has to be as free as possible.'

'Do you love me?'

'Kay, if you don't know it, my telling you won't make the slightest difference.'

She was so confused by him she had nothing to say. He left for a rehearsal. Apparently he wasn't staying in the hotel.

The waiter brought her some Scotch and said, 'His first night was a smash. He's the hottest thing in town.'

She took a bath, drank some champagne, established it was five o'clock New York time, exhaustion was setting in. She ate a smoked salmon sandwich. He called her at 5.15 and told her to take a taxi uptown to an apartment near the concert hall. 'We'll have a drink and go to the theatre together.' He began the show at the Lincoln Theatre at 8.30 that evening.

The apartment was beyond the Plaza, up in the East Seventies. The traffic was horrendous and in the end she decided to walk. She arrived at the apartment exhausted, her ankles swollen. The heat was murderous and she was now over an hour late.

She found the doorway. It certainly wasn't in the Spanish area. The hallway was unattended and she climbed two flights of ornate steps and knocked on the first door. There was no reply so she knocked again. The hall light went out. The sultry air was over-breathed, her face running with sweat and humidity. She checked the address in her bag and went downstairs to look at the street number. Her arrival on the sidewalk coincided with a first flare of lightning. She went back upstairs and banged loudly on the door, called his name. Silence. Then she heard a shocked, girlish laugh, which she, forever the optimist, took to be a television. The only way this trip would not be a mistake would be if she knew, absolutely, that she and the gypsy were meant by God to be together.

The girl who opened the door was hardly a good omen. She

was blonde, wearing a man's dressing gown and she was long-limbed and well-shaped, naked and barefoot. The dressing gown had been put on hurriedly and a cigarette hung at the corner of her lips. She looked like a tart. At the sight of her, Kay sat down suddenly on the nearest stair. There was no choice about it. 'I'm sorry, I must have the wrong apartment.'

'So who do you want?' She was American with a slight accent.

'Angel Lupez. Is he on this floor?'

'He's in this apartment.'

'In here?' Kay was amazed.

'Not here now. He's out.' She kept the door to behind her.

'I'm Kay Craven. He told me to come here.'

'Well I can't help that. He's busy somewhere and I'm sorry I can't let you in.' She started to shut the door but Kay leapt up and pushed it open. The girl resisted.

'So what do I do?' said Kay, almost frantic.

The girl laughed. 'How do *I* know?'

'But I've come from London to see him.'

'Honey, so many people do. Call later. He'll be in around eight to go to the theatre. He goes on at quarter to nine.'

From inside the apartment, Angel said, 'Let her in, for heaven's sake.'

The girl made an expression of mock helplessness and the door opened enough for Kay to enter.

Angel came out of the bedroom doing up his trousers. Behind him the low Japanese bed was unmade. It was obvious they'd been in bed when Kay arrived. Her face, as she looked at the bed, fell apart like a bad pie crust. In one move she had been ruined. He saw it all. He'd won.

The girl was saying something about a drink but Kay stayed staring at the bed in which he'd enacted at least some of her fantasies. She'd been kept waiting while he'd had his satisfaction. The sheets, like traitors, were only too willing to give her the whole story. He tried to move the duvet to cover the copious stains. She said, 'Who are you?' She didn't even look at *him* and her voice was unrecognisable.

'Me?' The girl was impudent. 'Me? His girlfriend, who else?' She walked, swaying her hips, into the living room. She was proud of her body, of showing it off. It was a good, tight body, used to movement. The sex had obviously begun in the living room. Kay saw his underpants, one sock. She picked the sock up and held it. It was the most intimate thing she'd ever done to him.

There was an uncertain silence.

'Shall we go out?' he said. 'The three of us. Have a drink downstairs. This storm finishes my head. I have to have something.' His face after making love was younger and smooth, the shadows under his eyes were deeper.

For something to do Kay went into the tiny kitchen and, using the sparse ingredients, made them all an omelette. Cooking soothed her, gave her back her identity. Behind her, the girl took off her dressing gown. She had an amazing body. Her breasts stood straight out. Her underclothes, tiny wisps of silk, were strewn, making a virtual path to the bedroom. Teasingly, Angel grabbed them, held them behind him so the girl had to try and get them back. He laughed as her breasts joggled about in front of his eyes.

How pleased he must be, Kay thought; he's got a married woman to leave everything and come running after him to America. Well they always said, 'Don't run off with the gypsies.'

The girl dressed very slowly, unwilling to cover herself up. He murmured something and she laughed, a rough smoker's laugh. As Kay cooked she realised the power a woman could have in the kitchen. You nourish the man; you could also poison him.

'Come and sit down,' he said to Kay and tried to persuade her into the living room. A glass of brandy was put in her hand as she sat, mute, like the victim of a road accident. He asked a question which she didn't even hear. He was irritated. 'I couldn't come to the door. I was in the middle of – well in the middle.' He shrugged and put on his shoes. The girl poured more drinks. The omelette burning aroused Kay and automatically she went back to the kitchen. He followed her, splashing his face with Cologne. It was not his usual perfume.

'Kay is my good friend.' He caressed her approvingly with his eyes. 'She looks after me. She has a generous heart.'

Oh, but I don't, she thought as she planned to kill him. She would use poison. She would never be at peace until this assault on her heart had been avenged.

'Add some herbs. Herbs, Kay, more salt. My God, what are you doing? In my country we do it like this,' and he tried to grab the spatula.

'Does your girlfriend like omelette well-cooked too?'

'Does she have a choice? This is the worse omelette in the world.' He cut some bread.

'You remember the French poisoner – what was her name?'

'I don't remember.' He frowned.

'How did you know about her?' asked Kay.

'I read about it in Paris. Come on, let's eat. Be quick!'

'I didn't know you were in Paris that long.'

'I was there years.' He wasn't thinking. 'I have to do the show in thirty minutes and my head is fucked. This food is fucked.'

'You always disliked the idea before – Paris.'

He scooped the omelette onto plates and found two forks. 'I'll eat with my hands.'

'I can't imagine you in libraries exactly. What were you doing?'

'What *do* people do? I was reading.' Then he realised what he was saying. 'I am fascinated by people's origins, their myths, their crimes. I like to know the history of the place I'm in.'

'Who are you?'

'Your guardian angel.' He took the first plate and gave it to the girl. He ate quickly. Kay just forked at her food. Her eyes met his over the plate. She knew he'd sacrificed the expected sexual pleasure with her for cruelty; it gave him more satisfaction. It was power he wanted, not love. By coming here she'd lost power and revealed her love. And lost.

The unmade bed was the one item he didn't have to let her see. Unless he wanted to break her heart. She now had to think fast. Panicky thoughts of Joel were beginning; would he divorce her?

They all went down into the street together. Angel was eating an apple. He was surprised when she wouldn't come to the theatre, angry even. 'But this is Alexis' show. It's for her.'

'Well, good luck.' Kay hailed a cab and went straight to the airport, carrying her bruised heart inside her like a wounded animal. Her return ticket and passport were in her handbag, the other stuff she simply left at the hotel.

She had a terrible journey home. The plane was delayed for five hours, the crossing turbulent. She couldn't get out of her head the girl's ridicule as she'd entered the apartment, and her spiteful amazement when Kay had taken a taxi instead of going to the theatre. She'd come all the way to New York and not even seen the show. This was one new kind of super-groupie!

· *Thirty* ·

The first thing Kay did on entering the house was find some information about the French poisoner. The second was to take her coat off. Joel was surprised to see her back; more surprised when she didn't speak. 'You look terrible,' he said. She went on reading. She couldn't remember when she had last washed, slept.

'What about dinner?'

'Dinner?' She couldn't remember when she had last eaten. Yes, the omelette. Two mouthfuls. 'I'm too exhausted to cook.'

'Yet you're not too exhausted to read.' He tried to see the book's title. The other books on the bed were also about poison.

It is incredible, Kay thought, but the Frenchwoman actually had a better and happier life than me.

'All I want is some supper. Is that too much to ask? I pay the bills, support you – '

'You sound like Roly,' Kay said. 'Perhaps I'd better get a tin trunk too.'

'All I ask is to be fed. Some good meals to keep me going, that's all.'

She didn't answer.

'Just a decent meal. Then I can get on with the business of earning money so you can buy clothes and take trips whenever you feel like it.' Joel could not face Kay's infidelity so he'd shut his eyes. If he had said one word he'd have to do something about it. Her illicit love would be admitted, would have to be challenged. Kay would have to make a choice, but he could not face losing her.

He walked out of the room, came back in to say, 'By the way, Tom's failed his exams. Disastrous!' He went downstairs and opened a tin of baked beans and gave Sophie money to get herself a hamburger.

Upstairs Kay wept with guilt. Although Tom's failure to pass had nothing to do with her, she blamed herself. Her sinful desire for the gypsy had caused – a family tragedy. Tom had failed once and Joel had used pressure to have the boy sit them again. He'd claimed Tom was ill the first time and produced a medical certificate to back it up. The second time the school had their doctor in to look him over but no illness then, just failure. No top university for Tom. He'd done no better than the Darby boys.

Kay stayed in bed reading books on poison. She planned ways to stuff the gypsy full of delicious foods all spiced with death. She was impressed with the French poisoner's story: Marie de Brinvilliers, born in 1630, the daughter of a French Councillor of State, was well brought up and extremely beautiful. She was a nymphomaniac and by the time she was thirteen she had slept with her brothers. She made a reasonable marriage when she was twenty-one to a baron and officer of the Norman regiment. Through him she met her downfall; her lover, a man of considerable intelligence and debauchery, St Croix. She paraded their affair in public and her father, appalled, had him thrown into the Bastille. He shared a cell with a poisoner.

On his release, St Croix and Marie began a career of poisoning for gain. They made a series of 'succession powders'. Her father was one of the first to fall ill and Marie dutifully nursed him to the end. She had a vast list of lovers, who she expected to stay faithful whatever she did. She was dominating and hated to be crossed. She had numerous children from different fathers, but she decided to murder her husband so she could marry St Croix who, not liking the idea, administered antidotes to the Baron. The mixture ruined his health. St Croix accidentally died while seeking the elixir of life in his laboratory and his widow found a black box in his possession which he'd instructed should be given, unopened, to Marie. The widow opened it and found a record of his crimes in which Marie was implicated. Marie fled to the Netherlands and entered a convent where, after three years, she was caught and sentenced to death. Before the execution she was taken in a cart to the principal door of the Church of Paris and there made a public confession of her sins. She was tortured by having large quantities of water poured through a funnel into her stomach, then the executioner severed her head with one stroke. Some of her relics were sold as charms and the story of her contrition and the dignity of her death made many consider her a saint.

Kay could see she had experienced a spiritual revelation, a sight of God.

As the poison idea took shape Kay was unable to eat, and Joel believed she was suffering from anorexia. It had taken six months to turn his family from a happy one into a bunch of losers.

Finally Liz was off. She came to say goodbye and the sight of Kay's face made her hesitate. Then she saw the book on poison. It was there, unmistakeably, amongst the newspapers on the unmade bed. She said automatically, 'What will happen?'

Kay gave up trying to deal with the day and flopped back into bed. Her head ached incessantly and her thoughts were sharp-edged and black. As though to herself she said, 'I am very alone. I have to choose whether or not to commit a major act. Usually life flows along; you get pregnant, have an animal put down, bury your parents – that's the big stuff. But this is so big it's out of my league.'

Liz with one eye on the book said, 'I wouldn't do it.'

' "Vengeance is mine," said the Lord. But is it?' Kay kicked aside the duvet and thought again about getting up. It was an unsatisfying bed for retreat.

Liz looked at the book out of the corner of her eye. Was the poison meant for Joel? 'Did you see our mutual friend in New York?'

'Of course.'

The 'of course' wasn't hopeful. Liz said, 'You've started to forget about him?'

'How can I, when all he does is think about me? He even slept with a woman in front of me – to exacerbate my nerves, my jealousy. To crucify me. There was no other reason. He will do anything, even refuse to perform, to get at me. He has stopped concerts in the middle of a hit run – think about it, Liz – because I wouldn't go to see him he deprived thousands of – ' She gasped and stopped.

Liz was thinking about it. Too many religious-type quotes. The 'crucify' worried her, that and Kay's expression. She tried a firmer approach. 'Put away the poison books and start reading one on obsession. That's what's wrong with you. Everything he does is a "sign". It has a special meaning, just for you. It's an illness. You've heard of that woman who thought that Edward the Seventh was in love with her? She would stand by the palace for hours and if a curtain moved in the third window on the right while she was there, if was a signal from him that he loved her. You should see a doctor. But you could get over it yourself. Why don't you write it all down?'

'Keep a diary you mean? And end up on Alexis' bridge? Is that what he suggests I do? He'd love that.'

Liz didn't like any of this. Kay looked the same, sterner but not mad.

'Has he telephoned you?'

'No,' said Liz.

'Then how do you plan to go to Cadiz tonight? Just walk into that house? I don't think so. The uncle isn't comprehensible in any language and he, my sweet, the flamenco gypsy, will do the money deal. I know him well enough for that. You pay, don't forget. First. They're gypsies. It's Angel's deal, he'll handle it.'

'Well yes,' said Liz. 'Yes, he did ring me about the rent.'

'So why did you say no? What did he say about me?'

He actually hadn't said anything, but Liz said, 'He asked how you were, and I said fine, how else would Kay be?' Liz thought it was the answer Kay would like. Next she tried to coax her friend away from morbidity by talking about her own problems. 'Every time I've been on the point of leaving, the kids sense it. They get sick. Jamie got picked up by the police. They've started acting out a whole scenario to keep me at home. People will do anything to avoid change – Angel's right.' That slipped out and how she regretted it.

Kay laughed mercilessly. 'So he sends you over to see if I'm suffering? And what I'm going to do? Tell him to come for Sunday lunch. I will have a very famous Russian musician here.' She named a conductor. 'He won't miss meeting him. He'd do anything to sit at the same table. At heart, Liz, he's a little crawler.'

Liz could see she'd have to cancel her travel plans. Now her best friend was playing out the stay-at-home scenario.

'All right, Kay, I won't leave you.'

Kay's life was clouded by obsession. On some days she saw its symptoms clearly. She could see the way it stubbornly kept alive against all the odds and how every move or non-move by the object of obsession was seen as a sign of love. This Kay in turn saw as an illness but could not free herself from it.

Liz decided to interfere. She tried getting Kay downstairs, back into life. She made her something to eat. It was noticeable how eggs always came into it when a soothing dish was required. This time scrambled eggs on toast, but the food was left untouched. Liz phoned Joel at his office and explained she could not leave for Spain while Kay was in such a mess.

'But what can I do?' he said, exasperated. 'She's very powerful in a submissive sort of way, I suppose that's her charm. But I have no influence. Who does?'

Liz knew the answer to that. She almost phoned Angel but she was dubious about getting involved in other people's affairs. However bad they were, outside intrusion only made them worse. It seemed to be something the participants had to go through on their own.

The phone call from Liz made Joel thoughtful. He blamed himself for his wife's predicament. Ambition had always come first and he'd left her too much alone. He needed to take time off to be with her.

Kay found this plan disastrous; it was the last thing she wanted. 'Don't you know why I'm like this?' She sounded quite cruel. 'Surely you want to ask me?'

As long as it wasn't mentioned he was safe. If she told him about her love then Joel would have to ask her to stop seeing the man and in her present mood she'd walk out. He couldn't bear to think of it so he shut up and said he'd do the cooking. After all, it would be a change.

'But, Joel, think of all those enemies who'll gloat over seeing you in an apron.'

'I love enemies, they keep me on my toes.' He went to the stove and turned things on. Then he went to the cupboard.

'No, I mean your *real* enemy.'

'And who's that, Kay?'

'Oh come now, my sweet! You know how I love sex. As you say yourself, I can't get enough of it. What was that expression – I love cock? That was it. I'd do anything for it. Yet these days I don't initiate a thing. Why? Your real enemy could be an insignificant little unnoticed guest from – '

'Shut up!'

Because the gypsy had been so cruel to her, she in turn was cruel to Joel.

'I'd do anything he wanted. You can't begin to imagine how far I'd go for him.'

Joel sat at the table, head in his hands, and she thought he was going to throw up. He started sobbing, and all around him the pans burned. She thought, Angel's done this to me, and no revenge was big enough for that.

She read bits of books on obsession but no amount of knowledge quietened her heart. She could see – the way she was going – she'd end up with Sarah Prince. Or over the railway bridge.

· Thirty-one ·

Laburnum seeds. They worked instantly. She'd got the idea from a TV serial. There were Laburnum trees all around apparently but she wasn't sure what they looked like. You got the pods and crushed the seeds with a mortar and pestle, put them in a soft concealing food like marzipan or a paella – instant death. TV had its uses.

She organised a splendid dinner party, full of the sorts of people Angel couldn't fail to want to know. The Russian conductor accepted. She got Liz to phone New York and confirm that Angel would come. He'd agreed to stop off in London on his way to Holland. How Kay understood and identified with the French poisoner! She believed she could not spiritually be saved while Angel lived.

Usually she hired a waiter and kept the cleaner on for a big occasion but this time she'd do everything herself. She didn't see it as quite the usual NWI soirée.

The meal was laid out. Nineteen guests assembled at the table but still he did not come. Joel, on his way to his place, saw an incongruous dish. He sniffed suspiciously. 'What's this?'

It was Angel's favourite. 'Paella,' Kay said simply.

'Never heard of it.'

'Oh, don't be silly.'

'Not in this house, darling. We're English don't forget.' He didn't bother to lower his voice.

'Leave it,' she insisted.

'Not with sole, darling, surely?' Joel removed the offending dish and wondered if her taste, along with the rest of her, had gone to pieces. Liz watched him scrape the paella into the rubbish and wondered if he was saving lives. Kay put away the phial of crushed laburnum seeds; into which dish would they now fit?

Still the gypsy did not come. He knows, she thought.

Joel went back to his seat. 'I like the right food to go with the right company.'

Sophie mimicked him. 'And I vote for Thatcher.'

'Could you make those fabulous fishcakes again?' whispered Roly to Kay. 'The ones with the creamy shrimp sauce? I can't get them out of my mind. D'you know that feeling?'

'I wish all I had in my mind was a fishcake,' she told him. Throughout the dinner she sat silent, moping, remembering how he'd set her up in New York, how intimate he'd looked with the girl. She couldn't get over the thought of the unmade bed. And then the thought of him in bed – and she'd had to travel thousands of miles to suffer.

The Russian, after a few assorted after-dinner drinks, eased open a bottle of vodka and brought up the subject of the gypsy. Most of the guests had gone; those remaining were either too drunk to move or lived nearby. The Russian said, 'I met a girl in Rome who'd slept with him. How narcissistic he is! What he likes to do is play with himself in front of a mirror and have one, or preferably two, girls watching. He likes to flaunt what they're missing, and he likes them to salivate a little. From then on it's all – perverse.'

'Is this the same gypsy?' asked Roly, who had a virulent loyalty towards the stars of his shows. 'There *are* several.' He was also mindful of what he was beginning to suspect about Kay.

'He's the best,' said the Russian. 'They say he has *duende*. How do I know what that is? His music isn't my music, you understand. I don't even consider what he does "music".'

'Do you like it?' asked Roly.

'It's a far cry from the great masters. But as a guitarist I will say that he is now the best alive. He was born knowing how to play. And some of his phrasing – it's divine. As a musician he is first class. But his private life is a concoction from hell: drugs, men, women, crime – '

'How do you know the girl in Rome was telling the truth?' asked Joel.

'Because she said it was such a waste seeing he is so pretty and she so – serviceable.'

'Is he into group sex?' asked Roly.

The Russian laughed. 'Not with me but I'm sure he does everything. He has a death wish.'

Kay didn't speak. She couldn't get her mind off what she had heard he liked doing in front of a mirror. It both disturbed and thrilled her.

'He had a seamy life in Paris,' said Liz. 'He knocked about the edges. Roly asked around.'

'Doing what?'

'Low life. Unsuccessful. He's older than we thought. He's at least thirty-six and he's been around. He's not a child star exactly. Was the paella meant for him or all of us?'

'Only him, Liz. He likes it. He'd have eaten the lot.'

'And?'

Kay didn't answer.

'What if someone else had fancied some?'

'They'd have enjoyed it. I'm a good paella cook, too. He taught me.'

She'd planned to tip the poison onto his plate. She'd sit next to him and supervise his meal. He wouldn't suspect, not on such a crowded occasion. What if someone had just reached over and taken a spoonful of his paella? The Russian, for instance? Kay saw the whole thing would have been a nightmare. She would have had to scream, take the plate, even confess. Unlike the French poisoner she could never let an innocent person suffer. It was between her and him. But how to get to him?

To find out his whereabouts she had to call his girlfriend in New York. The humiliation that caused was intense but the girl seemed only too pleased to hear from her. 'I'm so sorry you didn't come to the concert. It was in some ways his best. I could see you were suffering – ' She paused. 'Jetlag?'

Thoughts of poison filled Kay's head. Coldly she said, 'I want to meet him, but not in London. Will you tell him that. Tell him Alexis needs company.'

Reflecting on Marie de Brinvilliers' end, Kay decided to put herself into God's hands immediately. She went to the nearby church and asked for salvation. Through this means she might reclaim her earlier peace of mind. She asked for prayers to be said for her as she knelt in front of the priest. 'I am so miserable. I'm divided into so many pieces, like broken glass. I don't know who I am anymore. I must give up this whole terrible murderous idea.'

This time, on her return from the church, the phone did not ring.

Kay's image remained constant and people still saw her as a valued, mysterious woman, one they wished to meet. Behind the façade, her mind licked its lips as she thought of the best ways to get to him. A picnic? Sandwiches in a rowing boat? The filling would be fun. Or a dark Parisian bar and the snacks a little more piquant than he'd expect? The church around the corner was undoubtedly doing its best but if you wanted salvation you had to stop being evil and she doubted if prayer could contradict a person's will.

The American girlfriend called. 'I told him we'd spoken. He's in Holland. He said he'd let you know the location. Have a good time.'

There was so much Kay wanted to ask her: did he do it in front of a mirror? What was he like in bed? Out of bed? At breakfast? In the bath? Did they take one together? But she wouldn't give the girl the satisfaction of even asking her name.

She wrote an article about the Green movement. 'Saving the planet was paramount.' Couldn't industrialists see the world was in trouble? Behind the words she saw the gypsy, doubled up in pain, and sweating, a picnic sandwich half-eaten in his hand. As he writhed, dying, would he admit his love for her or his wish to destroy her? The more evil her thoughts, the more religious her practices. Each fantasy would be punctuated by a fervent prayer.

October was usually her favourite month but not this year. One night, in the last week of the month, with the weather still warm, she sat by the open kitchen door and suddenly the room was filled with his perfume. It was so strong she even checked to see he wasn't outside. She remembered how he had come to take her to the desert – whenever she had started to be free he came to reclaim her. Dramatically she gave in to the idea that he could never let her get away: she was his. One touch from him was more powerful than the full sexual act with another man. If he'd simply taken her and loved her as he should, instead of taunting her and making her lose everything, their lives could have continued.

He called the next morning. 'Kay, it's your turn now.'

'My turn?'

'To be on stage. You're always in the wings watching. Let's see what you can do. I will meet you in France.'

He arranged to pick her up in Dieppe which he said was the location of his earlier dreams.

'What dreams?'

'For a while when I was in Paris I used to hear about those surfboards flying across the waves, to the horizon, and I used to think about them. They summed it all up – freedom. So I want to go and see for myself.'

'Haven't you been, then?'

'I got too famous.'

Dieppe and the surfboards skimming to the sea; that was his most famous song.

'So you admit you lived in Paris?'

'There's no time for false pride anymore.' His voice was almost broken, as though by late nights, too much smoking and drink.

'So what did you do in Paris?' she asked softly.

'Got by.' He hung up.

She went to Camden High Street to buy her ticket. She went

out so rarely she felt assaulted by the open air. There seemed to be no barrier between her and the street, its noise, the people. Where was her skin? Why couldn't she keep all this out? She could see the neighbours were delighted; there was nothing like a lucky person's downfall to bring about secret jubilation. Kay had been too lucky.

Joel was waiting in the house. He wanted to confront her but said instead, 'You look – well, you look – ' He couldn't find the word.

She suggested one. 'Insubstantial? When I came out of Woolworths I saw a rainbow. I take that sort of thing personally.' Then she told him she was leaving.

This news coincided with his. After years of manipulating, scheming, being single-minded about his work, producing some original marketing projections and prodding the weakness of his enemy, he'd got his way. He was now chief of the company. His élitism hadn't done any harm, and neither had Kay's meals.

'I thought we could have a celebration, do something here, like the old days. Let's do it together.'

'Just have men, darling. Sit them along the table and give them plenty of the sort of food Mummy made. Men are pigs. And when they get together to eat and drink and the women aren't there – well, they're pigs at a trough. Haven't I seen them? With each course they get younger and sillier. Dirty jokes, food jokes, pig jokes, pranks, schoolboy laughter, a lot of noise. Then they start throwing the food around – '

'You obviously don't like men, Kay,' he said sharply.

She didn't want him to like her. Anymore. She didn't expect to come back. 'Just get in someone to dish the food up fast and shove it into their faces.'

'Who do you suggest? Paula?' he said provocatively.

'Don't threaten me, Joel.' The pain of that name intruded on all the other pain, reminding her she was about to lose her husband anyway. Hadn't the dead singer's diaries described a similar incident? 'The first time he said the name Paula I thought, Watch out!'

'It's up to you.' Joel padded lightly around the kitchen. 'I can't go on without some release.'

She didn't answer.

'Or do you want me to simply chuck the whole thing? Why should I take the promotion? Why? What's the point?'

'Because it's what you've aimed for ever since I've known you. Just because I'm in trouble doesn't mean you have to be self-destructive.'

'But we're in it together.'

'Not anymore. You've got good ideas. You get people's respect. You want to improve the quality of modern life and health and – ' She couldn't go on.

'So when are you going?'

'I'd better go now.'

'I just want to believe you're going to something better than a Spanish waiter or whatever he is.'

'That's the danger of being élitist and a snob, Joel. You've got the blinkers on and the enemy comes up behind.'

'He's just using you, Kay, to fight some cause for gypsies. And he *was* a waiter – I had him checked out. Anyway, go or stay, but remember – I made you what you are.'

'That's ludicrous.' If she'd been less depressed she'd have laughed.

'I'm responsible for your writing. Before me, darling, you were just a cook.'

She looked at him almost casually, this man with whom she'd performed every kind of sexual act. How well she knew him. They'd gone shuddering to the edges of ecstasy, near-perversion. She'd loved him, adored him, couldn't get enough of him. And here she was saying it hadn't meant a thing, it was over, it could never happen again, as though she were cancelling a delivery of wet fish from the Camden Fisheries. Her light tone surprised even her.

The gypsy had driven her mad. But there was no legal section that could keep her from doing what she craved.

As she left she said aloud, 'I'll have vengeance for Joel's pain and Sophie's. I'll make it up to Tom. I have to rid myself of the cause and then of myself.'

· *Thirty-two* ·

The phial of poison was in her bag. Passengers looked at her with admiration – the one thing she hadn't lost was her beauty and the sea air made her face glow. Kay realised how little she knew herself. For forty years she'd been predictable and then a complete stranger turned her into another sort of person altogether. How could this have happened?

The boat arrived late. There was no sign of her prey but as Kay left the dock, a Frenchwoman approached her. It was Rose, his film star companion. Kay had trouble recognising her; all movie stars seemed to be a lot smaller in real life. Well, I've played this scene before, it really doesn't matter, Kay thought. Whatever he thought up was just a waste of his energy and other people's time. But on this occasion, the mistress was not to be used for provocation. Rose said, 'He would have gone on waiting but your boat is late and Luc wanted him to go to score.' She invited Kay for a drink. 'It was a rough crossing?'

Kay thought it probably had been but even that didn't matter. She threw her return ticket into a rubbish bin.

Rose chose an old bar near the harbour. 'The fishermen drink here but they're asleep now. They go out at night and come back around five or six.'

They sat at a zinc-topped table and Rose ordered a bottle of wine. 'Angel says how marvellous you are – a woman of quality.' Then she bent forward, tears dripping between her fingers. 'I am having such a terrible time.' Quickly she wiped her face.

Kay thought, is it endemic, this unhappiness?

'He said he was coming to Dieppe. It was his first trip. He'd always wanted to come to Dieppe in the old days. So I said I would come too because I needed some sea air. I can't tell you what I've suffered.' She lit a cigarette. 'I know I can talk to you because you couldn't possibly feel like this about him. I am jealous of you because when he talks about you I can see it's something special. Although I have truly nagged him on the subject he says he doesn't sleep with you. I don't believe him but that's none of my business.' She paused. 'Does he?' Her eyes reminded Kay of Sophie's. Almost amused, she said no. Why not tell the truth? 'So I came to Dieppe with him because I was jealous. I am supposed to be big, I am shit. I can't even put myself in front of a camera, he's made me so unhappy. Luc wanted to come to Dieppe too. Luc is the top, has been for years. He likes me in his way. You've seen him in a million films, he looks like a cat.' Kay remembered his face. 'But Luc wants to do a drug deal here. He knows someone on the outskirts. Last night we stayed in a hotel overlooking the sea. We played poker and got drunk. The three of us. But Angel was restless and in a bad mood. Then he starts on me, really bad treatment. He said that compared with me, you were a goddess, that I should get the hell out of your way. Now he's gone with Luc to do the deal. A very voluptuous French housewife owns the house. I've seen her. Luc says he adores sleeping with her – all that flesh. He described her to Angel. The huge flesh I think excited Angel.'

But the housewife's availability depended on her truck-driver husband being absent and after another drink Rose decided Angel had agreed to go along to annoy Rose rather than enjoy a fleshy woman. She had another drink.

'Am I out of my mind? He wants a threesome with Luc! It's been staring me in the face all night!'

'How long did you live with him?' Kay asked.

'A night? A day? How long, how short? He ran around me like a dog for weeks but I told him to piss off. So he said OK. *Ça va*. It was all the same to him. I had to sing in my last movie and he said he'd teach me. Just watching him day after day, the way he performs, got to me. But I still didn't do anything. We went out together and the press did a big number; he was flavour of the week, and I think he liked that. He loathes, just loathes the French, especially the Parisians. So to take out their new star was a little *coup* for him. I decided I was getting too involved, that I must never sleep with him, to finish it once the singing lessons were over. It was as though he knew. He came rushing onto my boat quite unexpectedly and gave me the love session of my entire life. Then he was gone. Only the smell of him was left.'

Kay took a cigarette and the barman lit it for her. It was clear he preferred her to the young movie star. Her looks would remain in their own right; to the moment of her death she'd be lovely.

'It was so good between us that I could not believe he didn't want it to go on. Who walks away from something that fantastic? But last night – brush off. I think he only came back to me to check me out, make sure I was still crazy for him. He's sexually vain. He wants women in their place and that's a long way beneath him.'

'Does he have other women?'

'He's probably having one right now. A fat one. He swings both ways, Kay. You know that? His agent Marco has certainly slept with him, and I think Angel stood on a lot of street corners before Marco picked him up. That was his big break.'

Kay asked about the act in the mirror in front of two girls.

Rose said, 'There's a little of that about him. How lucky, how fortunate you are not to be hooked in that way.'

Kay didn't have a laugh left in her.

Rose suddenly screamed, 'I want to really get him. I want to find the truck driver and send him home early, catch Luc with his pants down. Put him away, both of them. All of them.' She was still threatening as to what she'd do as Kay went off towards the suburbs in the direction Angel had supposedly taken. She walked for an hour and could find no sign of Luc the famous actor's enviable car. She asked a few people about the fat housewife, but maybe in their eyes she wasn't fat, because they hadn't heard of her. Then she heard the sound of a guitar, unlike any other, and there was Angel sitting in a yard playing a *solea*.

Kay leaned over the wall and watched him. He stopped playing and turned slowly, as though ready to attack. Then he saw her. He struck the guitar dramatically. 'So there you are.' Something in her eyes made him look at her again. She saw that he saw that it could not go on, that he had made her obsessed and ill. Her eyes had a fixity that scared him. He recovered himself and said, 'Now it's your turn.'

'My turn?'

'I told you,' he helped her over the wall, 'it's all been easy for you. You've been the audience, now go on stage.'

Kay said, 'I'll win.'

He said, 'Why?'

'Because I am good.'

'Goodness wins!' The gypsy was amused. 'I don't think so.' When she didn't answer he said, 'So you believe in universal justice?'

Kay replied, 'I believe in God.'

The voluptuous Frenchwoman, half dressed, opened the back door and demanded in French who the hell the unwanted bitch was. Kay saw the way Angel looked at her, the way his eyes caressed all that flesh. A stab of jealousy made her say, 'Oh, don't worry about me, I'm just a friend. It's Rose you've got to worry about.'

'How did you get here?' the woman asked in English.

'Rose told me.'

The woman was appalled. 'How the fuck does she know where I live? *Does* she know?'

'Obviously,' said Kay. 'How do you think I got here?'

The gypsy watched Kay, amused. He put his arms around the Frenchwoman. 'Don't arouse yourself, not in this way. Save all that for later. Rose doesn't know.'

'She spotted the car,' said the woman.

'But it's a kilometre away. Kay heard me playing the guitar. That's right isn't it, Kay?'

'No.'

Luc appeared behind the woman. 'Rose will get the law – she's angry enough. I'm going to have to put the gear down *les chiottes*. I'm pulling the plug on the whole weekend.' He went back inside and sounds of the lavatory flushing, Luc began swearing. The woman, maddened, rushed between Luc and the gypsy. 'Has she got the police? That's all I want to know.' The men couldn't tell her. She looked at Kay.

'Yes,' said Kay.

The gypsy laughed. 'You're learning fast.'

The woman swore. 'What do we do?'

'Get rid of it all,' he said, 'just in case. All of it. They have sniffer dogs.'

'Thousands of francs. Shit! You and he will pay. Get that in your head.' The woman turned to Kay. 'Get inside.' Roughly she pushed her into a small kitchen and locked the back door. 'They may have us, but we have you. You do understand?'

Angel put a bottle of Cognac on the table and played a song. The woman closed the shutters, got dressed and sat, tense and still, for half an hour. 'Nothing,' she said. In the background sounds of the lavatory flushing continued.

Luc said, 'They're hardly going to arrive like this.' He made the sound of sirens, as he threw a pack of cards onto the table. 'When it's dark we fuck off.'

'How did she get the address,' said the woman. She landed Luc a blow on the face. 'You told her because you're jealous of *him*.' She gestured obscenely towards Angel. 'She'll come out here and knife him if she sees him with me, you know that. She's Arab. I told you to watch her.'

'I didn't tell her anything.' Luc shuffled the cards.

'Now all we need is my husband to come. *Voilà!* Full house.'

'When is your husband due back by the way, *chérie?*' Angel asked.

'Tomorrow night or the next morning.'

'Earlier,' muttered Kay. 'Rose is working on it.'

Angel laughed, genuinely amused, as the woman tried to deal

Luc another blow. He defended his face. 'Watch it? How else can I earn my living?'

'Show them your arse,' said the woman. 'Out of the two it's the younger looking.' For a while she considered the idea of Angel going back to Dieppe to placate Rose, but she didn't trust him. She decided they should all stick together for now. To cheer herself up she demanded her share of the money for the drugs. The men paid half each without too much concern. It was more money than Kay saw in a year.

Kay looked for signs of intimacy between the woman and Angel; she felt he had not had his turn but wanted it. There were no obvious signs of sexuality between Luc and the woman – if her flesh excited him he was keeping it to himself. After a while the woman took off most of her clothes. She seemed more comfortable with the evening air on her body. Kay said she was hungry. What about making some food?

'What d'you think this is? *Chez vous*? Make it yourself, I'm not your servant.' The woman tossed Kay a box of matches.

She prepared a meal of liver and beans and they all ate ravenously. All except Angel. The food seemed to worry him. He forked it around but nothing arrived at his mouth. He made excuses. 'You can't rely on anything these days.' He threw his bread down. 'Pass on the food.' He looked meaningfully at Kay then went outside into the yard. The woman grabbed his plate. 'My husband would kill for this.' She looked at Kay with a grudging respect. 'With food this good, you could have any man you want. Anyone can fuck.' She licked her fingers. Angel was still outside. 'Watch it, gypsy. That's all they want, an eyeful of your arse. You should never have brought him,' she said to Luc.

Luc went outside. 'Shit! He's here eating a packet of crisps like a fucking wolf. Yet gourmet food he won't stomach.'

At 2.00 am Kay made some cinnamon toast. She gave a piece to Angel.

'I will make my own.' He got up.

'No,' said Kay. 'This is for you.'

'Eat it and shut up,' said the woman.

Kay smiled at the gypsy. 'So the way to your heart isn't through your stomach.'

It was her rage that scared him, she knew that.

The French woman and Luc disappeared.

Angel said, 'You're not what you seem. The beneficent English lady taking your hamper to the hospital – Kay Craven visits the unfortunates. You do good, but for your own good.'

'I've told you, I wanted to help that woman. I hate injustice. My worse fear is to be trapped without choice.' She realised she'd been experiencing her worst fear for months. It was ironic.

'Go back to your husband, you don't belong here.' And with that he disappeared into the yard, leapt over the wall and was gone.

Kay shouted for the woman. Wearing her white slip she ran barefoot into the street. Luc, in underpants, went the other way, over the wall. Within two minutes the gypsy was brought back. There was no argument about it. The woman had a gun shoved hard in the small of his back.

'You enjoy taking the stuff. Why should I take the risks?' She took his guitar away from him and put it in a cupboard, and put the key between her breasts. 'At dawn we all go together, with the harbour workers. We see what Rose has been up to. My guess is nothing much. A false alarm.'

'It cost enough,' snarled Luc.

Kay put a salad on the table. 'I thought I'd make a rice pudding with nutmeg and vanilla for dessert.'

'Don't bother,' said the gypsy quickly. 'We'll be leaving before then. It's all a great drama you've brought here.'

She noticed he was looking at the others for signs of discomfort. He still wouldn't eat, yet the food was safe. An hour later they were all still alive, playing cards.

The woman told Kay, she had a lovely smile. Kay gave her some recipes. The woman laughed. 'You're so good in the kitchen you could be French.' She put the gun out of sight and went back to the card game. Angel sang one of Alexis' songs quietly.

'That is beautiful,' said the Frenchwoman. 'One of yours?'

'I wish it was.' Suddenly he was telling her, a complete stranger, about Alexis, about her life. Kay couldn't believe it. It was like a last confession.

'It sounds as though you arrived a day too late,' said the woman. 'A true love story.'

'She had a terrible life.' Kay was eager to be part of the story, to defuse its love. 'She was a victim of everyone's selfishness.'

'She was never a victim,' said Angel, furious. 'Don't you know anything? She was valued, she had grace, she was profound like a true gypsy.'

The woman watched them, amused.

He turned to her. 'Alexis gave me delight, made me sing.'

'But you didn't know her,' said Kay.

'She's in her songs.'

'And what about *her*?' The woman gestured towards Kay. 'Does *she* make you sing?'

The gypsy calmed down and started to beat a rhythm on the table.

'What time does it get light?' asked Luc.

'Six-thirty, seven.'

'She would have known joy beyond words,' said Angel.

The Frenchwoman asked who.

'Alexis.' He said it as though he was in love with her.

'Why did she kill herself if she was so happy?'

'Because she preferred not to be.' He turned on Kay. 'You'll never understand a woman like her.'

'But what did she do that was so particular?' asked the Frenchwoman.

'*Do*?' He couldn't be scathing enough. Again he turned on Kay. '*Do*? You couldn't see it any other way.'

Kay said, 'Why don't you tell us, instead of being so arrogant?'

In a mocking tone he said, 'Her perception and yours, for a start – completely different. She saw life as it was, so she saw beauty in it. Even in a pile of litter. She understood signs. The world spoke to her. Trees, lamplight . . . I understood her because she was a gypsy. If she'd been with me I would never have let her die. You think she ended her life because of that cheap mistress he had? But Alexis didn't belong to those people. She had *duende*.'

'What is that?' asked the Frenchwoman.

'You're born with it,' said the gypsy.

'Have I got it?' asked the Frenchwoman.

The gypsy paused, almost laughed. 'I can promise you faithfully you have not got it.'

The Frenchwoman wasn't sure if she should be pleased or not.

Angel said, 'You have it or you don't. You can't acquire it.'

'So it's a talent,' said the Frenchwoman.

'Not at all. And it doesn't occur as much as people think. *Duende* can be there only once in a gypsy's lifetime.'

'What does it do?'

'It freezes the blood, sends shivers through the soul. You never forget it. One or two moments in Alexis' songs are like that. You see, Kay she didn't write *about* it. She wrote *it*.' He tried to hide a cynical, teasing smile.

'You still don't tell me why she died,' said Kay. 'Why?'

'Wash that cup!' the Frenchwoman said suddenly to Luc. 'I can't keep washing up. All these fucking cups, life is too much sometimes.'

Kay felt chilled. She shivered, yet it was warm.

The gypsy said, 'Someone just walked over my grave.'

'Can anyone have *duende*?' asked Luc, not wanting to hear it was something he lacked.

'God no,' said Angel. 'Only a gypsy. Sometimes it's all he has.'

'Not you,' said Luc. 'You're as rich as me.'

'Why don't you eat your salad?' The Frenchwoman pushed the plate towards Angel.

He shook his head and looked away. It was obvious he was very hungry. 'I'm not arrogant, Kay, you are. Very. In fact it's his arrogance – your impossible husband's. You wear it around you like one of those mink coats he buys you.'

The Frenchwoman shuffled the cards. 'You two can use the bed if you want. But hurry.'

Kay gasped with an almost unbearable pleasure. The gypsy jolted as though shocked. Then he sat, too still. Almost shyly he looked at Kay. He took her hand and she thought, no, that opportunity has gone. The little death they talk about during orgasm wasn't the kind he'd be having. He put her hand onto his heart, to let her feel how it was beating, then he put the hand back in her lap chastely.

The woman said, 'You waste time with a lot of intellectual chatter and you could be enjoying yourself.' Looking at Kay, she said, 'What a waste, Angel.'

'She looks like a Madonna,' said Luc.

Angel swore in Spanish. 'There's nothing more fake than a woman who looks like a Madonna. They are the most deceptive. A flesh and blood Madonna.' He spat with contempt. 'Once you bring flesh into it you can kiss divinity goodbye. Flesh is your sentence, your mask of sin.'

'So you prefer your Madonna in plastic and clay?' said Luc.

'Or rubber,' said the gypsy. 'I can go a long way on a blow-up rubber Madonna.'

'It's a shame she's not a gypsy.' The woman waved a hand towards Kay. 'Then you'd have had her.'

Of course, that was it! Why hadn't Kay seen it before? The endless hostility, the pleasure he took in making her suffer. It was almost as if he was jealous.

The woman, as though emphasising what Kay had discovered, said, 'You can only go with your own kind, and you think you're beneath this one.'

Angel didn't like that.

'No, it's true,' said Luc. 'You're a gypsy yet you speak three languages. You read books. You can talk about ideas, not just money and fucking, or whatever the rest of them go on about. You wanted to better yourself. That's why you speak French.'

'And English,' said Kay.

Furious, Angel said, 'I have to learn English if I want to live in New York.' His eyes were blazing with rage.

'No, Luc is right,' said the Frenchwoman conclusively. 'You want to be considered an equal with the next man.'

'Better,' said Luc. 'Better than the next man. There's nothing so inferior as his blood.'

The gypsy jumped up, ready to hit Luc. The woman got the gun out and kept it near her. 'All right, Angel, let's just say you have a confident view of yourself. You want to be as good as the next person, and why not?'

Kay thought, Somewhere, someone has really put him down. 'Eat your salad,' she said, and put a forkful to his lips.

Angel pushed it away roughly. 'Everyone is on to me suddenly. What about you?' He turned to Kay. 'You don't have faults I suppose?'

'I'm your prey, darling. Remember, you sang about it in my house? During that dreadful lunch party.'

'We'll talk about it later.'

She didn't think there would be time.

'It's not a question of being as good as the next person, but of being as good as I can be.' He wanted Kay to understand. 'Why should I be some shabby gypsy, when I have this?' He touched his head. 'I love language. I learn easily. If I'd been a Spaniard I would have gone to university and been a scholar.'

'And no one would have heard of you,' said Luc.

With the beginning of daylight came the sound of the workers going to the harbour. Angel looked at the gun. 'Don't even try it,' said the woman. 'You can try me if you like, as you don't want to try her.'

Instead he went into the yard and sang songs of love and death, soul-death. They made Kay think of how she'd loved him, before he'd dealt her so many wounds.

It was time. She made the decisive meal, an omelette spiced with herbs and poison. Luc made the coffee, the woman poured orange juice.

In the light of the dawn Angel saw how Kay had suffered. Her face was hollowed and sad, beyond tears. He knew she would kill him for destroying her. He accepted death as he accepted fate. She gave him the omelette. She said, 'I'll eat it with you.' She got two forks. She looked into his eyes and he into hers. 'You're afraid,' she said.

He got up proudly. 'So you've suffered. Haven't I? Haven't I been excluded all my life? Except for my talent, which is part of my family's blood, you wouldn't even notice me.' He proudly stuck his fork into the omelette, prepared to die. 'We gypsies often bring about our own deaths. We plant the idea, then leave it to others to carry out.' He scooped up a generous helping.

The Frenchwoman came hurtling towards them, screaming. She kicked the plate and forks across the yard. 'Out! Get out! He's here. My old man.'

Kay looked at the omelette, all mingled with bits of broken plate. She was appalled. Luc rushed out naked, carrying his clothes, and vanished over the wall. He pulled the gypsy with him. Kay went on staring at the plate.

'I'll clean it up, get going! My old man.' And she got a broom and pushed Kay towards the wall. Then she started sweeping the yard.

Angel sang all the way into Dieppe. 'I am tired of being gazed at by life. Leave me in the halls of rest adorned with white lillies. So what if I don't come back?'

There was suddenly a lighthearted atmosphere. The sun came out.

Luc said, 'No police, no press, just me tossing 100,000 francs down the john. And your guitar locked in her cupboard.'

The gypsy laughed. 'I don't need it.'

· *Thirty-three* ·

In her hotel room Rose was lying across the bed. Angel checked her pulse, saw her feverish eyes, then turned on Kay. 'What have you done to her?'

Rose vomited.

'Get a doctor,' said Kay and put a cold flannel on the girl's burning head.

'Why do it to her?' said Angel. 'She's nothing to do with things.'

Kay looked after the girl, even when the doctor had left and she was sleeping, she sat stroking her head. Angel watched, quite moved by her. The bad oyster Rose had eaten, had stopped her taking her revenge; she'd been too sick to even get help for herself.

Mid-morning and Kay, trying to clear her head, walked down the shingle to the sea. She'd lost all sense of time. She turned and he was there beside her. Boys on surfboards were skimming across the waves. Angel sat on the stones and pulled her down beside him. 'It's a bad sea,' he said.

'Do you think you could do that? It looks very skilful. It would need practice.' They watched the boys keeping their balance with difficulty. A full westerly wind had started up.

'If you want to fly as much as I do, you can do it.'

A group of young men crunched by, carrying surfboards. They wore black oilskin suits. Angel turned, looking for the place to hire them. 'You were very kind to Rose. You have compassion.'

'Had.'

'No, it's still there. Your good qualities, which I so admire,

unfortunately work against us. You are right, I am jealous of you.
I challenge you because you are a superior woman, above me, and
you're not from my people. If you were a gypsy I would applaud
you. You obsessed me as much as I did you, I'm sure. I wanted to
know what made you so serene and sought-after. I had to taste it.
Then I could grab it and drop it and no one would value it again. I
didn't have a choice about what I was doing. If you'd been from
my family I'd have shown you mercy.'

'But why?'

'So, you see, you are not evil. You have blackness in you but I
brought it out.'

Again she said, 'But why?'

Impulsively he ran to the hut at the top of the beach and came
back with a surfboard and an oilskin suit.

'You must tell me *why*.' she said.

He took off his clothes and put on the suit. He was intrigued by
the surfboard, ready to go. He left his clothes in a heap beside
her.

'This is my big moment. I dreamed of this. Years ago I went to
Paris to try and work as a performer and I failed. This was before
flamenco really caught on. I didn't have any money left and was
discriminated against for being gypsy. I was beaten up, my papers
stolen, and I didn't even have the fare home. I ended up having to
work as a waiter in a third-class brasserie opposite the Gare St
Lazarre. The French manageress treated me like a pig – worse.
And how I despised the food I had to serve. That time scarred me
absolutely. After that I changed. I wanted to be better than
others. I learned a lot of my languages, my dear Kay, serving in
that cheap restaurant. The women were always propositioning
me, so I learned some colourful dialect in bed.'

'Were there many women?' Her questions were involuntary.

'Because I was good-looking they all wanted to have me. Men,
especially men. And couples. I had all sorts of things done to me.
It's a time I will never forget. Often I didn't even get paid. It has
coloured my attitude to foreign women. Now I will use any magic
trick to seduce them but my not-so-unconscious aim is to cause

pain. I have always had a sexual vanity and I hated being used. Hated it.'

'Why didn't you go home?'

'Like that? Are you crazy? And I was used to it, it was a way of life. During my time at the brasserie I was obliged to work seven days a week. My dream was to cross over the square to the station, take the train to Dieppe and go surfboarding across the sea. It symbolised everything, cleansing and freedom from that rat hole, from failure and debauchery. Paris never allowed me any of my dreams. I returned luckless to my village. I didn't want anyone to know of my shame, but gypsies see things. I was considered an ill omen. I'd worked in a third-rate brasserie for nothing, being touched up by insulting foreigners.' He spat. 'They wanted to kill me. Surprisingly my family didn't tell you. They like a little revenge. They held my shame over me. The washer-up for frogs who fucks as well. Perhaps in time they'll sing about it.' He sounded cynical. 'I was nineteen when I left to make my name. I was stuck in Paris for four years. They'd warned me not to go, that I would find nothing. They had seen it in the flames of the fire. Even the birds crowed about it. But I had so much to give, I couldn't just stay among animals. When I got back my father knifed me.'

She had already seen the scar. 'I wasn't allowed near any girl, I was on the outskirts of things for quite a while. And then the rage for flamenco helped turn me into an international performer and changed everything. They said I was the Mick Jagger of traditional flamenco. I am very wealthy but I still live at home in the manner of all gypsies.'

He picked up the surfboard. It was his gift to her, his humiliation. 'I have never told that to anyone. You see, Kay, you still have a good heart.'

'Have you ever been in love with – '

He shook his head decisively. 'I will never marry outside my own blood, if that's what you're asking.'

'That girl in New York – '

'A tart. I need to go with tarts because they're hard. There is absolutely no possibility that I could meet my own sorrow in one of those creatures, as gleaming and shallow as tin. With their perfect smiles, all false. Only their teeth are real.'

He ran to the water's edge and looked at the sea. Then he turned, looked at her.

'I hardly know you,' she said.

'If you want to know about me just listen to Alexis' songs.'

After a shaky start he took off, and managed to stay upright.

'Be careful,' she shouted.

'It's the best thing for you,' he shouted back. 'You will be *you* again.' He was caught up in the current and was literally flying over the water.

As she watched him carried farther away she felt her energy come back like the tide, coming in, healing all the wounds. As he flew across the water, beyond the harbour, she turned to walk back up the beach. His pile of clothes had a final look about them. She frowned at them, unsure what to do. She looked out to sea and there he was, just visible. She was sure he'd gone too far out. One minute he was there, then he was gone.

She called the lifeguards and they went out in boats, but they didn't find him. His body wasn't washed up on the shore either. The boy who loved flying had simply flown away.